ONE LITTLE MISTAKE

MIRANDA RIJKS

INKUBATOR
BOOKS

Published by Inkubator Books
www.inkubatorbooks.com

Copyright © 2025 by Miranda Rijks

ISBN (eBook): 978-1-83756-664-8
ISBN (Paperback): 978-1-83756-665-5
ISBN (Hardback): 978-1-83756-666-2

Miranda Rijks has asserted her right to be identified as the author of this work.

ONE LITTLE MISTAKE is a work of fiction. People, places, events, and situations are the product of the author's imagination. Any resemblance to actual persons, living or dead is entirely coincidental.

No part of this book may be reproduced, stored in any retrieval system, or transmitted by any means without the prior written permission of the publisher.

PROLOGUE

I guess we get lazy with our friends and family. Particularly the ones we've known forever. The class clown remains the person we choose to spend time with when we need a pick-me-up, regardless that her joviality has been a pretence for decades, and that these days she's secretly popping antidepressants. Or how about the nerdy friend who got a first in chemistry and now heads up an engineering firm? She's scarily intelligent and put-together, and we're still in awe of her and a little afraid of saying something stupid in her presence. So we wait for her to reach out to us first, despite the fact that she's desperately lonely and her husband is a controlling bastard.

It's the same with our close family. We take out our frustrations on our spouse because we know they'll forgive us. We blame our parents for our failures because, however hard they tried, it was never enough. You see, we all make judgements, and then we hold on to those judgements for years, decades even. So when one of the people you're closest to starts acting utterly out of character, it's hard to know how to respond.

Yet that is what's happening right now.

'I just need to understand why.'

'I've got nothing to say to you,' I snap. I don't lose my temper easily, but in this moment I'm seeing red. Just like my father. A deep thinker, he was logical and easy-going, until he was pushed too far. Then he exploded.

'I'm not leaving.' Arms in front of chest, legs planted wide.

I'm genuinely puzzled. How is it possible that this person whom I know so well, so intimately, is acting completely out of character?

'Get out!' I shout.

'Tell me the truth. I deserve to know it.'

I lose it then and grab the nearest thing to a weapon I can find. I wave it in front of me. 'Get out!'

Except there's more than one item that can be used as a weapon in here. I stumble slightly. And then I see they've picked up one too. It's moving high in the air as if in slow motion, rising towards the ceiling and then coming down so fast, creating the whooshing sound of a whip. I can't get out of the way, and I know it's going to hurt. I brace myself.

It hits me on the temple, and bright lights flash behind my eyes. How is it possible for someone who claims to love me to do this? My knees give way, and I'm falling, my hands reaching upwards in vain. Something sharp and solid catches the other side of my head. The pain is blinding, excruciating, unfathomable. And as blackness descends, I realise it's all over.

CHAPTER ONE

The app pings to let me know my taxi is waiting outside.

'You look gorgeous,' Jared says, eyeing me up and down. I'm wearing a new dress made from a silk fabric that looks like it's been brushed with pastel watercolours. I bought it from a designer shop on the King's Road, in the sale, but it was still ridiculously expensive. If I hadn't been with Stella, I wouldn't have ventured inside the fancy boutique. I glance in the hallway mirror, tugging my cream faux fur jacket closed, and shout goodbye to the kids. After blowing a kiss to my husband, I step outside.

I'm excited. My friend Lucia is getting married in a couple of weeks' time, and tonight it's her hen party in a Mayfair private members club. Lucia is an old university friend, part of our tight-knit group whose lives are intertwined so much, I doubt we could ever unravel ourselves. Not that Lucia lasted the full three years at university or gained a degree. She was scouted midway through our second year, and lured away with promises of global catwalks and obscene sums of money. With her pixie face and razor-sharp cheekbones, combined with impossibly long legs, Lucia became a top model and is now a social media influencer. The fact that her dream life came true has spurred the rest of us on to realise our own dreams. Not that we have; not really. I mean, who could keep up with Lucia? Nevertheless, she remained part of our group, and despite her crazy, high-octane life that involves jet-setting around the globe, she's still just Luce to us, ordinary Lucia, albeit exquisitely beautiful. I think we're her anchor; perhaps her only anchor. Her first marriage fizzled out after a mere two years, but I hope that her forthcoming marriage to Hamish will last. He's the owner of a chain of veterinary practices and has his feet firmly on the ground. The wedding will be sumptuous, to be held in a fabulous castle in Scotland with turrets and vaulted cellars and a ballroom too big to be captured on a photo. But that's to come. Right now, I'm sitting in a Nissan Leaf Uber, stuck in traffic on London's Park Lane. I've misjudged how long it will take to get from our home in Barnes to central London. That's the trouble with London, and that's why I normally take public transport, except this evening, in my finery, I treated myself. I hate being late. Absolutely hate it, and despite knowing that my incessant foot tapping and picking at the edges of my nails will do nothing to speed up the stalled traffic, I can't help myself. My stomach starts to churn, and I try, but largely fail, to remind myself that these are my friends; this is not some important business meeting. It really doesn't matter if I'm delayed.

Eventually, the car pulls up in front of a Georgian townhouse with imposing steps and flamboyant planters on either side of the door that are crammed with flowering plants in shades of purple and white. I thank the driver and step out inelegantly, unused to wearing high heels and a slippery silk dress. I notice a couple of men standing on the pavement, holding cameras with oversized telephoto lenses. They ignore me, but suddenly there's a frenzy and several more paparazzi appear, cameras clicking, lights flashing.

'Over here, Lucia!' one journalist shouts.

'Who else is joining you for your hen party?' another asks.

I stand to one side, temporarily frozen at the spectacle of Lucia unfurling herself from a navy Rolls-Royce. She's wearing a long silver dress with spaghetti straps, the fabric skimming her slender frame. Lucia must be freezing, but if so, she doesn't show it. She flicks her head back and poses for the cameras, one ankle in front of the other, vertiginous heels that make her well over six feet tall, her left hand poised so that her diamond engagement ring sparkles vibrantly. Today, her hair is dark and very short, its natural colour, and her eyes so blue, they're almost turquoise. Set against her smooth olive skin, she is dazzling. I remember someone at uni asking her if she was wearing coloured contact lenses. She wasn't.

It's only then that she notices me and her body relaxes, a smile sweeping across her flawless face.

'Kate,' she says, striding towards me, enveloping me in a floral-scented hug. 'I'm so glad you're here.' She links her arm through mine, despite the difference in our heights.

'Wouldn't miss it for the world,' I say.

I'm conscious of the cameras, awkward next to my stunning friend, but she doesn't hesitate as she leads me up the steps and into the foyer.

'You look stunning,' she says, glancing down at me.

'Nothing like you,' I mutter, but she just squeezes my shoulder.

'Ms Highsmith, welcome. May I lead you to your reception room?' The man is wearing tails and a black bow tie, his dark hair slicked back with too much gel, and is clearly the maître d' or some such member of staff. 'Many of your guests are already here.' He speaks in a clipped manner, as if he's trying to emulate the formal speech of the early twentieth century.

We follow him along a corridor lined with black and white photos of the many dignitaries and celebrities that have frequented this club over multiple decades, our heels sinking into the plush burgundy carpet. There's music coming from a room ahead, the dulcet sounds of a small jazz band, not the raucous Abba songs I had playing at my hen party in a pub over a decade ago. The maître d' stands back and holds his arm across an open door.

'In here, Ms Highsmith.'

A gaggle of about twenty women explodes with welcomes and cheers, genuine delight on their faces that the bride-to-be has arrived. The group is split into two. Lucia's old friends and female relatives, the 'ordinary' women who have dressed up in their best clothes but will never grace the pages of a magazine, and the supermodels, who stand at least four inches taller than everyone else and are impossibly slim and glamorous. Stella appears at my side, clutching a champagne flute. She has choppy blonde hair, a wide smile and is wearing a pink tiered dress that swamps her slight frame.

'How are you?' she asks, air-kissing me.

'Traffic was a nightmare,' I say.

'It's very glam, isn't it?' Stella murmurs. I glance around. We're in a beautiful room, with sparkling chandeliers, gold frescoes and a huge roaring fire in an oversized fireplace flanked by six-foot-tall floral displays in pale pinks, coffee hues and creams. At the far end is a long table, laid with a starched white cloth, silver cutlery and flowers in similar shades running the full length of the centre of the table. Flowers are interspersed with candlesticks of varying heights. The band sits near the door, while servers wander around with perfect little canapes on silver platters. A glass of champagne appears on a tray in front of me, and I thank the young woman, who simply nods in acknowledgement. If this is the hen party, I can't imagine what the actual wedding will be like. This is the ultimate in tastefulness. No balloons, or strippers or bespoke printed T-shirts here.

The band stops playing, and Lucia grabs a microphone; not strictly necessary as the room isn't big.

'Just wanted to say thank you all so much for coming. Maricela is over from Australia, Savannah from the US and Narin from Lithuania. And the old crowd.' She points at Stella, Dakota, Erin and me. 'You girls have kept me sane through all the crazy times, reminding me that models and influencers aren't special. We're just ordinary girls in the spotlight. Thank you. You're my sisters, and I love you from the bottom of my heart.'

I notice Lucia's actual sister, Bella, flinch slightly. But Lucia is right. We choose our friends; we don't choose our family. A heartening glow settles on me as it always does when Lucia throws a compliment my way. She talks a little about Hamish and how lucky she is to have found him, and how she's hoping for a more normal life going forward with children, perhaps. And then the music starts up again, and more champagne flows.

Stella and I drift towards Erin and Dakota. Stella might be my best friend, but I see the most of Erin. She's married to Kieren, a GP, who spends way too many hours each weekend and often after work with my husband, Jared. They're both golf fanatics and disappear for extended periods to play eighteen holes at various golf clubs in Greater London and the Home Counties. As a result, Erin and I are left with the kids. She has twin boys aged twelve, boisterous, uncontrollable lads, while Jared and I have Rosie, aged nine, and Albie, who is about to turn thirteen. Our children attend the same schools, and we live just two streets apart. Erin is serious and fragile. She's always been the quietest of the five of us, gaining a degree in English Literature at university, briefly holding down a job in publishing, although she's not working now. I worry about her. It seems as if she has the weight of the world on her shoulders permanently, even though she's never admitted it, I sense she's unhappy.

Dakota, on the other hand, is the polar opposite. With flawless ebony skin and large almond eyes, her beauty is on par with Lucia's. What she doesn't have is the height or the slim-line figure, but to my eyes, she's the most stunning of us all. A single mother to Violet (she's never admitted who Violet's father is), she's a solicitor and glides through life seemingly without a care in the world. I wish some of her laissez-faire attitude would rub off on me. Perhaps dealing with negativity daily thanks to her job, she allows it to glide over her.

'This place is gorgeous,' Dakota mutters. 'And the flowers are stunning.'

A server appears with a platter of exquisite canapes shaped to look like swans. Erin turns to Stella. 'Have you done the catering?'

Stella sighs. 'No, Lucia didn't ask me.'

'I don't suppose a place like this outsources catering. Are you doing the catering for the wedding?' Erin asks.

Stella sighs. 'Nope. How I wish she'd asked me.'

'I can't imagine Lucia has organised any of this herself,' Dakota says diplomatically. 'She's got a fancy wedding planner for Scotland, and her publicist probably arranged every aspect of this hen party.'

Dakota is right, but I say nothing. I have clients like Lucia, women who employ armies of staff and don't actually make any detailed decisions themselves. I have my own recruitment business, supplying staff to wealthy, jet-setting families. They come to me when they're looking for a new housekeeper, nanny or butler. Often, I'm invited to visit their mansions to discuss their detailed requirements. I've got used to being on the periphery of the uber-wealthy, accepting that they're a breed unto themselves, grateful sometimes that I don't have to manage five different homes all around the world.

'I didn't want to say anything,' Stella adds, taking a large swig of champagne, 'but I have to admit my nose is a bit out of joint. The publicity would have done me good. Anyway, who wants a top-up of champagne?' She beckons to one of the servers, who comes hurrying across.

'How are my girls?' Lucia appears suddenly, flinging both arms around the shoulders of Stella and Erin. 'I'm so glad you could make it tonight. Have you chosen what you're wearing for the wedding?'

'Something warm,' Dakota laughs. 'October in Scotland isn't likely to be baking. Couldn't you have flown us all to Bali or Mauritius?'

Lucia laughs. 'Hamish had his heart set on a full Scottish wedding. Bagpipes, kilts and all the paraphernalia, so I could hardly say no. The castle is stunning, and I'm sure you'll love it. Apparently, some rooms are haunted.'

'Don't put me in one of them,' Erin says, shivering melodramatically.

As we're ushered towards the table and take our seats in front of the sumptuous spread, I glance around the room. I'm so lucky, so incredibly lucky. I have amazing, generous friends, a successful husband and gorgeous children. Even my business is going well at the moment, despite all the economic instability. I've worked incredibly hard for all of this, eager to live up to the high standards expected of me, and for a brief moment, I bask in the success.

If I had known what Monday would bring, I might have indulged more. Drunk more champagne, laughed more riotously with my friends, accepted second helpings. There's always a before and after, that invisible line drawn in time, and we never know when it might arrive. For me, nothing would ever be the same after Lucia's glorious hen party.

CHAPTER TWO

I've still got a headache despite it being over thirty-six hours since Lucia's hen party. Yesterday was a write-off thanks to the hangover. I had hoped that drinking Bollinger all evening might reduce the effects of alcohol. Not so. I've definitely paid the price for over-indulging. This afternoon, I had a meeting that overran, and now I'm in danger of being late to collect Rosie from school. Albie, who has just started senior school, takes the bus after school, and walks – or rather lopes – the short distance from the bus stop to our home.

I park the car three streets away and jog towards the school gates. A crowd of parents and au pairs is already waiting, and I scan the familiar faces, hoping to chat to Erin or Dakota. Except there's something wrong. Whenever I smile at people I know, they glance away, frowns knotting foreheads. Eyes turn to look at me, narrowed. Women are staring and then turning their backs to me, whispering behind their hands. I glance over my shoulder, wondering if there's someone odd standing behind me. But no. I look down at my clothes; perhaps I haven't done my fly up or I've got a huge coffee stain down my front. I think I look all right. My cream trench coat is clean, and I'm wearing it over a navy trouser suit. It's weird. Really weird.

I catch sight of Dakota wearing a canary yellow jumper that offsets her dark complexion. Normally she's in a sharp suit, so she must have been working from home today. I try to weave between the waiting parents to reach her, but then the school bell rings. Almost immediately, flocks of children pour out of the gates. Dakota turns, and I know she sees me, except she immediately looks away and starts talking animatedly to a woman standing next to her. It's very odd and unsettling. I realise that not a single parent has said hello, or even returned a smile. It's like I've become an instant pariah, or worse, invisible. It's not like I'm one of the popular mums, but I have plenty of friends at the school gates and have got to know people as a result of having kids in two separate classes. What the hell is going on?

But then Rosie is at my side, dragging her school rucksack along the pavement. I heft it onto my shoulder and bend down to kiss her, except she deftly avoids me and strides on ahead with Tessa, one of her little friends, their heads bobbing together as they chatter.

'Tessa, come here, please!' her mother bellows over my shoulder. I turn to speak to Martina, whom I know reasonably well, but it's as if she's looking right through me. 'Tessa!' she exclaims again.

'Is everything alright?' I ask, but Martina cuts me off.

'We're in a hurry,' she says, grabbing her daughter's hand and tugging her away, her eyes skittish and looking everywhere except at me.

My heart sinks. What the hell is going on? What have I done that everyone is avoiding me?

I stride quickly towards the car, Rosie struggling to keep up with me. When we reach it, I fling her bag onto the back seat and hurry her inside. Once she's buckled up, I remove my phone from my handbag in order to charge it on the central console. And then I see it. Numerous WhatsApp messages from both the children's class WhatsApp groups, messages that are still pinging in, in rapid succession. I glance at them.

What the hell!

I can't believe this!

How could anyone do this? Glad I'm not on the list!!!

I want nothing to do with Kate Pedersen ever again!

I realise with a sinking heart that I must have done something, although what, I do not know. With trembling fingers, I scroll back through the messages, but there are scores and scores of them with several parents commenting repeatedly. What has happened? What have I done?

'Can we go, Mum?' Rosie asks.

'In a moment,' I reply distractedly.

And then I see the very first message. But it's not a message. It's a photo. For a couple of seconds, I can't register what I'm looking at. And then I let out a whimper.

It's my spreadsheet.

The spreadsheet where I listed the names of my friends and I ranked them from one to ten on various qualities, ranging from tardiness to sense of humour, attractiveness to common sense. My stomach clenches, and I feel nausea rising up in my gullet. I undo the seat belt, fling open the door and make it to the far side of the pavement just in time to vomit at the base of a hedge.

'Mummy!' Rosie screeches. There's nothing I can do to protect my little girl. When I stop heaving, I grab a tissue from my pocket and then look up at her, her little face pale with concern, eyes big.

'It's okay, darling,' I say, hurrying back into the car, slamming the door shut. 'I must have eaten something bad at lunchtime. Nothing to worry about.' But that's one of the biggest lies I've ever told my daughter, for deep down, I know that life will never be the same.

Perhaps I shouldn't have done it. No, of course I shouldn't have done it. In my gut, I know it's not normal to rank your friends, but it's not as if I'm the only one. I read an article just a few months ago about an A-list celebrity who told her assistant to only arrange meet-ups with friends she ranked highly. And it's nothing new, is it? Back when I was young, we had to choose our eight best friends on the social media app MySpace. Even earlier than that, when we first start nursery school, we're encouraged to find a best friend and then suffer horribly when our supposed best friend dumps us for someone else. As adults, we have to be selective, especially since most of us have such busy lives we simply don't have the time and emotional bandwidth to keep up with a large friendship group. And then there are the important events in our lives. Who makes the guest lists for weddings and hen parties? How do we choose one friend over another when selecting godparents for our children? We have friends who fulfil different needs. The person you choose to go out and party with is likely to differ from the friend you choose to call at 2 a.m. when you're miserable and need a shoulder to cry on. We all do it; make those judgments.

The difference is I wrote it down.

I like spreadsheets. I like personality profiling and databases. It's what I use for my work, and so it didn't feel like much of a stretch to use it in my personal life. Except that spreadsheet was meant for my eyes only. I've never shown it to anyone, not even my husband, Jared. Especially not my husband.

'Mummy, I'm hungry! Can we please go home!' Rosie wails from the back seat, and I glance at the time. If I don't get a move on, Albie will be waiting outside the house. I turn the engine on and we head back home, except I'm not concentrating. I don't move away fast enough at a red light, and the car behind me blares its horn aggressively. Rosie is talking, but I'm not listening, and then I have to apologise when she asks me the same question twice.

How the hell could this have happened? How could my private spreadsheet that not a soul was meant to see be leaked into the public domain? And what on earth can I do to mitigate the damage? Because right now, I look like a complete and utter bitch.

Back at home, I give Rosie a chocolate bar, just to keep her quiet. Albie arrives home from school five minutes later, and I give him some chocolate too. Terrible parenting, I know, and they both look at me as if I'm quite demented; after all, I'm normally so strict on diet.

'Go and do your homework, sweethearts,' I tell them both. 'I've got a couple of work calls to make.'

I hurry to our bedroom and kneel next to my side of the bed, reaching under the divan mattress for the thin folder that I always keep there, hidden from prying eyes. It's exactly where I expected it to be, where I left it this morning. The Excel printout is slipped inside the folder, and I pull it out, tears pricking at my eyes. It looks untouched. The names of my closest friends are in the rows under the first column. And heading the columns across the page are the ten things I consider most important in my friends. The traits I've chosen are reliability, kindness, sense of humour, attractiveness (I know, I know), trustworthiness, ambition, positive energy, loyalty, empathy and intelligence. I've graded everyone on each trait and then given them a total score out of one hundred. There are a few hand-scribbled notes down the side of the spreadsheet because having a pompous husband or monster children impacts the overall scores. It's not like our friends are our friends in isolation. And the scores have changed over the few months since I started the spreadsheet. I shove the folder back under the bed and rub my knuckles into my eyes. I wish the floor would open up and I could disappear never to return, or best of all, that no one would know that this is my spreadsheet. But stupidly, I printed it out on my company paper with my name, Kate Pedersen, printed on the top left and our distinctive logo of Pedersen Domestic Staff Agency on the top right.

How the hell did this get leaked into the public domain?

With a trembling hand, I take my phone out of my pocket. There must be several hundred comments now from both the kids' WhatsApp class groups. Everyone I know has something to say, even if their comments are just astonished or vomiting emojis.

> Mil123: I can't believe that she's listed her closest friends!

> JemmaP: And she's ranked them so low. Poor Erin... Ouch.
>
> PhoebeStagers: Guess they're no longer her friends.
>
> JJWithers: Unbloody believable! Glad I'm not her friend.

The only people I can't see commenting are my closest friends: the women that I've graded. Dakota and Erin are in the WhatsApp groups, but Lucia and Stella don't have children, so perhaps they're not yet aware of it. Hopefully, they never will be, except deep down I doubt that. Our lives are so intertwined, children or not.

I navigate to our private WhatsApp group, just for the five of us, the one that lights up several times a day with the incessant messages that we send each other. Except weirdly, I can't find it. It takes a few moments for me to realise that I've probably been booted off it. That my best friends are talking about me behind my back.

I call Stella. Lovely Stella, my best friend, who I graded 71 out of 100, the second highest on the list. She and I talk every day without fail. I don't know what I'm going to say to her, but I'll grovel and cry and beg her to forgive me. I just have to get her on my side. Except the call goes to voicemail. I try again, this time ringing on her mobile rather than through WhatsApp, and it cuts off almost immediately. It's possible that Stella is busy, but not likely. Normally she answers with a cheery, 'Sorry, babe, can't talk right now. I'll ring you back later.' Stella is a private chef, offering dining services to banks and city law firms, and most of her work is in the mornings, preparing five-course lunches. She's rarely busy at this time of day. If she has got some major event on, which seems to be increasingly rare, I'd certainly know about it.

I try calling Lucia, but she also doesn't answer. And now I'm not sure what to do. I type out a message to Erin, my brittle, barely keeping-it-together friend struggling with her boisterous twin boys. I know without looking that I scored Erin the lowest. A mere 43 out of 100 if I recall correctly. But everything I write sounds trite, as if I'm making an excuse for myself, trying to wriggle my way out of this horrible mess. In the end, I delete the whole long message and just type two words.

> I'm sorry

I press send before I can overthink it. I watch as the ticks turn blue and I wait. She's read the message, but there are no blinking dots, nothing to suggest that she's sending me a message back.

By the time Jared comes home from work, I'm in a complete state. I fed the kids a pizza from the freezer and ice cream with some chopped-up fruit. A far cry from my normal home-cooked meals. Both the children picked up on my nervous disposition, the way I tore at the side of a nail with my teeth, making specks of blood appear.

'That's gross, Mum,' Rosie said, turning up her nose. If it's possible, Albie was even more sullen and unresponsive than normal. I literally have no idea how he's doing at his new school. I had hoped that the descent into teenage behaviour might be gradual, but it's as if with every passing week he becomes less communicative. I'm starting to grieve for my eager-eyed, bouncy little boy. After their supper, I let them disappear to their rooms. I attempt to make Jared and me some food, but I'm distracted by all the messages about me, which have now moved onto Facebook, and I burn the rice. It takes every iota of willpower I have, but I turn off my phone.

Jared is a partner in a venture capital firm, which means several things. He earns obscene sums of money; he works literally every hour except for when he's playing golf (although I'm pretty sure he's still working when he's playing), and he's ridiculously ambitious not just for himself but for the rest of us. Jared is a perfectionist and your typical A-type personality. In the early years of our marriage, I loved that about him. His ambition and high standards were intoxicating. I felt so proud that this handsome, confident, incredibly ambitious man chose me to be his life partner. He supported me when I set up my business, and even today, we have our deepest conversations when we're discussing my balance sheet or when he's about to close a major business deal. It's what fires him up. But it's also exhausting being around him. Yes, he's critical and occasionally even mean. He takes me for granted and does next to nothing in our house, but when he notices me, I feel like the most desired woman in the world. And to cap it, he is an extraordinary lover, or at least he used to be, because I can't actually remember the last time we made love.

He dumps his briefcase in the hall and strides into the kitchen. His red tie is loose at his neck, and the top button of his white starched shirt is undone. Jared gives me a perfunctory kiss on the cheek as he always does and strides to the fridge.

'Good day?' he asks as he takes a beer out. Jared drinks beer only at home. When we're out, he's a wine snob, choosing the finest reds and impressing friends and clients with his extensive knowledge of viticulture.

'Not really,' I mumble. For a moment, Jared doesn't register my response. Normally we're both upbeat with each other and just repeat the same old words without truly thinking about them. It's only after he's opened the can and poured the beer into a glass that he notices my silence.

'What's the matter?' he asks, hovering by the door. I know he'll be itching to get out of his suit so he can take a long, hot shower.

'I've done something bad,' I say, my voice almost a whisper. I'm leaning against the granite kitchen island, my eyes on the ground.

'What do you mean?' Jared asks.

'Something I did has gone viral, and not in a good way.' I let out a little involuntary sob and try to turn it into a cough. Jared doesn't like weakness, and I'm dreading his response.

'What is it?' he asks, his fingers drumming on the side of the glass.

'I created a spreadsheet where I ranked my friends, and somehow, someone has photographed it, and now it's gone viral. All the mums at both schools have seen it, and Erin, Lucia, Dakota and Stella are ignoring me. Actually, worse than that, they've booted me off our WhatsApp group.'

'What spreadsheet?' Jared asks, his eyes narrowing. 'You need to show it to me.'

I sigh and nod. 'It's upstairs.'

I follow him up to our bedroom and bend down on the plush, beige carpet, handing him the folder after retrieving it from its hiding spot. Jared's initial reaction is to snort with laughter, but then something changes and he turns to me, dropping the paper onto the bed.

'Does Hamish know about this?'

'What's Hamish got to do with it?' Why is he bothered if Lucia's fiancé has seen it?

'Just answer, please,' Jared says. There's a stillness in him that's making me nervous.

'I don't know.'

'You need to call Lucia now.'

'Why?'

'Because they might disinvite us to the wedding. I told you about the huge business deal I was hoping to tie up with Hamish. His veterinary firm is ripe for investment, and the team has already started work on it. It's a vast, massively lucrative deal, and you could have just screwed it up!'

It takes me a moment to remember that Jared mentioned something about Hamish's chain of veterinary practices, something to do with a takeover. At the time, I had thought that was just Jared posturing, ever on the hunt for the next big deal. But perhaps it was more than that.

'Bloody call her, Kate!' he shouts at me, and I recoil. Jared rarely loses his temper, but when he does, it's explosive.

I dial Lucia's number, but it goes to voicemail.

'No answer,' I whisper.

'Leave her a message and tell her to call you back immediately.' Jared swivels around and walks out of the room, slamming the door behind him.

I simply don't understand who could have copied my list. Who found it hidden under my bed? Or has someone got access to my computer or phone?

I call Lucia again, and this time I leave a message. My voice sounds tremulous, and I'm finding it hard to swallow the tears. 'Hi, Luce, it's me. I'm so, so sorry. I assume you've seen the picture of the spreadsheet, and I know you must hate me. Honestly, I don't know why I did it, and obviously it was never meant for anyone else's eyes except my own. Guess it's just a reflection of my own insecurities. I hope you'll forgive me since the last thing I want to do is hurt the people I love the most, and that's you, Stella, Erin and Dakota, my oldest and very best friends. I'm so sorry, Luce. Please call me.'

CHAPTER THREE

Lucia doesn't call me, and neither do any of my other friends. I send them all grovelling, apologetic messages but get no response. In a way, I don't blame them. If the shoe were on the other foot, I'd be disgusted. As I lie next to Jared in bed, listening to his gentle snoring, I try to work out how my list got leaked. There are only two possibilities. Someone has come into our home and found it under my bed and photographed it, or someone has hacked into my laptop or phone. I think about the people who have access to our house, our bedroom in particular.

There's Pavlina, who cleans our house twice a week. She has a key and the alarm code, but she's been cleaning for us for nearly a decade. I trust her completely; I have to, since she knows everything about our family. The too many sleeping pill empty strips in our bin; the narcissistic messages left on the answer machine by my mother; the ready-to-cook meal wrappers pushed into the kitchen bin. Pavlina is mid-fifties, and I just can't imagine her looking through a folder and photographing a spreadsheet. She cleans for a couple of other families who attend the kids' schools, but I struggle to come up with a motive. She's always been discreet, never discussing the other households she cleans for, barely talking about her own children. Besides, I hardly ever see her. She lets herself into our house long after I've left for work in the mornings, and when I return in the afternoons, the place is immaculate.

Then there's Amara, who is twenty-three and occasionally helps with the children after school or babysits on the rare occasions Jared and I go out together. She's studying for a master's in nutrition and likes to test out her newfound skills on the children, preparing them meals that look like burgers and chips or chicken nuggets but are secretly packed full of healthy foods. She has grand ambitions of starting up her own food business one day. Amara is the youngest daughter of our neighbours, the Singhs, two doors down. They're a delightful family where everyone except Amara is a doctor. Being bright, young and highly computer literate, of course she'd have the wherewithal to upload and disseminate a spreadsheet, but I just can't see that it's in her nature. What would she get out of it? Besides, Amara hasn't been in our house for well over a week.

For a second, as Jared turns over in bed and inadvertently kicks my leg, I wonder if it was my husband. But no, that's a ridiculous thought. He was livid about the leaking of the list, worried about losing a business deal. And it really isn't his style. He doesn't do social media (except LinkedIn, where he has several thousand followers), and he certainly isn't on any school WhatsApp groups. My best guess is that my phone or laptop has been hacked.

I doze on and off, but by the time the alarm clock chimes, I'm feeling exhausted, not in the slightest bit ready to face the day. Jared has the annoying trait of being instantly awake and alert, and he strides to the bathroom. When I hear the shower going, I can't resist the temptation to turn on my mobile phone. I expect it to ping relentlessly, except it doesn't. Instead, there is just one message from a woman called Henrietta Gregson. She's the parent rep in Albie's class, and although I know her by sight, we've never spoken.

> Hello, Kate. I've decided to remove you from both of your children's WhatsApp class groups. I thought this would be best for your mental health. I suggest you don't search for your name on social media.
> Yours, Henrietta Gregson

What the hell? My mental health! I'm not sure how I feel about this. Is it worse knowing that everyone is talking about you behind your back or worse actually reading the messages? I think I'd rather know what they're saying, and now I'm feeling even more ostracised than I was before. And who gave her the right to make that decision? And telling me not to search for my name. It hadn't crossed my mind to do so, but now I'm tempted; it's what anyone in my situation would do.

'You're not up yet?' Jared says as he strides into our bedroom, buttoning up his starched shirt. There's a hint of disapproval in his voice. Judgement even, as if I'm some slouch.

'I'm getting up,' I say, swinging my legs out of our king-size bed. 'What's in your diary today?'

'The normal.'

He's obviously still annoyed with me, so I let it pass and make my way to the bathroom.

Two hours later, and I'm at my desk. Pedersen Domestic

Staff Agency, or PedDom as we affectionately call it, is based in an office on the second floor of a modern block at the Hammersmith end of Fulham Palace Road. When I first set up the agency a decade ago, I chose a smart central London location for my office, near Covent Garden. The single room cost me a fortune in rent and nearly crippled the business before it began. I quickly realised that mostly I, or my staff, would visit our clients in their homes, which largely were in the very smartest London residential areas: Knightsbridge, Holland Park or Hampstead. We weren't anywhere near Covent Garden, and our potential candidates weren't bothered where we were located, so long as they could reach us by public transport. Fulham Palace Road is an easy location for me, helped by the fact that I have two company parking spaces in the underground car park. The drive from our home in Barnes to the office is twenty minutes on a good day, although with London traffic, there aren't many of those. These days, PedDom has a staff of eighteen people, and my right-hand man is Cole, Stella's husband. He's our financial director and does so much more than just monitor the finances. But this morning, I've avoided him. I can't bear the thought of Cole having seen my list, of Stella sharing her disgust.

I've shut my office door and pulled down the blinds, something I rarely do. Normally, I would walk out of my office into the open-plan area where most of the staff sit, but today I place an internal call to Nigel, our IT guru. He manages our computers, the extensive database and CRM system.

'Would you mind popping into my office?' I ask.

A moment later, Nigel's head appears around my door. Mid-thirties, he's an aficionado of facial hair and is almost too hirsute. If he were customer-facing, I'd say something. But he's not. He sits at the far end of the open-plan office, his eyes permanently glued to his computer screen.

'Come in,' I say, gesturing for him to sit on the chair opposite my desk. I clear my voice before speaking. 'I'd appreciate if this were kept confidential.' Nigel sits up straighter. 'A private document of mine has made its way into the public domain, and I'm wondering if any of my devices might have been hacked. Would you be able to check?'

Nigel's bushy eyebrows rise almost to his hairline. 'We've got plenty of anti-virus software, and I'm not aware of any data leak.' He looks really worried.

'It's not to do with the business,' I reassure him. 'But would you be able to check my laptop and phone?'

'Of course. Has any money been stolen? Or client data?' He shuffles uncomfortably. He takes his job seriously and is forever instructing us to change our passwords and comply with every new regulation regarding GDPR and the like.

'No, don't worry. It's just a personal document, but can you check my devices anyway?'

'Sure thing. I'll be able to spot if you've got any viruses or malicious software. I'll also check for phishing emails and key loggers.'

I unplug my laptop and hand him my phone. 'How long will you need them for?'

'This morning. Is that okay?'

'Yes. I've got a new client meeting at 10, so I won't need them for a couple of hours.'

Nigel is walking out of my office when I say, 'Will you be going through my personal data?' I'm not sure I can cope with the embarrassment of Nigel judging me.

He swivels to face me, appearing affronted. 'Of course not. I'll just be checking for any spyware and the like.'

I thank him, and he hurries away.

I head towards the larger of our two meeting rooms, ready for the potential new client. It's been designed to look more like someone's living room than an office. I want both our clients and candidates to feel relaxed, so they're decorated in neutral tones, with beige sofas and sheepskin cushions in burnt umber and teal blue. Water is served in Dartington Crystal glasses and coffee in fine porcelain cups, items that our clients might have in their own homes. Fresh flowers are delivered twice a week and are always colour-coordinated and sweetly scented. We also have deliveries of petit fours, macaroons and exquisite miniature sandwiches from Fortnum and Mason. It's an enormous expense, but it sets us apart from our competitors and reassures our clients that we understand quality.

My assistant has printed me off a sheet with the name and basic details of the couple who are seeking a housekeeper and a nanny for their three children, all under the age of ten. They have a house on Egerton Crescent, a handsome curved street of large white stucco houses in Knightsbridge, where the starting price for a home is at least £10 million. They also have a weekend house in West Sussex and, no doubt, a home on the French Riviera or a chalet in Verbier or Gstaad as well. The woman's name is Melanie De Beaufort, and as I settle into an armchair, I remember the girl I shared a room with during my first term at university. She was also called Melanie, and unfortunately, she took an instant dislike to me. I never got to the bottom of her antipathy, but perhaps it was simply because I had arrived before her and bagged the best bed. That first term was miserable for me due to her incessant bullying. She'd invite friends over to our room, but the moment I walked in, they would fall silent and stare at me. If I dressed up to go out for an evening, she'd look me up and down and say things such as, 'Are you really going out looking like that?' I could never prove it, but food that I'd cooked and stored in the fridge would disappear, and once she poured a cup of coffee over both an essay I'd spent hours working on and the accompanying library book that cost me a fortune to replace. She told me I wasn't attractive enough to hook a boyfriend, that I was only at the university because my parents were rich and had bought me a place. She was quite a bitch.

If I hadn't met Stella, I'm not sure I would have stayed for a second term. And now, there's such irony. It's me who is the bully; it's me who has upset my friends and turned into the judgmental bitch. The thing is, despite all the trappings of success, the big house in Barnes, my business and family, I never feel like I'm good enough. I'm forever trying to keep up with Jared, who is the most ambitious and high-achieving man I've ever met. I try so hard to keep the perfect home, make sure the kids are doing well at school, bring in new business and be a good boss to my staff. But it's exhausting. There's never enough time, and the knot in my stomach rarely, if ever, fully unwinds. I know where all of this comes from, this relentless desire to be perfect. It's my parents. Yes, we all blame our parents, but mine were, and still are, utterly demanding and incapable of showing genuine affection. Mum was a judge, recently retired, and Dad had his own engineering firm. Their careers were far more important than their children, and my brother and I were packed off to boarding school at a young age. My self-worth hinged on my school grades, my popularity at school and approval from others. Yet that approval was always just out of reach, and I suspect it still is. I can justify why I created the list, why I feel the need to judge myself against my friends, but it doesn't undo the fact that I might have just ruined everything.

And as I welcome Melanie and Jeff De Beaufort, and take in his Rolex watch and her ten-carat diamond ring, I still feel like a second-class citizen. I know it's not healthy for me to be around so many wealthy, successful people, yet they are the ones I rely on for my business, and I can't walk away. So I smile and reassure them I understand exactly the type of person they want to employ, and an hour later, they have signed my contract and I have organised for one of my team to visit them in their sumptuous Knightsbridge house.

Back in my office, my laptop and phone are on my desk with a note from Nigel saying that he's found nothing untoward. I'm not sure whether that reassures me or makes me more uncomfortable. I suppose deep down, I'd hoped someone might have hacked my laptop because the alternative is far worse. That means someone has physically been into my bedroom and found the list. The more I think about it, the more the number of suspects increases. I've had friends over who could have nipped into my bedroom when they were upstairs using the bathroom, my parents visited at the weekend, and we've even had workmen in the house. A plumber visited ten days ago to fix a broken toilet, and a representative from the alarm company came to do its six-monthly service. I keep on returning to Pavlina and Amara, but struggle to believe it really could be either of them.

The rest of the day passes uneventfully, and I'm in good time to meet Rosie at school, but I don't get out of the car until the very last minute. I'm dreading facing the other parents. But then I see Stella striding past my car. I jump out and race towards her, tapping her on the shoulder.

She turns, and a scowl passes over her face.

'Can I have a word?' I ask quietly.

'Sorry, I haven't got time.' She turns her back to me, and my stomach clenches. I stand on the pavement, shocked, before eventually heading back towards the school. A moment later, the bell rings and, unusually, Rosie is one of the first kids out of the gates. Her cheeks are blotchy, and her eyes are red and swollen.

'What's up, darling?' I take her schoolbag and reach for her hand. Recently, she hasn't wanted to hold my hand, but today she grips it hard. Then she bursts into tears.

It isn't until we're in the safe solitude of my car that I understand what's happened. My little girl has been disinvited to Tessa's birthday party.

'I'm the only one in the class who isn't going,' Rosie sobs.

'Did Tessa explain why?' I ask.

Rosie shakes her head. 'Her mum says I'm not welcome. I don't know what I've done wrong.'

'Oh, darling,' I say. 'You have done nothing wrong.' I'm tempted to tell her it's me who has screwed up, that I've hurt some of the people I care for the most, but I'm not sure that she'll understand. 'You mustn't feel sad,' I say. 'Children fall out with each other all the time and then make up equally fast. It happened to me a lot when I was at school.' Except every word feels false.

'But it's not Tessa,' Rosie wails. 'It's her mum who says we can't be friends anymore.'

'I'll speak to her, sweetheart. And on the day of the party, let's go to the cinema and eat popcorn and have a lovely time.'

Back at home, when Rosie is upstairs in her room, I call Martina, Tessa's mum. The phone rings for a long time, and I wonder if she'll actually answer. But then she does.

'Kate,' she says, uttering my name as if it were ice.

'I'm just calling because Rosie is devastated that she's been uninvited to Tessa's party. I was wondering if this might be a mistake.'

'No, Kate. It's not a mistake.'

'I understand that I have offended people,' I say. 'And I'm very sorry about it. But please don't take it out on Rosie. This has nothing to do with our daughters.'

'Except it does, Kate. I don't want my daughter to be friends with a child whose mother is a bully. I don't want you or your daughter in my house. Goodbye.'

She hangs up on me, and I'm left staring at my phone in disbelief.

CHAPTER FOUR

I don't know how to make it better. I've sent grovelling messages to my friends, and I even considered posting a statement on my Facebook page apologising for the spreadsheet, except at the last minute, I decided it might be better to say nothing.

Rosie cried for an hour, and I simply didn't know what to say to her. I explained that I had done something stupid and that was the reason she had been uninvited to the party. She told me she hated me, and I had no retort. I hate myself, too.

Once again, this morning, I slinked into my office without talking to Cole. I'm sure Stella will have filled her husband in on my spreadsheet by now. Since I'm dodging him, I guess I'm both a coward and a bully. I'm busy working, and that at least is some solace as it takes my mind off the horrors of my private life. I've put together a shortlist of three candidates for the nanny position for a long-standing client. In fact, Isabella de Claassen is one of my favourite clients. She is married to a footballer, but doesn't have the pretension and entitlement that some of the other WAGs have. I genuinely feel she's permanently pinching herself that she is living such a privileged life. Over the past few years, the de Claassens' property portfolio has expanded dramatically, and I've provided the staff for most of their houses in the UK and abroad. She also has four children under the age of seven. Many women like her might gravitate towards a fully qualified nanny, but she's after someone who is completely down-to-earth and isn't bothered about formal childcare exams. The last nanny I placed with her is leaving after five years, as she's getting married and joining her army-fiancé in Germany. I'm confident that Isabella will like the three candidates I've selected, so after emailing her their CVs, I pick up the phone and call her.

'Kate,' she says, and then clears her throat.

'How are you, Isabella?' I ask.

There's a pause, and then she says, 'There's something I need to discuss with you.'

'I've just emailed the CVs of three candidates for your nanny position,' I say.

'Um, yes. I, ugh...' Weirdly, she's stumbling over her words, her Liverpudlian accent strong. 'I won't be using Pedersen Domestic Staff Agency anymore. I'm sorry.'

There's a long silence before I say, 'Can I ask why?'

'I heard of your indiscretion, Kate. How you rank your friends and how everyone knows about it. I am... well, this isn't the kind of behaviour I would expect of you or your firm. I'm sorry, but I don't want to work with you anymore.'

'But it was a mistake,' I say. 'Nothing to do with the business.'

'How do I know you don't rank your clients like that? It just makes you... well, untrustworthy. I'm sorry, Kate, but this is goodbye.'

I stare at my phone as the line is cut.

I can't believe that one of my best clients has ended our contract. And how the hell did Isabella de Claassen find out? Is it all over social media now? There's a sickening feeling in my stomach, and a clenching of my throat. Is it really possible that one stupid mistake might not only kill off my friendship group but also destroy my business? I get up from my desk and start pacing the office, running my fingers through my hair, trying to think straight. I might not have wanted to talk to Cole, but it seems I have no choice.

With heavy feet, I walk the short distance down the corridor and knock on his open door. 'Can I have a word?' I ask.

Cole is a good-looking man with mid-brown hair and kindly eyes. He has a penchant for brightly coloured socks, which often are mismatched. Considering his attention to detail – particularly for figures – is second to none, I find his quirky dressing amusing. There's something a little geeky about him, which I find endearing.

I shut the door behind me and sink into the chair opposite his desk.

'I've lost Isabella de Claassen as a client.'

He frowns. 'What happened?'

'She's become aware of the list.'

He raises an eyebrow.

'The list I wrote ranking my friends, including Stella. I assume she's told you about it?'

He lets out a snort. 'Oh, that.' He leans back in his chair, a grin on his face. I'm glad he finds it funny.

'Is Stella really upset?'

'She'll get over it. You know what she's like; explosive to begin with and then it's all forgotten a day later.'

'So you think she'll forgive me?' I sit up straighter as I feel a rush of hope.

'You rated her 71 out of 100, which was the second highest on the list, and she was only marked down for tardiness. And let's face it, being on time isn't Stella's strongest point. So yes, I'm sure she'll forgive you.'

'Thank heavens.'

'It's kind of funny, Kate.'

'Except most people don't think like you do. I have no idea how Isabella de Claassen found out about it. It's not like her kids go to the same school as mine.'

Cole turns to his computer and types in something. He peers at the screen and scrolls down.

'It's everywhere, Kate. All over Facebook, Reddit, forums left, right and centre, and unfortunately, your name is there for everyone to see. And...' he pauses for a moment. 'Bloody hell, these women are judgmental. They don't even know you.'

Cole is right, but then again, I have hurt some of the people I care about the most. I reckon I deserve some of the vitriol. 'I'm going to have to say something to the staff.'

Cole leans back in his chair and runs his hand over the stubble on his chin. 'There's talk about it out there. You know I'm not one for gossip, but even I can tell that the staff know about the list. Perhaps it's more serious than I thought.'

'Oh God,' I say. Can the humiliation get any worse?

'For what it's worth, I think it's hilarious. And it's the sort of thing that's big news today and will be forgotten tomorrow.'

'Not if we lose clients.'

'I suppose not. Look, I'll support you, whatever you decide.'

Ten minutes later, I've called a staff meeting and am standing in front of the doorway, all eyes on me.

'I'm sure most of you have seen the list I wrote, ranking my friends. It seems to be all over social media. I regret creating it and, most of all, I regret how I've treated my friends. It's a shame that someone found something private and put it into the public domain. I know it makes me look like a horribly judgmental person, and I'm sorry it's affecting your livelihood. We've just lost the de Claassens as clients as a result. I hope you will support me, and if any clients or candidates mention it, please say how desperately sorry I am for the hurt I've caused, or send them my way so I can apologise.'

The room is so quiet that when someone's telephone rings, we all jump.

'I'll let you get on,' I say, and return to my office, closing the door.

And now I wonder if that was the right thing to do. What if some of them hadn't known about it? What if I've completely lost their respect? Perhaps I should consider standing down as the managing director, let someone else step into my shoes for a few weeks or months? But has it really come to that?

I look at my phone, hoping that perhaps I've been reinstated to the class WhatsApp groups, but I haven't.

By lunchtime, I'm desperate to get out of the office. I grab my coat and bag and hurry downstairs, intending to walk to Pret a Manger to grab a salad. I've got my head down, weaving between other office workers out on their lunch break, when someone calls my name.

'Kate!'

I come to a halt and glance up. I take a moment to place

the woman in front of me. She's dressed casually in tight-fitting jeans and a navy anorak.

'It's Marilyn, from school,' she says, although I've already worked that out.

'Oh hi,' I say. Marilyn has a son in the same class as Albie and has been one of the school gate mums for the past seven years. Not that we're friends; barely acquaintances. 'How are you?' I ask.

'Actually, I wanted to ask how you are,' she says, peering at me.

'Yes, fine. You know,' I say, tensing myself, eager to walk away from her. Except Marilyn extends her hand and places it loosely around my wrist.

'I looked up your office address and wanted to reach out,' she says. She's staring at me earnestly from behind her thick, black-rimmed glasses. I suspect she thinks they make her look trendy, but they're much too big for her small face. 'Have you got time to join me for a coffee?'

I desperately want to say no, except her hand is still on my arm and she's looking at me so imploringly.

'You came to Hammersmith especially?' I ask.

'I thought you might need a friend, what with everything that's happened.'

She's right, I do need a friend, but this is weird. I'm not sure Marilyn and I have spoken a word to each other in three years.

'Just a coffee,' she says, as if she can sense how desperately I'm seeking to come up with an excuse.

'Alright,' I say eventually. 'There's a coffee shop just around the corner.' Only then does she let go of my wrist.

The coffee shop is small and already busy. I regret not

choosing Pret, but I was more likely to run into my staff there.

'What can I get you?' I ask as we queue at the counter.

'Oh, this is my treat. I'm the one interrupting your day.'

'Right, thank you,' I say, feeling awkward. 'Just a latte, please.' I've lost my appetite.

Carrying our coffees, we take the last remaining table at the back, near the toilets.

'So, how are you really?' Marilyn asks, staring at me over the top of her glasses. 'I'm so sorry you've been ostracised.'

'I probably deserve it,' I say, taking a sip of burning-hot coffee.

'No one deserves the backlash you're facing. People are so quick to pass judgment without really understanding what has happened. And I should know.'

I wonder if Marilyn is reaching out because she wasn't on the list. But then I recall an incident years ago when the boys were very little, how Erin accused Marilyn of flirting with her husband, Kieren, after some parents' do. How she was ostracised from our friendship group. How I went along with it.

I wait for her to continue, and after a couple of sips of coffee, she does.

'Do you remember what happened?' she asks.

I wish I could pretend I didn't, but I do.

'Your friend Erin said that I was making a pass at her husband. I'm sorry, but it was ridiculous. First, I'm happily married, and second, he really isn't my type. But it snowballed, and before I knew it, I was the school gate pariah.'

'I'm sorry,' I murmur.

'Anyway, I know how you're feeling. It's miserable being

on the outside, to have people turn their backs on you, to not get invited to evenings out where you're the only one not on the guest list. And it hurts your kids too. They sense their mama isn't liked, and the chances are that residual hatred is taken out on them too. They're not invited to birthday parties due to you, and how do you explain that to a six-year-old kid? All I'm praying for is that secondary school gives my boy Joey a chance to start over, to not be tarnished with the same brush he was at primary school. He's as good at footie as the next kid, but he's not asked to be on any team. And he's a bright boy, but I don't want him to pretend to be dim just to fit in. Let's hope that the kids from other schools who don't know him will give him a chance. We all need to be given the opportunity to reinvent ourselves sometimes, don't we?'

I study Marilyn with curiosity. It feels like she's needed to get this off her chest for some time, yet every word she's saying resonates. I'm going to be like her, and my little Rosie is already seeing the consequences of that. I think back to when Marilyn was banished from our friendship group, and I feel terrible that I never questioned it, that I immediately accepted Erin's outrage. Just because Marilyn wore skirts that were a little too short, that her cleavage was on display, that she came across as being 'not one of us' doesn't mean we had the right to shun her. Guilt lies heavily on me, knowing I was complicit in how she was treated.

'I'm sorry, Marilyn,' I murmur. 'I was thoughtless, and I'm sorry I hurt you.'

She sighs. 'It was a long time ago, but the feelings of worthlessness and being an outsider don't go away. I wanted to let you know that you're not alone.'

'You're very kind.'

'So what are you going to do about the list?' she asks.

I shrug. 'No idea. All I can do is apologise to the people I hurt and ignore everyone else. Any ideas?'

She shakes her head. I glance at my watch and realise I need to get back.

'Sorry, but I've got a meeting. I need to return to the office.'

'No problem. But let's stay in touch, shall we? What's your number?'

It seems churlish not to swap telephone numbers, so I read out my number and a second later she pings me hers.

'Perhaps you'd like to meet up one evening?' Marilyn suggests.

'Sure,' I say noncommittally, but really, I don't want to meet up with Marilyn. Just being around her makes me feel guilty, and beyond that, I want to make up with my old friends. Being associated with Marilyn will not help that. I know this makes me an even greater bitch than I already am, but it's the truth. I want my life to return to how it was two days ago.

I'm dreading collecting Rosie from school, and being the wimp that I am, I message Amara to ask if she might be free to do the school run. She replies almost immediately, saying she'll be at the school gates to collect Rosie. I promise to be home in time to make the kids' supper.

As it turns out, I'm finding it hard to concentrate, so I leave work early and head straight home. As I push open the front door, I see a small padded envelope lying on the doormat. My name is typewritten on the front in block capitals, and the envelope feels squidgy, as if it's filled with something malleable. I take it into the kitchen and use the kitchen scissors to open the seal. As soon as I do so, there's a revolting stench. I tip the envelope up and out slides a see-through plastic bag, like the ones I use to wrap the kids' lunchtime sandwiches. With disgust, I realise that it's filled up with dog poo. A card falls out too, with the word BITCH typed on the front in big capital letters. I gasp. I stare at them both, wondering who the hell would do something like this. But then the front door opens, and I hear Rosie's high-pitched voice chattering away to Amara. Hurriedly, I shove the bag of poo into the rubbish bin and hide the card and envelope under a pile of papers, then I wash my hands in the sink.

'Mum! Mum!' Rosie says excitedly as she runs into the kitchen. 'Amara wants me to be her model when she sells her food! I'm going to be famous!'

Amara appears behind her and laughs. 'Well, perhaps not famous, but I was hoping Rosie could be in my business plan if that's alright with you, Kate?'

'I don't see why not,' I say, relieved that Rosie seems happy.

'Do you need me to stay for a bit?' Amara asks.

'Not necessary, but thanks for collecting Rosie from school.' I take a note out of my wallet and hand it to Amara. 'This might sound weird, but have you been in our bedroom?' I ask.

Amara appears startled. 'No, I'm not even sure which your room is. I've been in Rosie's room and Albie's, but nowhere else. Is there a problem?'

'No,' I say with a smile. I've got no reason to accuse Amara, and I really can't afford to offend her. We say our goodbyes.

It isn't until later, when Albie is home and both the kids are in their bedrooms, that I take another look at the envelope and the card. There's nothing on the envelope to indicate where it's come from, no address or stamp, so it must have been hand-delivered. But who knows where we live? I sigh. Everyone who attends the kids' schools knows where we live, and the reality is, our address is easy to find. Jared registered a company he set up using our home address, so you only need to go onto the Companies House website to find it. The days of being ex-directory and hiding one's personal details are long gone. But if the envelope was hand-delivered, then the chances are our Ring doorbell has captured the person pushing it through the door.

I log onto my app and scroll back through the events of the day. And there it is. A person is approaching our door at 2.17 p.m. They're wearing a baseball cap and keeping their head down low so I can't see any facial features. A gloved hand darts forward and pushes the white envelope through the letterbox, and then the person swivels around so quickly, their head still down low, and jogs at speed out of the reach of the video cam. I watch it again, playing it in slow motion, but the person has been clever. There's no hair on display, and they're wearing a hoodie and jeans. From the shape of the person, I think it's a woman, but it's hard to be sure. It all happened so fast when the sun was shining directly at the door, casting shadows so that any identification would be impossible. I wonder if the person chose that time of day especially. But who would go to those lengths? Sure, I've upset people, offended them, but to post a threatening message like that through our door is outrageous and deeply unsettling. Am I scared? Not really, but it makes me want to scoop up the children and take them away from here.

Rosie scampers into the kitchen. 'When are we picking up my bridesmaid dress?'

I hesitate. I haven't spoken to Lucia, and I don't even know if we're still invited to the wedding, let alone if she'll still want Rosie to be one of her bridesmaids. Rosie has been looking forward to this for months. It's the first time she's been asked to be a bridesmaid, and we've already had two fittings for the dress. She's been counting down the days until the wedding.

'I need to have a chat with Lucia,' I say, trying to keep my voice light. The thought of telling my little girl that her dreams of being a bridesmaid might be over is too much to bear. Once again, I try calling Lucia. Once again, she doesn't answer.

CHAPTER FIVE

'We need to leave home by 9 a.m. tomorrow,' Jared says. He was so late getting home from work, we have barely spoken, and I haven't had the chance to tell him about the dog poo. We also haven't discussed 'the list' again, but that's the thing with Jared. If he's angry about something, there's a mini explosion of anger, but by the next day, it's normally forgotten.

'Tomorrow?' I ask.

'Please don't tell me you've forgotten,' he sighs, slipping under the duvet. 'The festival. I've discussed it with Kieren, and it's best we each make our own way there and meet up on site.'

I squeeze my eyes closed. I'd completely forgotten that it's tomorrow we're joining Erin and Kieren Medding at Goblins Music Festival. How could I have let that one slip? I'm normally on top of our diary, and I should have prepared the kids' belongings, put out their rainwear and their overnight things, yet I've done nothing. This has been on the calendar for nearly a year, and under normal circumstances, Erin and I would have spoken repeatedly to finalise the plans. Except she hasn't returned my calls, and even the kids seem to have forgotten about it.

'Yes, of course,' I say to Jared. I won't be telling him I've forgotten. Instead, I'll have to get up extra early and make sure we're ready.

'I trust you've made up with Erin, apologised to her for the mess you created with the list.'

'For God's sake, Jared. You're meant to be on my side. I've already said I'm sorry, and hopefully this weekend will allow us to paper over the cracks in our friendship.'

He grunts and turns off his bedside light.

'Jared,' I say softly, hoping we can continue the conversation, but my husband is already asleep. How does he do that? Fall asleep the moment his head hits the pillow.

I sleep badly again. I'm going over and over who might have leaked the list; how I can repair our friendships; and who might have shoved that horrible envelope through our front door. I know I've upset people, but to do something like that is completely over the top.

By the time it's 9 a.m., I've packed all of our overnight bags into Jared's Audi, and the kids are bouncing with excitement, ready to go. It seems like it's only me who lacks energy.

Jared switches on Spotify, and the kids are both listening to music on their phones. I've resisted their demands to watch films on iPads in the car, and sometimes I feel bad that I'm so much stricter with my kids than parents of friends are. The journey south is uneventful, and ninety minutes later, we're entering the gates into a vast field. I am relieved to see that they have already erected the teepees as we pull up next to our designated pitch. Jared is great at many things, but DIY and putting up tents aren't his thing.

'Is that where we're staying?' Rosie points excitedly at the white teepee. 'Are we all sleeping together with Teddy and Seth too?'

'No, silly,' Albie says. 'Teddy and Seth will sleep with their parents. We're in there with Mum and Dad.'

As if on cue, a Range Rover pulls up alongside us, and Kieren sounds his horn, as if we didn't already know they'd arrived. The boys are waving frantically.

I'm the last to get out of the car, and I note Erin is too. I steel myself and climb out, then walk around to their car. Kieren is patting Jared on the back and then he's leaning down to give me a kiss on the cheek. Clearly, he's forgiven me for the list, or perhaps he doesn't know about it.

'Who's excited?' he asks the kids. Even Albie, who is increasingly glum and introverted, has a big smile on his face. 'Right, let's get our things in the tents, and then how about checking out the first act of the day?' He mentions some pop singer I've never heard of, but the kids clearly know who he is.

'Hello,' I say awkwardly to Erin as she hauls a bag out of their open boot. She's wearing jeans, brown boots and a thick parka jacket, even though it's mild for the time of year.

'Hi,' she says, without looking at me.

I touch her on the back and she flinches slightly, but at least she turns around to look at me. I'm shocked at how pale and withdrawn she seems. Her hair is tied back in a ponytail, and it looks like it could do with a wash. She's not wearing any makeup and appears gaunter than usual. I wonder if she's ill. Normally I would ask her, but today it feels all wrong to comment on her appearance.

'I'm really sorry, Erin,' I say. 'The last thing I wanted to do was hurt you. I should never have created that list.'

'Yeah,' she says, still not meeting my eyes.

'Are you alright?'

She sighs. 'Just fine,' she mutters, although there is zero conviction to her words.

The day is long, and although the kids are having the time of their lives, I would rather be anywhere except here. There are music acts, magic and puppet shows for the children, and numerous stands, some selling rubbish, others offering activities normally found at fetes and fairs. The kids try archery, and Albie is surprisingly good at it. They go on a small rollercoaster and eat kebabs and candyfloss, which makes them hyper and silly. The place is heaving with families, and no one seems bothered by the light drizzle that starts later in the afternoon. By 6 p.m., there's nothing I want to do more than return to our tent for some peace and quiet, but the children still seem to have boundless energy. I've tried speaking to Erin, bringing up the list again, but she shuts me down, and our conversation is stilted and relates just to the activities here at the festival. I'm worried about her. She seems even more down than usual. Erin has never admitted it, but I know she's been struggling with depression for years. I've seen the strips of tablets in her bathroom (and yes, I was snooping), and once she told me she sees a therapist every week but then rapidly changed the subject. I've never understood why she's tried to hide her mental health struggles, but she does, and so it remains the big issue that's never discussed.

The headline act is due to start any minute, so we make our way to the main stage, Rosie sitting on Jared's shoulders, the three boys chattering away. There are thousands of people, and it makes me realise how uncomfortable I am in big crowds. It isn't until we're inside the enormous field, several rows back from the front, that I realise Erin isn't with us.

'Where's Erin?' I ask Kieren.

'She's gone back to the teepee. Has a headache,' he says.

I wish I could join her.

An hour later, and the children are at last beginning to flag. We trudge through muddy fields and then have to queue for ages to use the stinking toilets and sinks. I swear to myself never to attend one of these events again. I'm cold, tired and would do anything for a long soak in my bath.

The light has faded, and Rosie can barely stand up from exhaustion. Back in our teepee, she falls asleep almost instantly, and even Albie drifts off quite quickly. I have to admit that the teepee is surprisingly luxurious, with proper mattresses for beds and thick blankets to drape over our sleeping bags. I sink onto the mattress, and Jared puts his arm around my shoulders, tugging me towards him. We lay there contentedly, and I allow myself to fully relax for the first time in days. I'm just dozing off when the canvas door to our tepee swings open.

'Jared!' Kieren is standing there in the low light, wearing a thick jumper over his pyjamas. His paisley-patterned trousers have been hastily shoved into his wellington boots.

'What's up?' Jared sits up in bed.

Kieren glances at the children and beckons him outside. Jared pulls on his Barbour jacket, and I grab my puffer coat, pulling it over my pyjamas, shoving my bare feet into my muddy wellington boots. We follow Kieren out into the darkness. To my horror, there's an ambulance parked behind our cars, its engine running.

'What's happened?' I ask.

'Erin has taken something,' he mutters. 'Can you look after the boys?'

'What do you mean, she's taken something?' I ask. Jared looks on uncomprehending, dazed from sleep.

'An overdose.' He speaks in a whisper. 'I think she's overdosed. We need to get her to the hospital.' Kieren, who is normally so unflappable, is trembling, his eyes huge in the darkness. And then I notice their two boys huddled together, their faces pale and scared, trembling in their matching pyjamas. 'Can the boys stay with you?'

'Of course,' I say, stepping forward and reaching out for the twins. 'Come along, you two, let's get you tucked up into our bed.'

'But Mum,' Teddy says, glancing back at their teepee.

Kieren bends his knees to talk to them. 'Mum will be fine. She's eaten something that disagreed with her, and she's got to have her stomach pumped at the hospital, but she'll be absolutely fine. I promise. You boys need to be good for Kate and Jared, okay? And I'll be back here in the morning.'

The twins don't look convinced, but I manage to steer them into our tepee. I can hear Jared and Kieren talking in low voices, and then there's the slamming of doors and the revving of an engine. Eventually, Jared comes back into the tent.

I walk over to him and stand on tiptoes to whisper into his ear. 'Is she going to be okay?'

'He thinks so,' Jared replies, but even my husband looks shaken, and my Jared rarely shows his emotions. 'Kieren will message me with updates.'

I get the twins into our bed, fortunately without waking our two, but of course there's no mattress for Jared and me, and we can't sleep next door and leave the kids alone. Somehow, we manage to haul one mattress from the Meddings' tent into ours, smearing the bottom with mud and grass cuttings.

'Are we meant to sleep on that together?' I murmur, eyeing the single mattress.

'One of us can sleep next door.'

'I guess I'd better be the one staying here,' I say. Jared doesn't disagree.

The twins couldn't be better behaved and, despite being known for their boisterous behaviour, are soon fast asleep. In fact, it's only me who can't sleep, tossing and turning all night, worry for Erin knotting itself in my stomach.

I must drift off eventually, because I'm woken by men's voices. I take a moment to work out that it's Jared and Kieren. There's a pale grey light seeping into the tepee, and the birds are singing. I sit up in bed and, as my eyes adjust to the daylight, I see that the four children are all still asleep. Soundlessly, I get out of bed, pull on some clothes over my nightwear and pad out of the tent.

'How's Erin?' I ask as I join the two men who are standing next to our Audi.

'She'll live,' Kieren says.

'Did she overdose?' I ask.

Kieren scowls at me, which is very unlike him as he's normally of a gentle demeanour. That's what makes him such a popular GP. I see a range of emotions pass over his face. 'The thing is, Kate. You knew Erin had depression, but your bloody list. Well, that has completely pushed her over the edge. She hasn't had a wink of sleep since it was made public. She's a sensitive soul, and this has cut her so deeply. Erin feels completely betrayed by one of her closest friends. I told her to laugh it off, that it speaks more about you than it does her, but when you're already in a dark place, it's not so easy to let things like that bounce off you.' He runs his fingers through his hair.

'I'm so very sorry,' I say, but Kieren has already turned away from me and is pushing back the awning into our tepee. Jared just stands there, shaking his head and sighing, as if I'm some small child who has just smeared crayon all over the wall. Kieren breaks the silence.

'Right, boys,' I hear him say rather loudly. 'It's time to get up. We're going home.'

If I were feeling bad before, now I wish the ground would swallow me up. Of course, I knew Erin struggled, but for Kieren to lay the blame at my door for her overdose is completely gutting. How can one stupid piece of paper cause so much misery? What I would do to go back in time and destroy it, or even better, never have created it in the first place.

We also leave the festival early, heading back to Barnes straight after breakfast. Jared explains to the kids that Erin fell ill and that none of us are in the mood to continue with the festivities. The kids moan and complain, but it isn't until we've turned out of the field and are on a straight road leading away from the rolling Downs that Albie lets out a cry.

'I've lost my phone!' he exclaims.

'Oh, for God's sake,' Jared mutters.

'We need to go back. It could be in the tent.'

'We're not going back,' Jared says, pressing his foot harder on the accelerator. 'We'll call up the organisers and get them to check the tepee. They're bound to have a lost property department or something.'

'But I need it!' Albie cries. He sounds close to tears.

'You need it to listen to music and play games on. That's hardly a necessity.'

'Don't you think we should go back?' I ask Jared quietly. 'It's an expensive thing to lose.'

'No, he needs to learn his lesson. We can claim for it on insurance.'

'So I'll get another one?' Albie asks, his voice brimming with excitement.

'No. You won't get another one. If you can't look after your belongings, that's your fault,' Jared says.

I feel sorry for Albie, but Jared is right. Our children are spoiled, and they need to learn to look after their things. I just hope that the festival organisers find the phone and send it back to us. Albie moans and sulks all the way back to London, and at home he rushes into the house, stomps upstairs and slams his bedroom door.

He isn't the only one feeling rotten. I'm missing my friends, Stella in particular. I send her another message. Under normal circumstances, I would call her, we'd talk about Erin and probably make our way to the hospital to visit her. Except these aren't normal circumstances. I've been exiled.

Stella and I have been close friends for such a long time. I remember walking along the lengthy corridor in my halls of residence, followed closely by my parents, my heart pounding. Mum was still giving me grief about my choosing to go to Durham University, set in the heart of the fairytale northern city with its stunning castle and cathedral. She had wanted me to study law at Oxford or Cambridge, and when I shattered her dreams by saying I didn't even want to sit the entrance exam, she was livid. Apparently, I was a terrible disappointment to her, a slouch for not trying hard enough, and she was still going on about it, even on that first day of Freshers Week as they dropped me off. Dad, of course, said nothing. I was the first to arrive and chose what I thought to be the best bed. As I was unpacking, my parents standing to one side, looking on disapprovingly, there was a knock on the door. I went to open it.

'Hello,' I said coyly.

The girl smiled broadly as she walked in.

'Hi! I'm your next-door neighbour.' At that time, Stella had very short hair, boyish looks, and heavy eye makeup. She looked nothing like my privately educated friends, and I was in awe. Mum, however, took an instant dislike.

'My daughter shouldn't be here,' she muttered.

I don't recall the rest of the sarcastic comments, but when my parents had left, Stella said, 'God, your mum is a real bitch. You poor thing.'

I loved her from that moment forward.

Stella didn't find university easy and barely scraped through her degree, but she was fun, a breath of fresh air, and we became the firmest of friends. We shared a house in our second and third year, and that's when she fell in love with cooking. We, her eager housemates, were all too happy to be her culinary guinea pigs. She worked several jobs to fund her way and saved enough to do a prestigious cookery course when she graduated. And that's how she found herself in fine dining and why she's now a private chef.

Stella and Cole live three streets away from us. Their house is modest compared to ours, but then it's just the two of them. Of course, we shared our dreams of finding the perfect partners when we were young students, but I guess we never talked much about children. But when Stella and

Cole got married and she announced they wouldn't be having children, in fact they couldn't have children, I was surprised. When I asked why, she muttered about a medical issue but swiftly changed the subject. True to her word, they don't have a family, not even a pet.

It gives me a sense of warmth and security that the five of us, who were such firm friends at uni, are still a united little group. Lucia is the only one who lives a little farther away in Battersea, cocooned in a luxury penthouse overlooking the Thames. With her imminent marriage, there's talk about her moving out of London completely, as Hamish's chain of veterinary practices is located all around the southeast of England. I don't see Lucia as a country girl, but then again, she might not need to be. If Jared gets his way, Hamish will sell out soon and make millions, and as Lucia travels all over the world for her work, I guess they could live anywhere.

Jared and I were the first to move to Barnes and were swiftly followed by Erin and Kieren. Dakota, a single mum to Violet, followed soon after, thanks to the childcare support Erin and I could give her, and Stella and Cole joined us three years ago. It makes our London living feel rather village-y, the way we're in each other's lives to such a degree. Or at least we were until the list blew up.

After lunch – which is a miserable affair as a result of Albie's sulking over his missing phone, and my worry about Erin – I ask Jared if he wouldn't mind keeping an eye on the kids. I want to go over to Stella's to talk to her in person.

I do not know if Stella will be home, but it's worth the short walk. I pick up a beautiful bouquet at the local grocery store (which is possibly the most upmarket and expensive grocery store in the country), and walk the short distance to Mallory Road. Stella and Cole's house is a two-up, two-down with a kitchen extension at the back, which they added shortly after buying the property. Cole made it clear that it stretched them financially, but Stella loves her new home and has spent hours stripping back and painting the windows and walls. As I approach, I see that she's pruning the plants in large pots that stand on either side of the pale green front door. She's tied a red scarf around her head and is wearing baggy jeans and a navy hand-knitted jumper.

'Hello,' I say with some caution in my voice.

She straightens up, and for a moment I wonder if she's going to tell me to take a running jump.

'I'm really sorry, Stella.' I proffer the bouquet of flowers, but the scent from the lilies makes me sneeze. It breaks the tension, and Stella sniggers. Relief courses through me, making me feel slightly weak.

'You'd better come in,' she says, putting down the shears and removing her gardening gloves.

I follow her through the house and into the large kitchen, which is crammed full of stainless steel equipment. 'Coffee?' she asks.

'Please.' I place the bouquet on the island unit and sit down on a high stool. 'Cole's not here?'

'No, he's out on a bike ride with some mates.'

'I just want to reiterate that I hope I didn't hurt you. Well, I know I probably did, but I'm praying you'll forgive me.'

'As you rated me 71 out of 100 and I was only scored poorly due to tardiness, I think I got off lightly. But what the hell were you thinking, Kate?'

'I just... It was meant for my eyes only. I'm sorry,' I bluster.

'I get that a lot of you is pretence. All that surface confidence and eagerness for success is just a facade and deep down you're still that little girl desperate for her parents' approval, but a bloody spreadsheet rating your besties?'

Stella's appraisal of me is harsh, but I have to admit it's true.

'Ouch,' I say.

She switches the coffee machine on, and it gurgles away. When the noise stops, I ask, 'Have you heard from Erin or Kieren?'

'No. Oh, weren't you meant to be at that music festival this weekend?'

'We came back early. Erin overdosed last night and was taken to hospital.'

Stella places her coffee cup down heavily on the counter, and coffee slops over the top. 'What the hell? Is she alright?'

'Yes, I think so. Kieren came back this morning and collected the twins. I don't know how long they'll keep her in the hospital. The trouble is, Kieren is blaming me. He said that she was vulnerable and that my list pushed her over the edge. If I felt bad before, now I feel like an evil witch.'

Stella pauses for a moment. 'Oh, come on, that's really unfair. I'm sure Kieren didn't mean it; he was just lashing out because he's scared. Did you give her the pills she OD'd on?'

'Of course not.'

'There you go. If anyone is to blame, it's Kieren. He's the bloody doctor. He should have made sure that his wife didn't have access to medication that she could overdose on.' Stella wipes down the spillage with a damp cloth. 'I knew she was struggling, but this is bad.'

'I know,' I say, 'and I don't know what to do.'

Stella takes my hand and squeezes it. 'It's not your fault, Kate. Really, it isn't.'

I smile weakly at my best friend, grateful for her support, but my gut is screaming that it is my fault and that I might have started a chain reaction that's going to create even more havoc. Yet there's nothing I can do to stop it.

CHAPTER SIX

As I'm a persona non grata, I ask Jared to reach out to Kieren to find out how Erin is. She's been released from the hospital and is now at home, apparently. So, on Monday morning, after dropping the kids off at school, I decide to visit her. I buy another bouquet of flowers and, with some trepidation, walk to her house. Unusually, the curtains are pulled across the downstairs windows. I hesitate, for that's not normal, and just pray that everything is all right. Forcing my feet to move up their path, I press the buzzer, my heart pumping a little too hard. I hope Erin will answer the door, or perhaps her mother, who often stays at their home.

Kieren opens the door. He's wearing casual clothes, a polo shirt and jeans, and this normally benign and compassionate man scowls when he sees me.

'I was wondering if I could see Erin and give her these,' I say, holding the bouquet out in front of me.

'It's not a good time.'

'Right.' I'm not sure how to counter that. 'Could you give

her these and say how sorry I am, and that if there's anything I can do, anything at all, she mustn't hesitate to reach out.'

'She's already upset, Kate, so I think it's best you stay away for a while.'

'Do you need any help with the twins?' I ask, for whenever any of us has been unwell in the past, we've always stepped in to help each other.

'We're fine. See you around.' He moves as if to shut the door, and I shove the bouquet forward.

'At least take these, Kieren,' I say.

He nods then, his face softening slightly, and accepts the bouquet, then shuts the door in my face.

'Shit, shit, shit,' I mutter under my breath as I turn and walk down their short path to the pavement. I glance up at the house, and I'm sure I see the shadow of someone at the top window and the shifting of a curtain. For a moment, I wonder if Kieren is telling me the truth. Is he keeping me from Erin because that's what he thinks is best, or is this Erin's choice?

To compound my problems, Lucia still hasn't responded to my messages. We're just under two weeks away from her wedding, and with the final bridesmaid dress fitting coming up, it's seeming increasingly likely that we've been uninvited. I'm going to have to break the news to Rosie, and she will be devastated.

After an uneventful day at work, where fortunately I don't appear to have lost any further clients, I make my way to Rosie's school. As I walk towards the gates, I hope that I'm already yesterday's news, that I'm being ignored, rather than being stared at. That suits me. I keep my head down and pretend to type on my phone to avoid catching anyone's eyes. When I glance up, I see Marilyn heading towards me. What is she doing here? Her son is at the senior school, so there's no reason for her to be here. And I really don't want to talk to her, so I edge away and then pretend to be talking on my phone, having an imaginary conversation with a potential candidate. It strikes me I'm living up to my reputation as a bitch, but I can't bear the thought of Marilyn asking me about Erin. And then, to my relief, the children start pouring out of the gates.

Rosie is in fine spirits, telling me about an art collage she's working on. I've bought the ingredients to make a chocolate cake, and I'm hoping that a bit of food bribery, along with perhaps allowing her to watch a film, might distract her from the inevitable disappointment I'm about to inflict.

I tell her when we're back at home, sitting in the kitchen, before Albie has arrived.

'Darling, I'm sorry, but I've got some bad news. Lucia has changed her mind about her wedding, and she's not having bridesmaids anymore.' I'll deal with the fallout of my lie at a later date, but I don't want Rosie to think she's been singled out.

She stares at me with an expression of dismay, and then the tears well up in her eyes.

'But I so wanted to be a bridesmaid. Did I do something wrong?'

My heart feels like it's going to break, and I reach out for Rosie, pulling her into a hug. She's stiff in my arms. 'Of course not, darling. But sometimes adults change their minds. I'm really sorry.'

Rosie is sobbing now, as I knew she would, and there's nothing I can do to make it better. 'We'll do something special the weekend of the wedding, perhaps go to the seaside or Chessington World of Adventures. What do you think?'

'I just wanted to be a bridesmaid,' Rosie cries.

'I know, sweetheart, and I'm sure there'll be another occasion in the future.' I'm not certain that there will, though, because everyone we know is already married.

'Can I keep the dress?' she asks, sniffling now, her tears dampening my blouse.

'I'll ask Lucia,' I promise.

It takes a long while for Rosie to calm down, but eventually the cake baking followed by a Disney film seems to do the trick.

Albie had chess club after school, so he arrives back late.

'How was your day?' I ask.

He just shrugs and heads straight for the fridge. Our boy seems taller and more grown-up every day, and I feel a brief pang of loss for my innocent little lad.

'Just so you know, I had to break it to Rosie that she won't be a bridesmaid at Lucia's wedding,' I explain. 'So be gentle with her.'

'Why's she no longer a bridesmaid?' he asks.

I haven't actually told him about the list, and I'm not sure that I want to. Perhaps he's heard about it on the grapevine, but if so, he has said nothing. I think he's more obsessed with his phone-less state. I gave him a really old Nokia so he's able to telephone me if anything happens on his journey to and from home, and he stared at it in disgust, not even sure how it worked. I decide to change the subject.

'By the way, I've got the invitations to your party. You can hand them out tomorrow at school.' Albie's birthday is two days after Lucia's wedding, and although I've booked an escape room and sent out emails to all his friends' mums (fortunately, before the list was leaked), I haven't got around to giving Albie the physical invitation cards to hand to his friends.

'I don't want a party,' he says, turning his back to me.

'What?' I ask, taken aback. 'Since when don't you want a party? You're going to be thirteen. You need to celebrate.'

'I don't want a party,' he repeats.

'Have some boys been mean to you?' I ask, wondering if there have been repercussions Albie hasn't told me about.

'I'm not a little kid, Mum. I can stand up for myself.'

'I know, darling. But I thought you were looking forward to celebrating, to having a party in the escape room.'

'I'm not anymore. Please, can I have a new phone instead of a party?'

I hesitate before answering. 'I'll discuss that with Dad.'

With that, he hooks his rucksack onto his shoulder and leaves the room without glancing back at me.

I'm floored by Albie's change of mind about having a party. When we discussed it originally, Albie was all excited. He was going to be the first of his mates to have a party in an escape room, so what has made him change his mind? I decide to ask Jared to have a word with him, to uncover what's really going on. And regarding the phone, it's probably not a bad idea to give him one, as undoubtedly he'll be the only kid in his year who doesn't own a smartphone. But this time I'll put a tracker on it.

I finish making the kids' supper and call them to eat. Albie lopes into the kitchen and sits down at his place, hoovering up his food before Rosie appears.

'Rosie!' I shout. Except there's no answer. I hurry into the snug, where Rosie had been watching the film. Except she's not there, and the television is still playing.

'Have you seen your sister?' I ask Albie as I return to the kitchen with a brief pang of nervousness gripping my insides.

'Nope,' he says, as he carries on eating.

Rosie used to love hiding from us. When she was younger, she'd hide in her wardrobe or behind the sofa, only her giggles giving her away, or her inability to not reply when someone called her name. I hurry out of the kitchen and search the house, shouting for her. She always responds, even when she's in a bad mood or not feeling well. Rosie is an easy-going little girl, eager to please. I hurry upstairs to her bedroom, except she's not there either. With mounting panic, I run into every room of the house, pulling open cupboards, searching behind curtains.

'This isn't funny, Rosie,' I say, panic clear in my voice.

'Albie!' I shout down the stairs. He appears in the kitchen doorway, chewing a mouthful of shepherd's pie. 'I've lost your sister. Can you help look for her?'

'Cool,' Albie mutters. I have to restrain myself from retorting angrily. Cool, it is not. Rushing back into her bedroom, I stand still for a moment and look around. It's then that I notice Bunny is missing from her bed, that some of her clothes are tumbling out of her chest of drawers. I race into the bathroom and see that her toothbrush and toothpaste are gone. With sheer terror, I realise that our little nine-year-old girl must have run away.

One of the things Jared and I debated shortly after having the kids was whether it was safe to bring up children in London. It was the key reason we moved to Barnes, which we felt was a London suburb with lower crime rates. But it's always been at the back of my mind that living in the countryside might be better for the children. Every day we hear sirens, learn of knife stabbings or burglaries. And now the terror is hitting me straight in my solar plexus. I almost fall as I race down the stairs, through the kitchen and out to the utility room. The back door, which leads into the garden, is shut but unlocked.

'Albie!' I shout. 'I'm going outside to look for Rosie. Can you have another look around the house?'

I don't wait for an answer.

'Rosie!' I shout as loudly as I can. 'Rosie!' My voice sounds harsh and high-pitched. Our garden isn't big – about six hundred square feet, lined with borders filled with mature shrubs, and a studio room at the far end, which Jared uses as a gym. There's a small play area to the side, with a tiny Wendy house that is really too small for Rosie to use. She's been pestering us for a bigger den, except we don't have the space for it. I try the studio door first, but it's locked, as I assumed it would be. And then I crouch down and open the door to the little toy house, except it's empty, just full of cobwebs and startled spiders who have made it their home. If she's not in the garden, then has she actually run away? Terror grabs at me, and I wonder if I should call the police. I think of that envelope with the dog poo, and my mind goes into overdrive. What if someone has taken her?

Except then I spot the garden gate is slightly ajar. It's normally secured with a padlock, but the kids know where we keep the key, and Rosie is big enough to take the key from the hook and unlock it herself. I race out of the gate onto the footpath that runs along the back of the gardens. I'm still shouting Rosie's name.

'Kate!' I jump as my neighbour appears. Janice is seventy and lives two doors down. She's a lovely lady, an ex-academic obsessed with yoga who lost her husband a couple of years back. As her grandchildren live in Australia, she's taken a shine to our kids and is forever inviting them over to feed them cake and sweets.

'I've lost Rosie!' I exclaim.

'She decided to run away,' Janice says with a wry smile. 'She told me she was unhappy and asked if she could come and live with me for a bit. I told her yes, for a couple of hours maybe, but only if we got your permission.'

I feel like sinking down onto my haunches with relief. I grab the fence to steady myself. 'Thank goodness,' I mutter.

'It's quite impressive how prepared she is. She even packed her toothbrush and toothpaste. You've brought her up well.'

Not well enough, I think.

'How about she stays with me until 8 p.m., and then I'll bring her home? Is that too late for a school night?'

'No,' I say with a smile. 'I think that's a lovely idea. Thank you so much. But she hasn't even had her supper yet.'

'Not a problem. I can give her something to eat.'

'The thing is, she's upset because I've told her she's no longer a bridesmaid at my friend's wedding.'

Janice raises an eyebrow.

'It's a long story.'

'Fair enough. We'll see you a little later. And don't worry, Kate.'

'Thank you so much, Janice.'

As I walk slowly back into the garden, I feel absolutely terrible. My little girl ran away, and it's all due to me and the damned list. And although I can't put my finger on it, I sense that this is only the beginning. That the repercussions are going to run so very much deeper.

CHAPTER SEVEN

The next day, to my immense relief, Lucia sends me a text message.

> Are you free to meet up for a drink tomorrow after work?

Even if I weren't, I'd move heaven and earth to make sure I could meet her. I arrange for Amara to collect Rosie from school, and she seems thrilled at the prospect of giving the kids supper. Her eagerness dispels any thought that she might have snooped in our bedroom and photographed the list.

I'm early at the wine bar Lucia has chosen. We're in Battersea, wedged between independent designer clothes shops and boutiques selling Scandinavian housewares. At 6 p.m., the place is full of the in-crowd. Young people dressed in trendy gear, talking a little too loudly, drinking cocktails and swaying to the dulcet tones of a female singer who is playing 1940s music on a battered piano at the back of the room.

I order myself a gin and tonic at the bar and take the glass to a table next to the brick wall with a good view of the room. Lucia is late, but then Lucia is rarely punctual. It's one of the reasons I scored her lower than Dakota and Stella.

Fifteen minutes later, she breezes through the door and glides over to my table.

'I'm so sorry, darling,' she says, leaning down, gazelle-like, to kiss me on both cheeks. 'Bloody car got caught up in traffic, and it's been one hell of a day. Can I get you another of whatever you're drinking?'

'No, I'm fine, thanks,' I say, so relieved that Lucia is acting completely normally. She dumps her Prada raincoat and Mulberry bag on her chair and strides towards the bar. Lucia is wearing high-heeled crocodile-skin boots that come up over her knee, and a tan suede skirt that barely covers her upper thighs. She may be 38, but Lucia looks as fabulous as she always did, with her cream cashmere jumper slipping down to expose a bare shoulder.

She's back at the table swiftly, for Lucia can always push herself to the front of any queue. She's holding a glass filled with what looks like orange juice, and may well be. Lucia tends not to drink alcohol.

'I'm really sorry,' I say, as she settles into the chair. 'The list and everything. I know it's caused so much upset, and I'm gutted that I've hurt you and the other girls.'

To my relief, she waves her hand as if to bat away my statement. 'A lot of fuss over nothing.'

'Really?' I ask.

'If I took every comment made about me to heart, I'd have slit my throat years ago.'

I swallow hard, because clearly she hasn't heard the news about Erin.

'It's what comes with being a celebrity.' She makes air quotes with her fingers when she says the word celebrity. 'People want to tear you down. I don't know whether they're jealous or whether they think they can get away with it as they're anonymous online. But seriously, you should let it go. We all make mistakes, sending an email to the wrong person, bitching about someone and them finding out about it.' She takes a delicate sip of her drink.

'So you're not upset?'

'The only thing on my mind is my wedding. Is Rosie getting excited?'

I nod because I can't tell her that last night I told my daughter that she was no longer invited. Lucia is going to think I'm a complete idiot. Why didn't I just wait until she contacted me? Of all of us, Lucia is the busiest. She's probably been on a photo shoot halfway across the world and has just flown in via private jet with her phone switched off.

'Look, I know there's been a lot of upsets about your silly list, but we're all grown women and the others just need to get over it.'

'You're not bothered about the score I gave you?' I ask.

She laughs. 'You marked me low in intelligence and organisation skills.'

'Well, only lower than Dakota, who, let's face it, is the brightest woman any of us know. And a little lower than Stella.'

'Of course I should be lower than them. I didn't even get my degree. And I'm crap at organisation. Everyone knows that, and that's why I've got an assistant and why I've employed a wedding planner. It's not a big deal.'

'I'm so relieved,' I say. It feels like an enormous weight

has been lifted from my shoulders. Both Lucia and Stella have forgiven me.

'Did you know Erin tried to overdose on Saturday night?'

Lucia's already enormous eyes widen. 'No. That's awful. Is she alright?'

'I think so, but Kieren is blaming me and doesn't want me to see her.'

'Why's it your fault?'

'The list. She was really upset by it, apparently.'

'God, she's so fragile,' Lucia mutters, which I think is a little harsh, but I let it go. 'I'll get my assistant to send her some flowers. Hope she'll be better for the wedding.'

I say nothing.

Lucia leans forward, and I inhale her signature scent of orange blossom and something slightly spicy. 'Use the wedding to make amends with everyone. It'll be so special for us all to be together, and I'm sure any resentment will be quickly forgotten.'

'Thanks, Lucia,' I say. The relief is enormous.

It feels like a sense of normality has returned during the last few days. There have been no more threatening notes, and although I haven't been added back to the WhatsApp groups, the sense that I'm being talked about has receded. Perhaps I was worrying about nothing.

Our Saturday mornings are always hectic, but this one is especially busy as I'm taking Rosie to her final bridesmaid dress fitting and Jared is taking Albie to football club. My little girl sobbed happy tears when I told her she was going to be a bridesmaid after all. She promised that she'd never run away again, and I promised her I wasn't angry. I just wish I hadn't subjected her to disappointment in the first place.

Lucia's dress is being made by a leading dress designer in

Chelsea, but Rosie's dress has been sewn by a dressmaker local to us, chosen by Lucia – or most probably, Lucia's wedding planner. We ring the doorbell, and when the lady answers, Rosie literally cannot stand still. We're led up the stairs to the woman's sewing studio with a little fitting room adjacent. Rosie's bridesmaid dress is on a hanger, and it's the first thing we see. Rosie jumps up and down and claps her hands, and so she should. It's beautiful. The dress is made of blush taffeta silk, and it has tiny sequins sewn around the neckline and on the cuffs of the puff sleeves, which catch the light and sparkle. Fortunately, it fits Rosie like a glove, and she really does look like a little princess. She also has matching ballet pumps made of taffeta and dyed the same blush pink. Finally, the dressmaker produces a fine silk mohair shawl, which she wraps around Rosie's shoulders and fastens with a sparkling brooch.

'That's in case it's chilly in Scotland. Ms. Highsmith selected this especially.' She stands back to look at Rosie and nods with approval. 'When's the wedding?' she asks me.

'Next week.'

'Good. So, young lady, you're not allowed to grow this coming week because it all fits you perfectly.'

'I won't!' Rosie says as she dances around the small room.

It's a challenge getting Rosie to take off the outfit, and a further challenge to put the carefully wrapped garments in the boot of the car. Rosie wants the dress to be on the back seat so she can touch it.

'Shall we catch the end of Albie's match, and perhaps we can all go out for lunch?' I suggest.

'Yes,' Rosie says, clapping her hands.

The playing fields edge the River Thames and small sections of woodland. It's an attractive area, and easy to forget that we're in London. Albie has been playing with the club since he was seven and enjoys his Saturday morning practice and the chance to play games against other clubs. Jared encourages him and, to be fair to my husband, he's normally the parent standing on the sidelines supporting the boys. He's there this morning, no doubt hollering encouragement from the edge of the pitch.

I find a parking space, and Rosie and I walk towards the field. To my surprise, as we approach, the boys are standing still, huddled in small groups. The coach, a big man called Justin Last, is walking towards the line-up of parents standing on the edge of the pitch. I hold Rosie's hand as we stride towards Jared, but as we approach him, I realise that Justin Last is also aiming for Jared.

'What's going on?' I ask as I notice the grave faces of both men. And then I see Albie, who is standing away from the groups of other boys, his head hanging low, his legs all muddy. Justin turns to look at Albie and beckons him over.

'I need a word with you both,' Justin says, in a worryingly stern voice. 'Can you send Albie to wait in your car or somewhere?' he asks.

Albie approaches us slowly, his eyes on his feet. 'Come along, lad,' Justin shouts. Albie does as he's told and starts jogging towards us.

When he's alongside us, Jared says, 'Albie, take Rosie and go to the car.' He throws Albie the car keys, and Albie catches them.

'I don't want to go,' Rosie moans.

'Come on, Nosey Rosie,' Albie says, holding out his hand.

'Straight to the car and wait for us there,' Jared shouts after them.

'What's happened?' I ask. I notice that the other parents have moved away from us as if we're contaminated somehow, and it reminds me of how I felt at the school gates straight after the list was made public.

'Albie's been bullying one of the less athletic boys,' Justin Last says. 'He was laying into the lad, shouting in his face, and I got there just in time to stop Albie from throwing a punch. As you know, there's no place for that kind of behaviour in this club. We have zero tolerance of bullying.' He cracks his knuckles. 'I'm sorry, but I'm banning Albie for the next fortnight.'

'Did you see what happened?' I ask Jared, finding it hard to believe that Albie might have started any fight.

My husband looks pale and tight-lipped. 'There was some sort of altercation, but I was too far away to see what was happening. I agree with you, Justin, that it's totally unacceptable, and we'll be punishing Albie accordingly. Please pass on our apologies to the boy affected, and we'll make sure Albie apologises too.'

The coach nods and then turns and jogs back to the waiting boys.

'What the hell?' I ask as Jared starts striding towards the car. I struggle to keep up with him.

'That was completely humiliating,' he mutters. 'No bloody son of mine gets sent off accused of bullying.'

'But Albie wouldn't do something like that,' I say. 'You just accepted that our son was to blame without even questioning it.'

Jared stops still just as we're exiting the gate. 'Oh, really?' he says, with an edge of sarcasm. He's crossed his arms over his chest. 'It's no surprise that Albie is a bully.'

'What do you mean? He's a gentle boy, and has never been accused of anything like this before.'

'Well, you've set a great example, haven't you? Isn't your list a form of bullying, Kate?'

My breath catches, not just from the tone of Jared's voice but also from his words. In a way, he's right, except I never meant to be a bully. I never meant to hurt anyone. I follow him as he paces towards his parked car. He pulls open the driver's door and then lets rip at Albie. When Jared tells him he won't be playing any more football for the rest of the season, Albie bursts into tears. It's been a long time since I've seen our boy cry, and my heart bleeds for him.

'Rosie, you go home with Mum,' Jared says, as he climbs into the driver's seat. 'We'll see you at home.'

Rosie's lower lip trembles, but she gets out of the car. I take her hand.

'Why's Daddy so angry?' she asks.

I sigh. 'Albie got into some trouble playing football. It's nothing for you to worry about.' Rosie looks unconvinced.

I expect Jared and Albie to be home before us, but they're not. I just hope that Jared isn't driving around the block shouting at Albie. He's the sort of man who is cool and collected in stressful situations, but when something really triggers him, he gets extremely angry. Jared would never get physical, but he certainly knows how to shout. Poor Albie.

'Can I carry my dress?' Rosie asks.

'Probably safer if I bring it in,' I say. 'But we can hang it in your bedroom so you can look at it.'

As I push open the door, my phone pings. I carry Rosie's dress upstairs and hang the coat hanger over the top of her wardrobe. I look at my phone as I walk into Jared's and my bedroom, expecting it to be from Jared. It's not.

When I read the message, I let the phone slip between my fingers onto the carpeted floor.

> Did you get my present, bitch? I hear one of your poor friends tried to kill herself. I hope you're happy now. You don't deserve to have friends. In fact, you don't deserve to live. Watch your back! I'm coming for you...

CHAPTER EIGHT

The atmosphere in the kitchen is truly awful. Albie is sulking because Jared has banned him from football. Jared is furious that his son has been described as a bully. I'm utterly terrified about the anonymous text, so it's only Rosie who is keeping us together with her constant chatter and excitement about the upcoming wedding.

When I'm clearing the plates, I drop one. It smashes into smithereens on the stone kitchen floor, and honestly, it just reflects my mood. I'm nervous, unable to concentrate. I want to make things better for Albie, but he refuses to talk to me, saying the incident at football was not his fault, and no, he won't apologise to the other boy. In fact, he won't even tell me the lad's name. Short of contacting Justin Last, which I'm reluctant to do, I can't force him.

I wait until the kids have gone to bed before telling Jared about the messages. We're watching a psychological thriller on Netflix, although Jared doesn't seem that engaged, as he's constantly looking at his mobile phone, a smile edging at his lips as he types a message.

'Something's happened,' I say.

He takes a moment to look up and acknowledge my words, and I feel like swiping the phone from his hand.

'I didn't tell you, but an envelope was pushed through the door the other day, and it contained dog shit and a note that said, *bitch*. And then this afternoon, I got a text from a number I don't recognise.'

Now I have his attention. 'Show me,' he says. I pass him the phone with the message displayed.

'Imaginative,' he says before handing it back. 'It's obviously to do with your bloody friend ranking list. You've pissed off a lot of people.'

'I get that, but this is really disproportionate, don't you think? Scary and threatening.'

'Do you want to report it to the police?'

I sigh. 'I don't know. How did this person get my phone number and know where we live?'

'It's widely accessible online, isn't it? Or it could be one of your so-called friends.'

I shake my head vigorously. Stella and Lucia have forgiven me. Erin is in no fit state to do something like this, and Dakota, well, this really isn't her style. She's a high-flying lawyer, and I can't imagine for one second she would risk sending such messages. It has to be a stranger, someone who is offended. Or another mum from school. But why? Why would someone show me so much hatred when I've done nothing to directly upset them?

'I think it's a stranger, or someone on the periphery of our lives,' I say. 'I checked the Ring video cam and I think the person who delivered the envelope was a woman.'

'Could just be a delivery person and not the actual sender,' Jared says. 'The thing is, you stirred up quite the hornet's nest with this bloody list, but gossipy stuff like this will be forgotten soon enough. I don't think it's anything major.'

'I suppose you're right. It will be some random woman who has taken the moral high ground and wants to punish me for being judgmental.'

'Exactly,' Jared replies. 'And you have been a bitch.'

'You're supposed to be on my side,' I say, stung by Jared's words.

'I am. Well, most of the time anyway.' He throws me that cheeky grin that still makes my insides melt.

'Besides, we're going away, and it's not like this person will be at the wedding, so I really wouldn't worry. We can set the alarm at night if you like, and you remember to set it every time you leave home, don't you?'

'Of course,' I say.

'What are we going to do about Albie?' I ask.

Jared yawns and stands up. 'I've said my bit. It's over to you now. I'm going to bed.'

He hands me the remote control and slinks out of the room. I listen to him pour a glass of water in the kitchen and then pad upstairs. Switching off the television, I remain on the sofa. I'm glad that Jared isn't as spooked by the text as I am. I've searched the telephone number that the text came from online, but nothing has come up. I also tried calling the number, but the phone is obviously switched off, and I didn't leave a message. What twisted person would send a message saying that I don't deserve to live? And what worries me too is that the person knows Erin took an overdose. That most certainly isn't public knowledge, although I guess various parents from the twins' school might have heard the news, plus the Meddings' family and neighbours. In reality, that could be a large group of people, the extent of which I will never know. I wish I could share this with Erin, but I know that's the last thing I can do. I only hope that Erin will be at Lucia's wedding, and that I'll have the chance to make up with her.

Eventually, I head for bed. Jared is already asleep, but I can't settle. What if the death threat is the real deal? Could I really be in danger? I'm just an ordinary middle-class mum, a nobody. I might have upset some people in my job, turning down candidates for positions, letting go of an employee or two over the years, but I don't think I'm a bad person. Just a bit insecure, as Lucia rightly pointed out. Surely a list where I've ranked my friends isn't worthy of a death threat? In the darkness, my mind wanders to many horrible places. How will the kids cope if I die? What evil and painful methods does this anonymous person plan to use to bump me off? By the time it reaches 3 a.m., I take a sleeping pill and drift off into a welcome, dreamless sleep.

DUE TO THE SLEEPING PILL, I'm really drowsy, so Jared does the bulk of the driving. It's a heck of a long way, and as it's been ages since I've been to the Scottish Highlands, I'd forgotten what a lengthy journey it is. We leave early and avoid any traffic coming out of London or on the southern motorways, but hit roadworks on the M6 and then again skirting Glasgow. By the time we reach the scenic Scottish scenery, Jared is tired, so I offer to take over the driving. The kids have been watching back-to-back films on our iPads, all my screen-time rules relaxed for this long road trip.

It's early October, and the colours are changing. Vast swathes of the mountains are covered in burnished oranges and yellows, some hillsides still a vibrant green but mostly muted now. Trees are gloriously multi-hued in autumnal shades, dark granite outcrops jagged against the pale grey sky. We skirt magnificent lakes, the hills and mountains reflected almost perfectly in the water. At one point, I open my car window to breathe in the sharp, cold air, so very pure and different to the air we breathe at home in London. I only shut the window when the kids complain that they're cold. Guided by the SatNav, I follow the route, turning off an A road, onto a narrow, almost single-lane track. Jared is asleep, and the kids engrossed in their screens. It's then that I notice a large black SUV approaching from behind, driving considerably faster than I am. I put my foot on the accelerator to gain speed, but the road is winding, and I'm not used to driving Jared's Audi, even though it's sturdy and holds the road well. The big black car is right behind me now, its lights on full beam, despite the fact it's 6 p.m. and there's plenty of natural daylight. My heart pumps a little faster, and I grip the steering wheel. It's as if the SUV is trying to push me forward, making me drive more speedily.

And then I think of the text. What if the person who sent it is deadly serious? What if they are seated at the wheel of the vehicle behind us, or some hitman that they've employed is? Would they happily kill my whole family? There are steep rocks rising high above us on my left-hand side, and one wrong move would send us careering into them. Horrific images of the car toppling over, bouncing against the rocks on one side and then toppling into the lake on the other make me grip the wheel even tighter.

'Jared,' I say in a hushed but urgent tone, hoping he'll awaken without worrying the children. 'Jared!'

He comes to slowly, rubbing his eyes, stretching his arms outwards. 'What's up?'

'Behind us,' I mutter. But just as Jared swivels in his seat to look through the back window, I glance in the mirror and realise that the vehicle has gone. Did it turn off in that split second I woke Jared? I let out an audible breath.

'What's the matter?'

'Nothing,' I say. 'There was a car tailgating us, but it's gone now.'

Jared sighs heavily. 'You were probably driving too slowly.'

I grit my teeth. Where is my supportive husband? Why does he automatically assume I'm in the wrong? It makes me think. How long has he been so negative towards me? It's definitely ramped up since the list fiasco, but I'm not sure either of us has been very kind to the other for a long, long time.

'Were you worried it was going to bump you?' Jared asks rather mockingly.

'It crossed my mind.' I grit my teeth. 'It's been rather difficult not to think the worst since receiving the text.'

'I don't think that your anonymous texter has followed you all the way to Scotland. You're letting your imagination get the better of you. Think we'd better get a few drinks in you when we arrive.'

If the children weren't in the car, I would let rip. Jared and I need an argument to clear the air. On the whole, we do arguments well. Shouting at each other, letting out all our frustrations until one or the other of us walks out of the room. And then an hour or even several hours later, one of us – increasingly me, I realise – will apologise and all will be forgotten. Fortunately, we're not the type of couple to leave things to fester for days or weeks. At least we didn't used to be. Of course, I'm no psychologist, so perhaps this isn't healthy behaviour after all.

The road gets increasingly narrower and windier. Rosie says she feels sick, and the last thing I can cope with is her throwing up when we're just minutes away from the hotel. I drive slower, and the scenery becomes even more breathtaking if that's possible. The mountains are more jagged, sweeping down to shimmering lakes in stunning autumnal shades. A bird of prey hovers over the car, and Albie exclaims with excitement.

'Look! Look! It's the width of the car, and we can see the bird's claws through the roof window.'

'It's scary,' Rosie says.

'It really is beautiful around here,' Jared murmurs. He's right. I think how we choose to travel the world, staying in luxury hotels, yet the scenery in our own land is quite exquisite. And then a large sign appears up ahead:

Welcome to Glencraven Castle, Luxury Hotel.

'It's a proper castle!' Rosie exclaims as the car tyres crunch over the long, straight, gravel drive, which must be at least half a mile long. She's right. Glencraven Castle has numerous turrets, some square, others conical, some with unusual crow-stepped gables, all in a breathtaking baronial style.

'It looks like something out of a fairy tale,' Rosie says with wonder in her voice.

'More like a creepy castle,' Albie adds.

The building is made from dark grey stone, giving it an ancient feel, heavy and weighted in the landscape, both imposing and spectacular. Ivy, which is turning deep red, climbs up one of the end turrets. Surrounding the front of the castle is a moat with a wooden drawbridge across it. There are mountains on all sides with a lake to our right. As we approach the castle, there's a sign directing cars around to the side and a surprisingly small car park that is already almost full. The kids are out of the car before I switch off the engine.

As I step outside, I shiver as I inhale the fresh, cold air and shake out my tired limbs.

'Can we go inside?' Rosie is jumping up and down.

'Sure. I'll collect the bags later,' Jared says. Rosie reaches for one of my hands and one of Jared's, and we swing her between us, something we haven't done in ages. Even Albie, who was far from keen on attending this wedding, seems impressed. We follow a discreet sign that says, Reception, and then we're walking over a smaller drawbridge. Rosie stops to look at the moat, admiring some gliding ducks, and then Jared is pushing open the heavy, carved door, and we step inside.

The interior is dark, panelled in wood from the floor to the ceiling, and covered with antique spears. There's a scent of furniture polish mixed with burning wood and sweet florals. Large antelope heads peer down at us on either side of a vast stone fireplace, and I shiver. There are several oak tables scattered around the space, with lamps that let out a low glow. Our shoes echo on the ornate parquet floor as we all gaze at the extraordinary interior.

'Good evening!' A woman appears, wearing a starched white blouse and a kilt in dark greens and blues, her mid-brown hair held up in a neat bun. 'Welcome to Glencraven Castle. If you'd like to follow me to the desk over there, I can check you in. My name is Morag. Have you had a pleasant journey?' She speaks with a heavy Scottish accent and smiles broadly as she points to a large oak table with a computer screen pushed to one side. 'So you're here for the wedding of Lucia and Hamish?'

'We are indeed,' I say. 'Have they rented the entire castle?'

'Yes, they have. We only run weddings here, so all the guests are attending the nuptials. It makes it much more intimate.'

Morag types our names into the computer and asks Jared to sign a form, and then she produces the biggest key I've ever seen. 'Would you like to take this?' she asks Rosie, whose eyes are wide and sparkling in the low light.

'Yes, please,' Rosie says, her small hand barely able to clasp the key.

'That's a rather large key to be carrying around,' Jared notes.

'The keys are mostly for show. Guests attending our private functions don't tend to bother locking their rooms,' Morag explains. 'Would you like me to show you around?'

'Sure,' I say.

Morag shows us the ground floor areas first, although she explains that the great hall is off limits for now as it's being prepared for Lucia's wedding. There's a gym and indoor swimming pool in a modern extension with glorious views of the mountains, and I promise to take the kids swimming once we're settled. Most of the reception rooms are wood-panelled, grand in proportion but made luxurious and cosy through soft furnishings and filled with big comfy sofas and sheepskin throws.

'Now to your suite,' Morag says with a grin. 'You have

two adjoining rooms and a bathroom. The larger of the two bedrooms has a magnificent four-poster bed, and it's particularly special.' She turns towards Albie and Rosie. 'Can you guess why?'

'Queen Mary of Scots stayed there,' Albie suggests.

'You know your history,' Morag laughs. 'I'm impressed. But no, that's not the reason.'

We're walking along a wide corridor now on the first floor, our feet quiet on the dark red carpet, intimidating oil portraits of men and women in old-fashioned clothes lining the walls. 'This is it,' Morag says. 'Can I borrow the key?' she asks Rosie.

We've stopped in front of a large wooden door with the number 13 on the side. I'm not superstitious, but I suppose I'd rather not be staying in room 13. Morag slips the key into the big lock and eases open the door. She stands back to let us in. She's right, it is a fabulous room with an enormous dark wood four-poster bed. A sofa covered in tartan sits underneath a curved window with vistas onto the loch beyond. The view is like something from a postcard; almost unreal in its beauty.

'Can I sleep on this bed?' Rosie says, jumping up to sit on it.

'Your bed is next door,' Morag says. 'Do you want to see it?' We follow her through a door from the primary bedroom into a cosy room with two single beds. On the bed nearest to the door sits a doll dressed in the exact replica of Rosie's bridesmaid dress. She rushes towards it and cradles it in her arms.

'The doll is for Rosie, and you, Albie, have been given a lesson in archery. Lucia has organised this, so I hope you'll enjoy it.' Albie looks impressed. Although Rosie has outgrown dolls, the fact this one is dressed in her bridesmaid dress has certainly impressed her.

'What's so special about the room?' Rosie asks, cradling the doll.

'Well, where your Mum and Dad are sleeping is said to be the most haunted room in the castle. We've got a number of ghosts at Glencraven, but the ghost in this room is the cheekiest of them all. He loves to play tricks on our guests.'

I walk towards the window. The last bloody thing I need is to be sleeping in a haunted room. It's not that I actually believe in ghosts, and I've certainly never seen one, but with my nerves as shredded as they are, this is something I could do without. I consider asking Morag if we could move to another bedroom, but then I'd be making a fuss in front of the children, and I don't want them to pick up on my fears.

Jared makes a silly *whoo-hoo* noise, and everyone except me laughs.

'As most of the guests are settling in this evening, we're offering you supper in your room. Breakfast will be in the main dining room tomorrow morning and then, as you know, the festivities will begin. There's a schedule of events on the dressing table. Please enjoy your stay and don't hesitate to ring through to reception if you have any questions.'

When Morag has left, Jared says, 'Hamish and Lucia have really pulled out all the stops.' On the wedding invitation, they made it quite clear that this was an all-expenses-paid trip. They didn't want wedding presents either, just donations to a cancer charity and an animal welfare organisation. Jared saunters over to where I'm standing and puts an arm around my shoulders. 'What a view,' he murmurs.

After unpacking our luggage and sorting out our rooms, I take the children swimming. The pool is warm, and we're the only people using it. In fact, we don't see any other guests, and it feels as if we've got the castle to ourselves. If things had been normal with my friends, we would have probably done the journey in convoy or at least agreed where and when we were going to meet up for pit stops, but even Stella suggested nothing. I just hope that Lucia is right, and that I really can use her wedding to patch things up with my best friends.

We have a delicious supper in the haunted room, and although the kids go on and on about ghosts, I try to zone out. As night falls, the room feels really cold, which is strange, as the radiators are blazing out heat. Perhaps there are draughts coming through the windows, or perhaps it's just me feeling exhausted. I use the kettle in the room and fill up a tartan-covered hot-water bottle, clutching it to me as I try to warm up in bed. Jared and I make love for the first time in months, but it all feels rather perfunctory.

As normal, he's fast asleep within moments, and I'm lying there, my mind racing. I think about Jared and our marriage and how it feels like it's being kept together by the finest of threads. The business with the list has made me feel vulnerable, and I'm craving Jared's support, possibly for the first time. I've spent so many years trying to be perfect, the best mother, the ideal wife, the dutiful daughter and kind friend. So much energy has been put into making sure our children have every opportunity in life and that my business is successful. And it's exhausting. I'm exhausted. But more than that, despite my family and a wide circle of friends, I'm actually incredibly lonely. Perhaps I'm feeling this loneliness because for the first time, I'm allowing myself to be vulnerable. Actually, I'm not okay. I'm really sad and adrift. I think back over the years, the times when I've struggled, and the only person I've shared my concerns with has been Stella. I'm tempted to pick up my phone and message her, ask if she's arrived, if she feels like a midnight drink. I take my arm out from under the thick duvet as if to reach for my phone on the bedside table, except my arm instantly feels freezing. The little hairs are standing up. Hurriedly, I snuggle back under the duvet, edging closer to Jared to absorb some of his heat. Perhaps this room really is haunted, or perhaps I am unravelling.

CHAPTER NINE

Silvery light has flooded our room, and whereas I was so cold last night, now I'm too hot. I push the heavy duvet off me and see that Jared isn't there. There are chattering voices from next door, and I realise that he's up with the kids. I lie there for a moment, enjoying the solitude, and then I hear running water coming from the bathroom. A few minutes later, Jared appears, his hair wet and flat against his head, wearing a white, fluffy hotel robe that's too short for him.

'Sleep well?' he asks.

'In the end,' I say.

'Thought I'd take the kids downstairs for breakfast so you can get ready in peace.'

'Thanks, that's kind.'

'Mummy!' Rosie comes hurtling into our bedroom. She's already dressed in leggings and a pink sweater. 'I saw a ghost last night. It was a little girl with long blonde hair that went all the way to her bottom, and she was wearing a white nightie, and she sat at the end of my bed.'

'What?'

Rosie disappears again into her bedroom. 'What did you say, Rosie?' I shout.

But Jared is dressed now and tells the kids to hurry up, that he's taking them for breakfast, and after some clattering from next door, the three of them walk out of our bedroom door.

'See you soon, Mummy,' Rosie says. She's clutching her doll. And then the door closes heavily behind them and I'm left in silence.

I'm shocked that Rosie says she saw a ghost. She might have been making it up, or with our conversation about ghosts, perhaps she had a dream and hasn't distinguished it from reality. But it's strange, and it leaves me feeling even more unsettled. I have a quick, burning-hot shower and get dressed quickly in jeans and a thick jumper. Our first formal meal will be tonight for the pre-wedding supper, but for now, I'm hoping to explore the grounds and breathe in some fresh air.

I'm among the last to arrive for breakfast. The dining room is full, probably with a hundred people, with quite a few faces I recognise, although Lucia and Hamish are not present. Some are Lucia's old friends and family; others are famous faces from the modelling world. Stella, Cole, Dakota, Erin and Kieren are seated together, along with the twins. I note that there's no space for us. Instead, Jared and the kids are at a table for four on the far side of the dining room. I wave at Stella, who glances up when she sees me, nodding faintly, but she doesn't wave in return. The frostiness is evident, and I feel such sadness and regret. But I will not make a fuss. I'm going to be warm and friendly and apologetic to everyone. I'm determined to tough this out, not only for Lucia's sake but also for the children. This is going to be a glorious weekend for everyone.

After breakfast, we return to our suite. Albie is in the kids' bedroom and I'm in the bathroom, washing Rosie's hair. As we walk into their bedroom, I hear a knock on our door.

'Hi, Jared. Can I come in?'

'Sure, Hamish. This is a magnificent place. You've been incredibly generous. It's going to be an amazing wedding.'

'Let's hope so.' Hamish's voice becomes louder as he walks into the bedroom. 'Look, I just wanted to have a word with you about the business partnership. I don't want to lead you up the garden path, so thought I'd best tell it as it is.'

'Right,' Jared says.

'I don't think it's going to work out between us. I'm really sorry. Happy to be friends and everything, but the business deal is off the table.'

There's a long pause.

'Any reason why?' Jared asks eventually.

'You know, just the old rumour mill, and we don't want to mix friends and business, do we? Friendship is way more important.'

I know for a fact that Jared would disagree with that. He lives for the deal, the money, the achievements.

'Right. Well, thank you for letting me know. I'll stand the team down.' I can tell that my husband is absolutely livid. His voice is emotionless. I take a step towards the door between the two bedrooms and see that Jared is standing there, his back to me, his hands clenched tightly at his sides. Oh dear. Let's hope this won't ruin the weekend.

Hamish pats Jared on the shoulder. 'Enjoy the celebrations, mate, and let's go out for a beer when we're all back in London.'

I listen as Hamish walks out of the room and the door closes with a click. Then I wait a further couple of minutes before reentering our bedroom. Jared is pacing the room, his face white with fury.

He swivels to face me. 'I've lost the deal of the year, and it's your bloody fault!' He jabs his index finger towards me.

'Excuse me?' I say, stepping backwards.

'I know you heard that conversation with Hamish. The rumour mill, Kate. That's you and your screw-up, and now it's affected me. I've lost millions, not to mention losing face in the firm. He was going to use me to sell his veterinary practice and fuck it–'

'Please keep your voice down.' I gesture towards the kids' bedroom.

'Oh, just piss off.' He strides towards the bedroom door, opens it and lets it slam shut on his way out. I'm seething, but I need to keep it together for the children. I take a deep breath and walk back into their room.

'Right, let's go for a walk and explore the grounds. If we're lucky, we might see some deer. And Albie, you've got your archery lesson in half an hour.'

'What was Dad so angry about?' Albie asks. Not much passes him by these days.

'Just a business deal that's gone sour. Nothing to worry about.'

It's chilly outside, but we're all wrapped up warmly, and I like how our breaths make little puffs of steam as we walk. It's a perfect day, the sky the palest of blues without a cloud in sight, and once again, I marvel at the beauty of the landscape. We find the archery set up in a neatly mown field to the side of the castle, and Rosie and I leave Albie in the capable hands of a sturdy, bearded man wearing tweed plus fours.

'Do they have a maze here?' Rosie asks.

'I don't know, but let's have a look.'

We follow a path that leads into a French potager garden. It's beautifully laid out in geometric patterns, with vegetables and flowers that have died back. 'Look, Mummy!' Rosie is pointing at a bed of large, plump squash, and I follow her to inspect it.

'Hello, Kate.' I jump out of my skin hearing the female voice behind me. I turn around and, to my surprise, see it's Marilyn. What on earth is she doing here? She hasn't suddenly become a friend of Lucia's, has she? And I'm embarrassed because, despite Marilyn sending me a couple of texts suggesting we meet up again, I haven't replied. But it seemed a bit too eager to meet again within a week of our first coffee. I'm mentally making excuses, so I force a smile.

'How lovely to see you here,' I say and hope it doesn't sound too fake and forced. 'I didn't know you were invited to the wedding. Is your son here too?'

'No,' she laughs. 'I'm not a guest. Lucia asked me to do her wedding makeup.'

'Oh,' I say for I realise now how little I know about Marilyn. Did I know she was a makeup artist? And if Lucia is using her, she must be good. I'm sure I wasn't aware of that. It's an unusual profession, and it would have stuck with me. But it also makes me feel bad for not enquiring about Marilyn's life. 'Have you done Lucia's makeup before, for some of her shoots?'

'Actually, yes. I was the lead makeup artist on a shoot she did last month for a clothing ad. We got chatting, and she mentioned she was looking for someone to come up to Scotland to do the makeup at her wedding as her normal artist is off on holiday. I offered, and well, here I am!' She extends her arms and does an awkward jig. 'Such a gorgeous place, isn't it?'

'It certainly is.' I search for something else to say but, unusually, can't think of anything other than it's weird for Marilyn to be here.

'Have the ladies forgiven you?' She leans in towards me conspiratorially.

Rosie interrupts us, any interest in the growing vegetables already gone. 'Can I play with the ducks?'

'You mustn't get too close to them, but you can look at them,' I say. She runs off towards the moat. 'Don't go too far!' I shout. 'I need to be able to see you.'

'Well, I guess they must have forgiven you, because here you are!' Marilyn adds.

'We're taking baby steps,' I say. There's an awkward silence, which eventually she breaks.

'I must be getting on. I'm meeting with our beautiful bride shortly.'

'It's lovely to see you,' I say, as Marilyn waves and walks away. I'm not sure it is lovely to see her, yet I can't quite work out why.

Rosie and I are walking in through the reception area when we run into Erin and the twins. For the second time this morning, I feel strangely tongue-tied.

'How are you?' I ask, leaning in to give her an air-kiss, but she takes a step backwards, leaving me to hover awkwardly.

'Alright, thanks. I'm just taking the kids to the pickleball courts.'

'Can I go too?' Rosie asks.

The twins throw her a disdainful look, and I'm not surprised that they're unimpressed at being joined by a nine-year-old girl.

'You can watch,' I say. 'But you don't know how to play. Or you could be a ball girl, perhaps? Is that okay, Teddy, Seth?' I ask the twins. The boys shrug, but Rosie takes that as a yes, and Erin and I stand in silence as the children wander off.

'I just wanted to reiterate how desperately sorry I am. About the list, and causing you so much misery. I'm really glad you've recovered and are well enough to be here.' I feel like I'm wittering, unsure what to say.

'Yes, well,' Erin mutters.

'I didn't realise you...' I let my words fade away.

'They've upped my meds,' Erin states. 'And Kieren won't let me out of his sight. But yes, you hurt me, Kate. Really hurt me.'

'I'm so, so sorry. I don't expect you to forgive me—'

She butts in. 'You see, just by saying that, you do expect me to forgive you, and it's not that easy. It's going to take a long time, a lot of therapy, and we'll have to see where we end up.'

'Okay,' I say. 'I hope one day we can get back to where we were before.'

She stands completely still and says nothing. I break the silence. 'Shall we go and check up on the kids?'

Later, Rosie and I are back in our suite. Jared is nowhere to be seen, and Albie is hanging out with the twins somewhere. 'I think you should have a rest,' I suggest. 'So you're not overtired for tonight.'

Rosie agrees reluctantly. She peels off some of her

clothes and gets into bed, while I pull the heavy curtains to block out the daylight.

'I hope you don't see the ghost again,' I say, and then immediately regret my words for fear I've just planted the thought into her head.

To my surprise, Rosie sniggers.

'What?' I ask.

'Ghosts aren't real, Mum,' she says in a superior voice. 'Daddy told me to pretend to you I saw a ghost. Did you actually believe me?'

For a moment I'm speechless. 'Dad told you to lie to me about the ghost?' I ask.

'He thought it was funny. And it is funny, isn't it?' I can sense that Rosie is unsure about my reaction, worried that she's upset me somehow.

'Yes, it's funny,' I confirm. Except it absolutely is not. Not only has Jared encouraged our daughter to lie to me, something she did worryingly well, but knowing my current fragility, why would a loving husband and father do something like that? It's not even remotely amusing. In fact, it's extremely hurtful. If Jared is capable of doing something like that, what else might he be doing? An uneasy sensation settles in my stomach.

I try to distract myself, spending a long time getting ready. I take a lengthy bath, soaking in bath salts and trying to read a book, then I blow-dry my hair, carefully apply my make-up and slip on a navy satin dress that I've had for a long time but often garners compliments. I'm hoping that it fits in with the dress code for the night, which is clothes suitable for a reel. Jared point-blank refused to rent a kilt, so he'll be in a dark jacket and trousers with a tartan tie that I bought especially for tonight.

Both Albie and Jared arrive back in our suite together, and I awaken Rosie. She chatters incessantly, which makes up for the fact that Albie scarcely says a word and Jared is answering my questions in monosyllables. It seems ironic that we're here in this exquisite castle to celebrate Lucia and Hamish when my family seems to be disintegrating. As we leave the suite, I try to plaster a smile on my face, to conjure up a feeling of happiness, if not for me, for my friends. But it feels so fake, as if my smile is frozen on my face, as if there's someone permanently watching me, ready to take a fatal shot.

CHAPTER TEN

The pre-wedding dinner is fabulous. We're seated in the main dining room, so we still haven't had sight of the grand hall. The staff replaced smaller tables with larger ones, seating ten people around each. It's the first time I've seen Lucia, and while the rest of us were instructed to wear cocktail dresses, she is in a full-length evening dress, a red gown encrusted with sparkling sequins. A kilted man is playing bagpipes, which makes conversation a little difficult. I think of our late Queen Elizabeth, who apparently loved the bagpipes, but to me, the sound is deafeningly loud and droning rather than haunting and ethereal.

To my relief, we're seated at a table of strangers. At least no one is going to notice the tense atmosphere between Jared and me, and my husband can whitter on about his business, bigging himself up. The children are well behaved, and the two men sat either side of me are charming. I feel myself relaxing for the first time in days. The only fly in the ointment is that Jared and I haven't had a moment alone to clear the air. It's clear that he's still furious with me for the cancelled business deal, and I'm angry with him for encouraging Rosie to tell such a major, hurtful fib. What could have been a bit of silliness seems to have been designed by Jared as another way to wind me up.

After the meal, there's Scottish dancing. This is something I've been dreading. Along with the wedding invitation, Lucia sent us a link to some classes to learn some of the basic dances, such as The Flying Scotsman and The Dashing White Sergeant. Jared and I never got around to attending any classes, although I checked out the dances online. To my surprise, my husband is up and ready to dance as soon as the music starts. When did he learn how to do this? Jared doesn't even like dancing.

'Are you going to join Daddy?' Rosie asks, noticing that I'm making no effort to get up.

'Maybe,' I say. And then lovely Cole appears and stretches a hand out for me.

'Jared not on your dance card?' he asks with a grin.

'I'm not sure this is my thing,' I say.

'I'll guide you. It's not difficult; you just need to follow everyone else.'

After the first dance, which I just about manage, I find myself face-to-face with my husband.

'We need to talk,' I whisper.

'About what?' he asks. There's a coldness about him that I don't recognise.

'Us. The fallout, the lie about the ghost.'

'Oh, for fuck's sake, Kate. Just let it all go.' And then he disappears, swept up into the line of people preparing to start the next dance.

By 10 p.m. most of the guests are drunk and reeling more and more energetically.

'Time to go to bed,' I say to Rosie. She is flagging, her head on the table, and Albie is off somewhere with the twins. I reckon they can't come to too much harm wandering around the hotel, especially as the staff-to-guest ratio is so high. Just as long as they don't remove any of those spears from the walls...

After I've put Rosie to bed, I don't rejoin the guests. Albie slinks into the room just after 11 p.m., holding a phone.

'Whose phone is that?' I ask.

'Dad's. He said I can use it. The twins have gone to bed.'

'Ten minutes and then turn it off,' I say.

I also get into bed, taking the opportunity to read my book. When my eyes start to close, I switch off the light and drift off to sleep clutching the hot-water bottle.

I awake to Rosie jumping onto the bed. The sun is shining, and to my surprise, it's gone 8.30 a.m.

Jared isn't here. It looks like he hasn't slept in the bed. The pillow is still plumped up, and the duvet is pristine and crease-free on his side. What the hell? I grab my phone to check for a message from him, but there's nothing. And then I remember he gave his phone to Albie. Where did he sleep last night? Or perhaps the party is still going on? Would that really happen on the night before a wedding?

'Where's Dad?' Rosie asks, articulating my thoughts.

'With his friends,' I say. 'Get dressed and we'll go downstairs for breakfast.'

'Can I wear my princess dress?' she asks.

I laugh. 'Not until later. You need to keep it clean.' Both of our dresses are in their covers, but I take them out of the wardrobe and hang them on the cupboard doorknobs. I also remove Albie and Jared's suits and lay them on the beds.

Rosie is almost beside herself that today is the day. Albie looks at his suit disdainfully.

Downstairs in the dining room, most of the guests are already gathered, a buzz of excitement for the impending nuptials. I look around for Jared, except he's not there. I'm selecting cereals for myself and Rosie when Stella appears next to me.

'Are you alright? What's with the frown? You look worried.'

'I am a bit. Have you got time for a quick word after breakfast?'

'Sure.' She rubs my back, and I feel such relief that my best friend is back.

I settle the kids in a drawing room that is stashed full of boxes of games and puzzles and tell them to keep themselves occupied and I'll be back in a few minutes. Neither seems particularly thrilled, but I need the time to talk to Stella alone.

'Hey,' she says. 'Let's go into the little library; there's no one there.'

It's a small room, panelled with wooden bookshelves filled with rows and rows of antique-looking books. I breathe in the wonderful bookish scent. We sit in small tub armchairs close to each other.

'Jared is furious with me, and he didn't come to our room last night.'

'What? Why?'

'He didn't sleep in our bed, and I don't know where he is. He loaned Albie his phone, so I can't reach him.'

She pauses for a moment. 'I don't think you should be too worried. He can't have gone far, and I'm sure he'll tip up for the wedding. After all, that's the reason we're all here.'

'We've been arguing. He's absolutely livid about the list. Hamish and Jared were going to do some big business deal, but Hamish has pulled out, and Jared is blaming me and the rumours. You know how he is with his reputation. And there was an incident with Albie at football club, and he blamed me for being a bully.'

'Oh, Kate.' Stella sighs. 'He's over-reacting a bit, isn't he?'

'That's what I think, but my nerves are frayed. It's like I've upset everyone, but Jared is being completely over the top about it.' I don't mention that threatening note and text message, but it's weighing heavily on my mind.

'He'll get over it. And he probably crashed on a sofa last night after drinking too much.'

'Did you see him?'

Stella shakes her head. 'But a lot of the guys were drinking heavily, and when I left, they were still dancing even though most of the women had gone to bed. I wouldn't worry.'

I'm debating whether to tell her about the threatening messages when Rosie comes hurtling into the library. 'Have you seen my dress, Aunty Stella? And my new doll?'

'No, I haven't,' she says.

'Can I show them to you?'

I glance at my watch. 'Only two hours to go until the wedding. Why don't we go upstairs and you can put it on for Aunty Stella?'

'Yippee!' Rosie says.

We follow the children up the grand wooden staircase, past the swords and the creepy portraits, and head to our room. I'm hoping that Jared might be inside, perhaps snoozing on the bed, full of apologies for overdoing it last night.

Except he's not there.

Rosie and Albie disappear into their room, but it's only as I'm turning to close the door and glance at the wardrobe that I notice my dress. I bought it especially for Lucia's wedding – the second expensive dress I've invested in for her nuptials. It's pale blue silk with tiny buttons down the front and gauzy fabric that skims my ankles. I am pairing it with silver stilettos, a matching bag and a white feather shrug. Except when I left the dress hanging in its see-through plastic wrapper before we left for breakfast, the dress was hanging straight, and now it's crooked, drooping strangely down towards the left, as if someone has dislodged it from the hanger. Room service has been, so perhaps they knocked it.

I lift the dress off the wardrobe knob and remove the cover. And that's when I see it.

The dress is slashed right down the middle.

I gasp, letting it slip between my fingers. 'Oh, my God!' I exclaim.

Stella is with Rosie in the adjoining room, but she pokes her head around the door. 'Everything alright?'

'No, it's not! My dress has been ripped in two.'

'What?' Stella hurries towards me and picks up the dress, which I've let drop to the floor in a silken heap. 'Shit, Kate,' she says, as she runs her fingers down it. 'The fabric isn't torn. It looks like someone has taken a pair of scissors to it.'

I take another look and realise that Stella is right. This is not an accident. There's no way that perhaps a member of staff has stood on it by mistake and it's ripped. The dress has definitely been cut with scissors. This is deliberate. I sink onto the edge of the bed.

'It didn't get caught in the car door or anything, did it?' The tone of Stella's voice suggests she doesn't think that for one second.

'No, absolutely not!' My voice sounds faintly hysterical. 'Someone has done this.'

'Was your door locked?'

'No.' I let out a groan. 'That woman, Morag, said that as all the guests are known to each other, there was no need to lock our door. Besides, the key is so vast you can hardly shove it in your handbag.'

'So anyone could have walked in?'

My shoulders sag. Stella is right. Literally anyone could have come into our room.

'Is anything else missing or damaged?' Stella asks.

I jump off the bed and rifle through our things. Jared's suit is lying on the bed untouched. The dress I wore last night is hanging in the wardrobe. I check our bedside tables, and my Kindle is there, as is Jared's iPad. The pearl necklace and earrings I brought to wear with the pale blue dress are in my bedside table drawer. The only thing missing is my husband.

Rosie appears in her bridesmaid dress, and to my relief, it looks perfect. She does a twirl, and both Stella and I gush about how pretty she looks. When she returns to her bedroom, I say, 'Nothing valuable has been touched. This was done deliberately to upset me.'

Stella lets out a puff of breath. 'That's awful.'

I sit for a moment, my head in my hands. Is this related to the list? Probably. And that means it has to be one of my 'friends', unless it's another guest or member of staff. That's ridiculous; a stranger wouldn't have done this. No. This is targeted and personal. This has been done by someone with an axe to grind, and that means at the top of the list are Erin, Dakota, Stella and Lucia. Except I simply can't imagine any of them doing something as petty and unpleasant as this. There might be some resentment towards me, but not enough to cut up a dress. But then I remember Marilyn is here too. Could it be her? She's tried to be friendly towards me, but I haven't exactly been warm in return, and that could give her a motive.

'What are you thinking?' Stella interrupts my thoughts.

'I'm going to go to reception to see if anyone has asked which room we are staying in.'

'Good idea,' Stella says.

'Could you keep an eye on the kids? Get Rosie to take the dress off very carefully as she's bound to get it dirty and creased it if she keeps it on for the next couple of hours.'

'Of course,' Stella reassures me.

Morag is in the reception area, talking earnestly to a six-foot woman I vaguely recognise. A model friend of Lucia's, no doubt. The woman is complaining that her bath towels aren't large enough. On the assumption that she's been treated to this weekend, like we have, I reckon she should count herself lucky she's got any bath towels at all. I wait patiently until the woman leaves.

Morag turns to me. 'Mrs Pedersen, how can I help you?'

I'm impressed that she's remembered my name, considering how many guests are staying here.

'Has anyone asked which room I'm staying in?'

Morag tilts her head slightly and frowns. 'Not that I'm aware, and we wouldn't give out room numbers even in a private function such as this. Is there a problem?'

'No, it's fine,' I say, although it's anything but. 'You haven't seen my husband, have you?'

She shakes her head.

'Right. Thank you for your help.'

My footsteps feel leaden as I climb up the wide staircase. I don't think for one second that all these things are isolated. Whoever has slashed my dress has done this on purpose to upset me, to scare me, and they've certainly succeeded. And that means the sender of the threatening text might well be here too.

'Any joy?' Stella asks as I enter the bedroom.

'No. I haven't got a clue who did this. My fundamental problem is I have nothing to wear to the wedding. I've only got the navy blue dress I wore last night.'

'I don't have anything spare either,' Stella adds. Not that I could get into any of Stella's dresses. She's petite, just five feet four inches and barely a size eight.

'You looked lovely last night,' Stella says. 'I'm sure no one will notice.'

I disagree but say nothing. I don't think the feather shrug will work over the navy dress either as the sleeves are all wrong. I'll look a boring frump, but decide that is the least of my worries. Stella looks at her watch.

'I'd better get going if I want to be ready on time. Message me when Jared turns up, okay?'

I nod.

Five minutes after she's gone, the bedroom door opens and Jared stomps in. Other than the fact he's still wearing last night's clothes, he's not looking as exhausted and hung over as I had expected. In fact, he's fresh-faced, as if he's showered and shaved.

'Where have you been?' I can't help snapping at him.

'Good morning to you too,' he says sarcastically, edging past me and striding towards the bathroom.

'You didn't come back to the room last night and I've been left to deal with the kids by myself. Don't I get an explanation?'

He keeps his back to me, and I see his shoulders rise and stiffen. 'No, Kate. You don't get an explanation.' He strides into the bathroom, and I listen as he locks the door behind him.

The irony that today is meant to be one of the happiest ever days celebrating the marriage of Lucia and Hamish isn't lost on me. Because I think my marriage is unravelling at the speed of knots, and I have no idea what to do about it.

CHAPTER ELEVEN

The time has come.

The four of us descend to the reception area, and for a moment, I stop still on one step and take in all the glamorous people. Most of the women are wearing designer dresses with matching fascinators, carrying little handbags, hair carefully coiffured and their makeup flawless. Many of the men are sporting kilts with a sporran, along with dark jackets, waistcoats and ties to match their kilts. Their outfits are finished with long socks and shiny dark shoes. I wish Jared had made more of an effort and was similarly clothed, but most of all I wish I wasn't in yesterday's dress. I look dowdy, more like a member of staff than a glamorous guest.

But then I'm distracted by a commotion at the main door. There are two men, casually dressed, holding large cameras, talking animatedly to Morag and a couple of other hotel staff. I shouldn't be surprised that the paparazzi are here, but it seems rather distasteful to gatecrash a private wedding.

I hurry down the steps as the guests are now being

ushered forward. Jared and Albie mingle with the other guests, but Rosie and I have been instructed to stay behind. When most people have entered the baronial hall, I take Rosie's hand and we peek through the large open door. It's a breathtaking space, with dark wooden panelling on the lower half of the walls and high mullion-style windows leading up to a curved ceiling made from thick stones. Vast crystal and gold chandeliers hang from the high ceiling, and at the far end is the largest stone fireplace I've ever seen, with a fire burning inside, the sweet scent of pinewood and rose drifting through the air. The entire space is filled with pale pink and white roses, in huge pedestal displays on either side of the fireplace, along the aisle, between and on the backs of the chairs and trailing down the walls from the windows. The scene is the height of luxury and good taste. A harpist is playing songs I don't recognise. Guests are seated in rows, and Hamish is standing in front of the fireplace, next to a woman wearing a dark skirt suit, presumably the registrar. Lucia had told us that as neither she nor Hamish is religious, they would have a non-denominational ceremony. Hamish bounces from one foot to the other, fiddling with his buttons, repeatedly glancing at his watch while he chats quietly to his best man, who is dressed similarly in the same tartan. In the baronial hall there are two official photographers; one with a camera, the other with a video camera.

The two other bridesmaids and one page boy join Rosie and me, alongside Bella, Lucia's sister, who is her maid of honour. Rosie is the eldest of the youngsters, and she's taking her role seriously, excited for Lucia to emerge.

And now, here she is. She looks exquisite, wearing a strapless white silk taffeta gown, a string of diamonds around her neck, the long trail of her gown sweeping out behind her.

She's holding a large posy of blush pink roses, which matches the colour of the bridesmaids' dresses. Bella helps the children lift up the train. Lucia throws me a quick, rather nervous glance. I smile at her warmly and mouth, 'You look beautiful.' Then I tiptoe into the room, taking my place on the aisle near the back. I don't even know where Jared and Albie are sitting.

The wedding ceremony goes without a hitch, and before long, Hamish and Lucia are kissing, and everyone is cheering. It's a relief that Rosie has performed her role flawlessly, and I feel I can relax. A little, anyway. Champagne and canapes are served in the main reception area, with some of the hardier guests spilling outside. Rosie has been whisked off to a room to join the other children, accompanied by a professionally trained nanny who is entertaining the kids for the evening so that the parents can enjoy themselves in peace. I still can't spot Jared or Albie, but I see Dakota and make a beeline for her. Of the four of my friends, I haven't had the chance to talk to her directly, to apologise properly.

'Dakota,' I say, putting an arm on hers. She's wearing a fabulous orange dress made from taffeta, with an enormous bow on her left shoulder. When she sees me, she visibly flinches. This isn't good. 'I wanted to apologise in person for the list.'

'It's an embarrassing shitshow,' she says, with surprising hostility.

I'm taken aback. Even Erin seems to have mellowed toward me, so I'm not expecting this.

'I'm really sorry.'

'You know it's affecting me professionally as well. It's all over social media, and my name is so unusual here in the UK, I was easily identified as your supposed friend. I've spent years trying to build up my professional image, and this...' She throws out the hand that isn't holding a glass of champagne. 'This is destroying it overnight. I'm a laughing-stock, although thankfully not as much as you are.'

'I don't know what to say,' I add. 'Except I'm really sorry. Will you forgive me?'

'No!' Dakota says extremely loudly. Several people near us turn to stare. 'No, Kate. You can't just expect me to say it's fine when it really isn't.'

Heat rises into my cheeks. 'I didn't mean to hurt you.'

'Except you did. Who in their right mind ranks their friends and gives them scores?'

I wish she'd keep her voice down. A group of guests standing next to us are staring at me with curiosity. 'Shall we have a chat in one of the private rooms?' I suggest to Dakota.

'No, Kate. I've got nothing further to say to you. I need time to get over what you've done, and right now all I want to focus on is Lucia's happy day.' She turns her back on me and strides away.

'What did you do to upset her so much?' A man in a purple tartan kilt asks me. I've no idea who he is and have zero desire to engage in conversation, so I excuse myself and weave between the guests, hoping to find Stella.

But then we're called into the great hall again, where magically the room has been transformed into a dining room, with a long table up near the fireplace and circular tables filling the rest of the room. A string quartet, consisting of four young women dressed in long, tartan dresses, is playing, and if there seemed to be a lot of roses before, now they are everywhere. Candles flicker on the tables and on tall candelabras dressed with trailing roses and ivy. It's such a breathtaking sight. I check the table plan and find our names. Table number two, up near the front of the room. I'm honoured. As I approach our table, I see Jared is already there. He doesn't even look at me as I take my seat, and it makes my blood boil. I don't know any of the people on our table, although initial introductions suggest that most of them are Hamish's relatives.

The meal is delicious, starting with Scottish smoked salmon wrapped around a salmon pate. The main course is grouse, a poultry I rarely eat, but it is tasty. And then a bell rings, and a man seated at the top table stands up.

'Good evening, everyone, and thank you for attending the glorious wedding of Lucia and Hamish. Hamish and I have known each other since we were five years old, and I have so many stories to tell, I could bore you for several hours and definitely make Lucia regret her two-hour-long marriage. But I'll be kind and just stick to the less humiliating yarns. Luckily for me, I'm at the top of Hamish's friendship spreadsheet.'

There's a tinkle of laughter, but I freeze. *Oh, no. Please, no.*

'Some of you might know our blushing bride didn't fare quite so well.' He glances down at the card he's holding in his hand; his notes, no doubt. 'Lucia came second to last, scoring a paltry 65 out of 100. Ouch. And yet it goes to show what a forgiving and beautiful soul Lucia is for the author of that list is here amongst us.'

Right now, I want the floor to sink open. People are glancing around, trying to work out who the culprit this man is referring to is. If I felt bad before, now I feel like I want to throw up. My cheeks are hot and likely scarlet, and I glance at Jared, who is throwing me daggers. In contrast, his face is pale, his fingers white as they clasp a glass of wine so tightly,

I'm worried he's going to shatter the stem. Stella is staring at her plate, clearly uncomfortable too, and I'm just glad I can't see Dakota or Erin.

'Is it you?' Hamish's uncle asks me in a much too loud whisper. Now I can sense all eyes on me, and I have never felt so ashamed.

And then there's the scraping of a chair, yet I can't bring myself to look up.

'Come on, George, that's not fair,' Lucia says. I glance up now and realise that Lucia is staring at me and mouthing 'sorry'. Oh God, can this get any worse? 'Kate's my best friend and we've all forgiven her, so let's move on, okay?'

'Sorry, Lucia,' George says, bowing contritely. 'So let's talk about Hamish. He was a naughty little chap at school...'

I zone out. The blood is pounding so hard in my ears I literally hear nothing. I'm grateful to Lucia for supporting me and even more grateful that she's described me as her best friend, because I'm not sure I really am, but in doing so, she confirmed it was me who is the culprit. I feel like I have a target on my back screaming Bully, that whoever is gunning for me is now going to be supported by an entire army of Lucia and Hamish's guests. I just want to get out of here, except I can't.

The speeches seem interminable, and I'm the only person not rolling around with laughter as the best man, Lucia's father and Hamish himself tell joke after joke. When everyone finally stands to toast the bride and groom and then sits down again, relief makes me weak. I'd like to get up, take myself to the toilets and hide, except I know people will stare at me. Instead, I accept the dessert, which is a medley of chocolate puddings. I keep my head down, my appetite having deserted me.

'Mummy.' I'm startled. Rosie is standing next to me.

'What are you doing here, sweetheart?'

'The lady who's looking after us sent me to get you. Albie is sick.'

'What do you mean, sick?'

'He's throwing up. It's gross, and he can't stop. He's crying too, says he feels really ill.'

Jared leans across the table. 'Is everything alright?'

'Albie's ill,' I say.

'He's throwing up,' Rosie adds, a little too loudly.

'Oh dear,' Jared says, but I note he doesn't make a move to leave the table.

'I'd better find out what's going on,' I say, pushing my plate to one side and placing my white, starched napkin on my chair.

'Did you eat grouse?' I ask Rosie.

'What's that?'

'It's like a tiny chicken.'

'Yes, I think so,' she says, frowning.

I take Rosie's hand and let her lead me through the great hall and back to the reception area. I sense eyes on me, but hope that's only my imagination.

'Where is he, sweetheart?'

'In our room, puking in the bathroom. It's gross.'

'He can't help it,' I say. We hurry up the stairs and into our room, where a young woman is standing near the door, looking extremely worried.

'I don't know what's going on,' she says. 'Do you need us to call a doctor?'

'Has anyone else fallen ill?' I ask.

She shakes her head. 'No, only Albie. I think he might

have food poisoning but I don't know if he's eaten anything different from the rest of us.'

'Okay, let me check.'

Albie is in a bad way, lying on the bathroom floor, shivering with a sheen of sweat on his forehead. 'Poor you,' I say, stroking his forehead. I reach up and pour him a glass of water. 'Do you think you can keep this down?'

He says nothing, but with a trembling hand, takes the glass from me. And then I hear the ping of an incoming message on my phone, which is in my small clutch bag, placed next to the sink. As Albie sits up, I reach for the phone.

My breath catches. It's another message from a number I don't recognise.

> Poor, poor Albie. Has he eaten something that's disagreed with him?

At face value, the message isn't sinister, except it is. Who knows that Albie is ill? And how do they know? Has my boy been poisoned, or is this an opportunist? Has the anonymous texter hurt my boy? I try calling the number, but as before, it goes straight to voicemail. But this time I'm fuelled by fury and the overwhelming need to protect my children.

'What did you eat, darling?' I ask.

Albie shrugs. 'The same as everyone else.'

I suppose it could be a bug, but how would the texter know that? Would one of my friends hurt Albie and be so cruel as to send a message like this? Dakota is furious with me, but I just can't imagine her doing this. My gut feeling is that someone has done something to Albie, and I'm terrified.

'I'm going to call reception and ask them to call a doctor,' I say. 'When was the last time you threw up?'

'Dunno, about fifteen minutes ago,' Albie says.

'And do you still feel sick?'

'Less so now. I want to go to bed.'

I help Albie into bed and, as it's way past her bedtime, I cajole Rosie to get ready too. Except she point-blank refuses to share a bedroom with her sick brother, so I give in and tuck her into my bed. I pace the bedroom.

I want to go home. Clearly, there's someone here at Glencraven Castle who wants to harm me and my children. It's one thing putting myself at risk, but there's no way that I'm going to put the children in danger. I need to talk to Jared.

I try calling his mobile, but unsurprisingly, he doesn't pick up. I don't want to leave the kids, so I call the reception desk.

'I'd like to call a doctor. My son is ill.'

'Right,' the woman says. 'How serious is it? Just thinking if we need to call an ambulance.'

'No, it's not that serious. He's been vomiting. Is there a doctor nearby?'

She pauses for a while. 'I'm afraid that our normal doctor, who lives just five miles down the road, is on holiday. There's a locum, but he's a good thirty miles away, and being a Saturday night, I think it'll be a long time until he gets here. I can try though.' She doesn't sound hopeful.

'If you could put the call in, I'd be grateful, and if my son improves, then we can cancel the callout.'

'Right,' she says.

'And would you mind locating my husband, Jared Pedersen? He's probably on the dance floor.'

'Of course, Mrs Pedersen. What would you like me to say to him?'

'Please ask him to come to our room.'

'I'll make a call to the doctor and send a member of staff to find your husband.'

I wait ten minutes and Jared still hasn't appeared, and just as I'm about to call reception again, the hotel phone rings.

'What's up?' Jared asks.

'Albie has been sick, and I want to go home.'

'Just because the boy has overdone it and thrown up? He's probably got hold of a bottle of vodka.'

'It's serious, Jared. I received another threatening text message.'

'Saying what?'

I read it out to him.

'It's not exactly threatening, is it? You're over-reacting.'

That incenses me. Doesn't Jared care?

'Please, can you take us home?'

'Don't be ridiculous. You're being melodramatic, Kate. It'll just be someone having a laugh. Besides, I've drunk way too much to drive.'

'So I'll drive.'

'No. We're staying put. The party has only just started. Get the kids to sleep and then come back and join the fun.'

'You don't seem to get it. Someone is threatening me. Us. This is serious, Jared!'

He sighs loudly. 'You're getting hysterical. Albie threw up. It's hardly a medical emergency.'

I can tell that Jared is not going to budge. I'm disgusted with him, feel completely unsupported and let down. I hang up on my husband.

I look at my sleeping children. Albie's complexion is much better now, and Rosie is flat out, her arms and legs stretched in a starfish. They will not be happy if I tell them we're leaving, but at least they'll sleep on the long journey. I start packing up, putting the kids' belongings and my stuff into the big suitcase, leaving Jared's clothes hanging in the wardrobe. He can make his own bloody way home.

Fortunately, I get little resistance from either Albie or Rosie. They're both so tired, they want to sleep. After stopping at reception to cancel the doctor, I bundle them in the car and glance at the clock. It's 10.17 p.m. I plug in our home address and study the SatNav. Eleven hours of driving to get home.

CHAPTER TWELVE

We get home at midday. I literally do not know how I did it; driving so very far through the night without endangering any of our lives. It wasn't sensible, I know, but we stopped regularly, even if the children slept through most of the stops. I took the occasional catnap and drank cups of coffee bought from uninspiring service stations. To avoid any distractions, I kept the ringer turned off on my phone, but now we're back at home, I take it out of my bag. I have five missed calls from Jared, three text messages and four voicemails.

> Kate, call me.

> Kate. What the hell are you playing at? You've emptied the room out, taken the children, and I've just looked on my car app and can see that you're driving south. Call me.

> For fuck's sake, Kate. You've driven home and just left me here! I've had to hitch a lift off Erin and Kieren. How bloody humiliating is that? Your behaviour is completely erratic, and frankly, I think you need to see someone.

It hits me that not once has he asked after Albie. He knew Albie was sick, that I was worried he had been poisoned, and yet all he's thinking about is himself and how my taking the car affects him. How can he just shrug off something like that? What if Albie really was poisoned?

For the first time, I realise that there's a whole side to Jared that I don't like. Have I always known that but chosen to ignore it, or is this something new? Ever since the list was leaked, he's been unsupportive and angry. Of course, he has every right to be disappointed in me, but surely he should have moved on, forgiven me like Stella and Lucia have. Jared has always been self-centred, hugely ambitious and focused on his own needs, except I thought he loved me, that he just found it hard to show his feelings. But now I wonder. Am I married to a narcissist? Is this the tipping point for our marriage? Something has to give, and something has to change. There's only so much apologising that I can do, and it's Jared's turn to show some compassion now.

He arrives home early evening, announcing his arrival by slamming the front door, then stomping into the kitchen where I'm making supper.

'How dare you leave me behind in Scotland! What the hell were you thinking?'

I've had plenty of time to think about this and have decided to – as much as I can – remain calm and in control.

'You said you didn't want to leave, and I considered it in

the best interests of the children to come home. It wasn't like you were stranded. There were plenty of friends for you to hitch a ride with.'

'You took my car!' He's pacing up and down the kitchen now, increasingly agitated.

'It's our car,' I say. 'This house is ours. Both cars are ours. We're married, and we share our assets.'

'I've no idea what's come over you, but I don't like it,' he says. 'You've turned into this bullying bitch, and I don't recognise my wife. And I don't like the effect it's having on the children either. You've turned Albie into a bully.'

'That's ridiculous,' I retort. 'Albie isn't a bully. And honestly, Jared, the things that have happened over the past couple of weeks have just brought everything to a head. You and I have been passing ships in the night for months. No, years, probably. We're so focused on achievements, we're never in the present.'

'I'm perfectly happy with my successes.'

'But it's not just about business success or money. We need to be happy. Have time for each other and for the children.'

'That's hypocritical coming from you, the woman who rates her friends. I'm not the one sticking numbers on everything.'

'Please sit down. Let's have a calm conversation about everything.'

He rolls his eyes at me and ignores the suggestion. 'It's not possible to have a sensible conversation with a woman who is hysterical, imagining dangers where there aren't any. It's completely delusional to think Albie was poisoned. Have you actually asked him if he stole a bottle of vodka, as I bet that's probably what it was?'

'And the note, the text messages?'

'Here we go again.'

Why is Jared being so dismissive, so cruel? For a moment, I wonder if he has been sending the messages. But why? It makes little sense. He's ashamed of the list and wants to pretend it didn't happen. He's furious that he lost the business deal with Hamish. We might be going through a rough patch, but Jared has no reason to make me doubt my sanity.

'I think we should go to couples counselling,' I say.

He snorts with a fake laugh. 'You have to be bloody joking.'

'I'm not joking. I think it could save our marriage.'

'Our marriage? There's nothing wrong with our marriage, other than you've been annoying the shit out of me for the past few weeks.'

I'm disgusted with Jared's response. Can he really be happy in this relationship? The more I think about it, the more I realise I'm deeply unhappy. He's mean, unsupportive and now he's trying to gaslight me, to make out that our arguments are my fault. I pretend that my self-esteem is high. Oh yes, I'm very good at pretending, but it's not. I permanently feel like I'm not good enough, but if he's going to bring out the passive-aggressive behaviour, then he's chosen the wrong woman. I will walk away.

'I want to go to counselling,' I repeat in a low, calm voice.

'Over my dead body.'

A vein is pulsating on the side of his forehead, and there are red patches on his face, beneath the heavy stubble and rings under his eyes.

I take a deep breath. I know that what I'm about to say could be the first thread that completely unravels our marriage and potentially destroys our children's lives, but I cannot go on like this. 'If you're not prepared to make that investment in our marriage, then perhaps we should think about calling it a day.'

Jared stares at me, his eyes narrowed, and for one horrible moment, I wonder if he has it in him to hit me. He clenches and unclenches his fists and then he turns around and storms out of the kitchen. I hear his heavy footsteps running upstairs and then there's clattering from the floor above. His footsteps run back down again, and the door to the basement slams shut. Briefly, he returns to the kitchen and strides into the utility room, grabbing keys from the hook behind the door. He doesn't even glance at me as he rushes past. I walk after him and see that he has placed the suitcase that we used to go to Scotland next to his golf clubs by the front door. He takes two coats out of the hall cupboard and then picks up the case and the club bag.

'Where are you going?' I ask.

He doesn't reply. He strides out of the front door, slamming it behind him. I hurry into the living room, where I can see out to the road, and watch as Jared strides towards his car. Opening the boot, he puts both bags inside and then climbs into the driver's seat, not once glancing back at the house. After he starts the car, he slams his foot on the accelerator, and the car almost skids as he pulls away from the pavement. I sink down onto a chair, tears welling in my eyes. Jared has gone, and from what he's taken with him, it doesn't look like he's planning on coming home anytime soon.

I put my head in my hands and let the tears flow.

'Mum?' I glance up, hastily wiping my wet cheeks with the back of my hands. 'Mum. What's going on?' Albie asks. His face is pale, and his brows are knotted together. 'Where's Dad gone?'

'I don't know, love. Dad and I had an argument, but I'm sure he'll be back soon.'

'I heard you,' he says, his voice squeaky and weak.

'I'm sorry.' I reach out to take his hand, but he steps away from me.

'Is it my fault?' Albie asks.

'Your fault?' I frown. 'Of course not. Why would it be your fault?'

'Due to what happened at the football club. Dad was so disappointed in me.' His head is hanging low.

'It's nothing to do with that, darling. You did something you shouldn't have done, but it doesn't mean Dad and I love you any less. Grownups argue sometimes, and being away from each other for a day or two can clear the air.'

'Are you going to get divorced?'

'No. You have nothing to worry about.' Although as the words slip out of my mouth, I wonder. I always swore I'd never get divorced, never take steps to break up our family, but Jared and my relationship is unsustainable. I'd much rather we were both happy and divorced than bring up the children in an argumentative and tense home.

'It's my birthday tomorrow,' Albie says softly.

'I know, darling. And we're going to have a lovely day.'

I send Jared a message.

> Where are you staying?

I can see that he's read it, but he doesn't reply. I expect he's with Kieren and Erin, bitching about me.

IT'S MONDAY MORNING, the first day of half-term and, most importantly, Albie's thirteenth birthday. I stayed up after he went to bed and blew up balloons and put up banners saying, 'Happy Birthday!' I wrapped up his presents, including the new iPhone. And now his gifts are piled up on the kitchen table, along with a birthday cake in his favourite chocolate sponge.

Normally during school holidays, Albie gets up late, but today he's up at 7.30 a.m., fully dressed.

'Happy birthday!' I say as he appears in the kitchen for breakfast. Rosie seems equally excited and begs him to open all of his presents. She hasn't clocked that Jared is missing, and I don't say anything.

'Isn't Dad here?' he asks.

I shake my head. 'I'm sure he'll be back later, and you can celebrate with him then. As you didn't want a party, I've booked for you to have a driving experience. We're going this afternoon.'

'Seriously, Mum?' His eyes brighten and he grins. I'm glad that the effects of being ill have completely worn off and he seems back to normal.

'You're going to drive a supercar,' I explain. 'You can choose between an Aston Martin, a Ferrari or a Lamborghini.'

'No way! That's the best gift ever. Thank you so much!'

'As good a gift as this?' I hand him the small box with the phone, and he rips it open.

'What is it? What is it?' Rosie bounces up and down. When he holds up the phone box, she groans and sinks into her chair. 'Boring.'

'It's not boring. Thanks, Mum. And I promise I won't lose it this time.'

I smile. 'It's got the same number as the phone you lost, so I'm sure Dad will call you to wish you a happy birthday.'

I've organised to have the day off work, so the kids and I potter around the house during the morning, Albie spending most of the time on his new phone. I hear nothing from Jared, so I send him a message, reminding him it's Albie's birthday and that we're going to the track event late afternoon, although I can't believe he would actually forget. We discussed it before going to Scotland, and he promised he'd leave work early to be there for Albie.

When my messages go unread, I get nervous. Albie will be devastated if Jared doesn't turn up. Eventually, a few minutes before we have to leave, I call him at work.

'Mrs Pedersen! How are you?' Jared's assistant asks as if it's made her day that I've rung. We make chitchat for a few moments, and then she puts me through.

'Pedersen,' Jared answers the phone abruptly.

'It's me.'

'I'm busy.'

'So am I, but I'm calling because it's Albie's birthday.'

'I know.'

'So you'll meet us at the racetrack, or do you want us to all go together?'

'I haven't got time.'

'It's your son's birthday!' I exclaim. 'He's thirteen.'

'And old enough to understand that it's his father who is paying for his fancy days out and expensive gifts, and that I have an important dinner that I can't get out of this evening.'

I refuse to argue with Jared. If this is how he wants to play it, then fine, but I will not cover for him with Albie. Albie will be devastated, but Jared will have to pick up the pieces. I refuse to make any excuses for my errant husband.

'I'll see the kids at the weekend,' Jared says.

'That's five days away!' The rare times Jared has been away from home for that long were when he's had to make business trips to Australia. 'I'm taking them to my parents' tomorrow for a couple of nights, so it would be kind if you could see them before they go.'

Jared ignores that comment. 'I'll send him a present.'

'We've already given him a present. The driving experience and an iPhone,' I say flatly. 'Where are you staying?'

'I'm not sure that's any of your business, since you were the one who suggested we call time on our marriage.'

I'm about to fire off a retort, but I hold my tongue. There is no point in having yet another argument.

'And in case of an emergency?'

He chortles. 'Oh, another of your emergencies? A scary text message? You can reach me on my phone.' With that, he hangs up.

I stifle a sob. It sounds as if Jared hates me. And right now, I think I hate him too.

I take Albie to the racing track, and he chooses to drive a red Ferrari. Rosie and I watch from the spectators' gallery. I tell him that Jared was detained at work on some urgent business and I see the sadness on Albie's face, but he says nothing. We eat at a pizza restaurant, and we're not home until gone 8 p.m. As I approach the front door, I see a large parcel on the doorstep. For a moment, my heart sinks. Please don't let it be something horrible.

Except Albie is walking in front of me, and his eyes light up. 'It's addressed to me!' he exclaims. I can't think of who would have sent him a gift. He's opened everything from family. He heaves the heavy box into the hallway and starts tearing the cardboard.

'It's a game console!' he exclaims. 'And a virtual reality headset!'

I look at it. It's the exact model that Albie had requested for his birthday, but when I looked at the price and the age suggestions for the games he was talking about, I told him it was out of the question. It was much, much too expensive and completely unsuitable for a thirteen-year-old boy. Albie accepted my pushback with no sulking or retorts, and I realised he was only trying his luck.

'And these games! My friends are going to love me!' Albie says. I pick up a few of them, and they have names like *Battlefield* and *Bulletstorm*, with gory pictures on the front featuring lots of guns and blood. They are completely inappropriate for his age.

'Does it say who sent you all this?' I ask.

He pulls out a piece of paper. 'Dad!' Albie exclaims. 'Dad gave me this! Oh my God, he's the coolest.'

I have to walk away. I'm seething with anger. How could Jared buy Albie such an unsuitable present? It's obviously a guilt gift and something that will back me into a corner. He knows I will have to ban Albie from playing these games, and in the process he'll look like the great guy, the fun parent, and I will be the bad one. How on earth am I meant to manage this?

CHAPTER THIRTEEN

I have a complicated relationship with my parents. I'm honestly not sure why Mum and Dad had me and my brother. We were a complication in their lives, and I'm pretty sure they only had children because that was the 'done' thing. Work was their everything, along with their standing in society. Mum had – still has – a brilliant mind, and she rose in the legal ranks, becoming a judge in her forties. Her legal practice and her clients were way more important than her children. Dad had his own engineering firm, which he sold for many millions a decade ago. The height of privilege, you might think. My parents worked hard, and my brother, James, and I wanted for nothing. Materially, at least. We had a live-in nanny until I was ten and James was eleven, and then we were both sent off to boarding school. Looking back at my childhood, it was akin to something out of a distant era. I spent years being miserable and desperately homesick, not for my parents, but for the sprawling house and the freedom of the fields and my pony, and the friends I'd grown up with when we attended the little primary school five miles away. I know my current friends – especially Dakota and Stella – look at where I came from with some envy, but they don't understand that I would have given up all the trappings of wealth for love and affection from my parents, and their unwavering interest in me as an individual. All Mum and Dad cared about were our school reports, the grades we got in musical instrument exams and James' sporting achievements. Whether or not they did it knowingly, we were benchmarked from a young age against the children of their friends. 'Simone got eleven A-stars at GSCE. Mina got a distinction in her grade eight piano, and she's only ten.'

And so I spent my childhood striving. I worked so hard, even though the academic work didn't come easily. At some unconscious level, I genuinely believed that if I got the highest possible grades, Mum might choose to spend more time with me. Of course, it never happened. Firstly, I wasn't clever enough to get top grades, and secondly, even if I had been, Mum would still have chosen her work.

Today, as I bundle the kids into the car, I realise I married a man who is fundamentally similar to my mother. Why I haven't thought about that before, I really don't know. I've probably been so busy on the old hamster wheel, I haven't taken the time for any self-analysis. And no, I don't want the same for my children. I want them to have parents who are present, who don't spoil them, giving them gifts rather than their time. I want us to focus on what our kids are good at and enjoy, rather than concentrating on grades and achievements.

And so it begs the question as to why I'm happy for Albie and Rosie to spend time with their grandparents. It's since Mum and Dad, now that they're retired, are showering my kids with the fun and attention that James and I never received. It's also because James is dead, and deep down they know it's their fault.

My beautiful, tender-hearted brother died aged twenty-seven of a drug overdose. So no, we weren't the perfect family. Not in any sense. While I just about coped with the pressures Mum and Dad placed on me, James didn't. He got addicted to drugs and alcohol at a young age, despite the fancy school he attended – or perhaps because of it. By the time he was twenty-one, he was a wreck. Of course, my parents chucked money at the problem, and he was in and out of rehab for years. It didn't work. James' death broke my heart and, eventually, it softened my parents. I know better than anyone that wealth does not bring happiness.

My parents live in a sprawling house in the Surrey hills. They have fabulous views from the back of their house, right across Surrey and Sussex to the South Downs beyond. It's an idyllic spot that gives my children the chance to breathe in fresh air and frolic in nature as I did when I was very young. If Mum similarly pressured them as she used to me, I wouldn't send them there, but she doesn't. She genuinely adores her only grandchildren. So we have an agreement: when we're not off abroad on holiday, they go to stay with them for a few days at half-term.

The big fly in the ointment is Jared. They think he's the perfect husband and that I got so lucky that he chose me. It would never cross their minds that he might be the lucky one because I chose him. If I told my parents that my marriage was on the rocks, I'm almost sure that they would side with Jared. And I simply can't risk that. I'm trying to be so strong, but the fallout from that would likely push me over the edge.

As we approach Dorking, I do what I've been trying not to do, and lie to the children.

'Darlings, I don't want you to mention to Grandma and Grandpa that Dad isn't at home right now. Just tell them he's staying with a friend as he's working on an intense business deal and hasn't got time to come home every night.'

Albie glowers at me, for he's not stupid, but it's the story I've been telling Rosie and she seems to accept it. 'Please, Albie,' I add, catching his eye in the rearview mirror.

He's angry with me, not just because he knows Jared has left home but also because I've stopped him from playing the 18+ games that came with the PlayStation. I was tempted to send the whole thing back, but why should Albie suffer from his father's grandiose guilt trip?

'When is Daddy coming home?' Rosie asks.

'I'm sure he'll be back by the time you're home from Grandma and Grandpa's.'

'I miss him,' Rosie says plaintively. It makes my heart crack a little.

As we pull up into their driveway, I see Dad seated on his sit-upon mower. It's one of his favourite pastimes, and he loves creating perfect lines on the lawn. Mum hurries to the front door, and I suspect she's been sitting at the window waiting for my car to pull up.

'Darlings!' she says, rushing out to greet us.

Rosie, who is young enough not to sense any of the undercurrents, rushes out to her grandmother, happy to be swept into a flamboyant hug. Albie busies himself hauling the bags out of the car.

'I've made you lemonade and a chocolate sponge cake,' Mum says. I raise my eyes for I'm not sure she ever switched the oven on during my childhood. 'Would you like a coffee, Kate?'

'Thanks, Mum, but I've got to hurry back to London.' I bite my lip as Mum walks back into the house, an arm around Albie's shoulder and holding Rosie's hand. How I wish I could share my worries with her. How I wish she wouldn't judge or blame me. Except I know if I shared my fears, we would revert to type, and I can't bear that.

'That's a shame,' she says, as I walk just behind her. 'Is it work?'

'Yes,' I say, as that's the one thing Mum respects.

'Well, I'm glad it's going well,' she adds.

I haven't told her whether it is or isn't, so I smile wryly. I hug the kids goodbye and tell them to be good, and then immediately regret it for sounding like my mother. So I hug them again, and Albie looks at me as if I'm demented.

'Have fun!' I say.

Dad is off his lawnmower now and is stooping slightly as he walks towards me. He's aged a lot in the last couple of years.

'Not staying?' he asks. We've never been a physical family, so he doesn't reach out for me, and I feel a deep yearning to give him a hug. Of course, I don't.

'I need to get back. I'll stay longer when I collect the kids.'

He nods and smiles. For a second, I hesitate. Dad is a better listener than Mum. Perhaps I could share my worries with him and receive the wisdom of age and experience. Except he turns away and walks towards the open front door.

I cry in the car. In fact, I cry so much, I have to pull over into a lay-by and switch the engine off. It's the first time I've really sobbed like this in – well, I can't remember. It's the loneliness. Having the kids at home and working all day has kept me busy, but now I face a completely empty house. No children, no husband, and no friends. I tell myself that isn't the case. I can still reach out to Stella and even Lucia, who I know is in London as she and Hamish had to delay their honeymoon as she has an important photoshoot. Perhaps Erin and Dakota might give me a second chance too. And the children are only gone for a few days. But Jared is another matter. Can I really give up on our marriage that easily? I want to talk to him, to be civil, to recoup a little of what we've lost. I call him, but of course, he doesn't answer.

Instead, I call Stella.

'Hiya. How's it going?' She sounds breezy and a little breathless.

'Are you around at all?'

'I'm doing Pilates but have nothing planned for the rest of the day. Well, I was going to clean the house, but frankly, any excuse not to do that!'

'Have you got time to come over to my place for a coffee or a glass of wine?'

An hour later, and Stella and I are sipping coffees at my kitchen table. The children's things are still scattered around the room, and I feel a deep ache in my chest.

'I think my marriage is over,' I say. The words catch in my throat.

'Oh, Kate,' Stella says, eyeing me with a look of concern.

'Jared walked out on Sunday night and hasn't been home since. He didn't even turn up for Albie's birthday. I don't suppose you know where he is, do you?'

Stella blinks rapidly, a flicker of surprise across her face. 'No. Why would I know?'

I shrug. 'You might have heard. I tried calling Erin, but she didn't answer or return my call.'

'He's probably staying with them. Jared and Kieren are really tight, aren't they?'

'Yes, but Erin is my friend too. I just thought...' I let my voice taper away. 'They're still angry with me over the list, aren't they?'

'Honestly, I haven't spoken to Erin since Lucia's wedding, and she seemed okay then. What brought everything to a head? That Jared slept somewhere else at the hotel?'

'It's not just that,' I say.

'Do you think he's having an affair?'

I pause for a moment, for yes, of course it has crossed my mind. Except I haven't actually voiced it, and now that Stella has, it winds me.

'Maybe,' I mumble.

'Bastard,' Stella mutters. 'Men can't be alone for five minutes before tumbling into the arms of some other woman. Did you ever find out where he slept when he didn't come back to your room at the castle?'

I shake my head. Stella gets up and walks over to the kitchen cupboards, opening one and removing my biscuit tin. I like that she's so familiar with my house, so comfortable here.

'You need one of these,' she says, producing one of the chocolate-covered biscuits I give to the kids as treats. I smile weakly as she sits down again. 'If he's having an affair, then you need to find out who with.'

'It's not just that,' I say and suddenly feel so exhausted. 'Stuff has happened since the list was leaked. I've got threats. You saw how my dress was slashed. Someone pushed dog poo through the door and sent me threatening texts. The reason I left the Highlands in such a hurry was that I received a text suggesting that Albie had been poisoned. It scared me shitless. I asked Jared to leave, but he refused.'

'Bloody hell,' Stella says, her jaw dropping open and her eyes wide. 'Have you been to the police?'

'No, Jared and I assumed it was some nutter who took offence at the list. But it must have been someone who was at Lucia's wedding, otherwise how did they know about Albie being sick?'

'Oh my goodness,' Stella says.

'I think it might be Marilyn.'

There's a long pause until Stella asks, 'Marilyn?'

'She's a mum from school who we ostracised. She was Lucia's makeup artist and was up in Scotland. Do you know who I mean?'

'I think I do, but I don't know her. So what are you going to do about it?'

I shrug again. 'Get drunk?' I suggest. I get up and walk to the fridge, taking out a bottle of white wine. Stella looks at her watch and then sighs. 'Why not? I've got nothing better to do.'

An hour later, and we're halfway through the bottle, which I think is very restrained of both of us. But Cole is out tonight, and we've decided to watch trash TV on Netflix, so we have a long evening stretched ahead.

When my phone pings with a message, I grab it easily, assuming it's from Mum with an update on the kids. It's not.

'Shit,' I say, as my hand trembles.

It's from yet another unknown number.

> Have your husband and children left you? Are you going to be all alone tonight in your big house? You might not want to go to sleep...

I feel like I might faint, so I rest my head back against the sofa. I assume I've gone very pale, since Stella leans forward and peers at me.

'I've received another text.' I hand her my phone.

'Bloody hell, Kate,' Stella says, standing up. 'This is horrible and really scary. Who knows that you're here alone?'

'No one except Jared and you.'

'Well, it's hardly me,' she snorts. 'Besides the fact I'm your best friend, I'm right here with you.' Of course it isn't Stella.

'But why would Jared do something like that?' I ask mainly to myself.

'You can't be here alone,' Stella says. 'I'll stay here with you. Cole won't mind.'

'No. I don't want to put you in any danger. I'm going to the police.'

She jumps up, her glass in hand. 'Good idea.'

'Should I call 999 or go to the police station?' I ask, staring at my phone even though the screen has now gone black.

'Go in person so you don't get fobbed off.'

'What's it like going to a police station to report a crime?' I ask.

Stella shrugs her shoulders. 'Haven't got a clue. My only involvement with the police was when I was stopped for speeding – 34 miles per hour in a 30 zone.'

I do a search online and realise that the nearest 24-hour

police station is in Hammersmith, on Shepherds Bush Road, which isn't too far from my office. Except I can't drive. I'm too tired and have drunk too much. 'I'll get an Uber,' I say.

'I'll come with you,' Stella says, picking up our wine glasses and putting them in the sink.

'No point in your having to hang around a police station for hours. Go home, and I'll call you when I'm back.'

Stella frowns and bites the edge of her fingernail. 'Are you sure?'

I give her a brief hug. 'You're being a great friend, but I really need to sort this.'

'Promise you'll call me as soon as you leave Hammersmith.'

'I promise.'

Hammersmith police station is heaving, which is not surprising for this time of the evening. I try to avoid the drunks and the homeless and then feel guilty about it. There is a front counter, which comprises two large glass windows with officers seated on the other side. There's a ticket machine that gives out numbers. I'm number 267 and, according to the display above the front counters, they are currently dealing with number 248. I wonder how long I'll have to wait. It's not pleasant, and I feel uncomfortable and so obviously out of my depth. I stand up, leaning against a wall next to a board filled with posters advertising help for addicts, The Samaritans and the like. No one looks at it. I take care not to catch anyone's eye and keep looking at my phone. Whenever there's a commotion, I shrink further back into the wall. It seems like forever, and forty-five minutes later, it's my turn. I hurry to the counter.

'How can we help?' the officer asks. He looks weary, with rings under his eyes and receding hair.

'I've been receiving threatening messages, messages that scare me, and I'd like to report it in case my life is in danger.'

The uniformed officer raises an eyebrow but duly takes down my name, address and other contact details. 'If you'd like to wait to the side of the counter, someone will come and talk to you.'

Five minutes later, another man appears from a side door and shouts out my name. I hurry towards him. He looks so young, early to mid-twenties at most, and is dressed in black trousers and a short-sleeved shirt.

'Good evening. I'm Constable Maryk. Please follow me.'

He leads me through a corridor painted in pale green and then into a small interview room with plastic-looking furniture. I sit down opposite him.

'How can I help?'

I explain everything. The letter with the dog poo, and I show him the card with the word bitch and the three text messages.

'Any reason why you think you've received these?' he asks.

And then I have to tell him about the list; how I ranked my friends and how someone leaked it onto social media. I think I see the edge of his upper lip twitch slightly, as if he's trying to stop a snigger. Really, I don't blame him. What must he think of me, a middle-aged, middle-class woman complaining about something that in the scheme of things is so very silly? Except that it triggered these messages, and there's nothing funny about those.

'So your deduction is that these have been sent by someone you know.'

I nod. 'Otherwise, they wouldn't have known that my son had been sick.'

'Right.' He jots some notes down in a notebook, positioning his arm so I can't read what he's writing. Eventually, he looks up at me. 'It might be a good idea if you stay with a friend.'

'Will you be investigating this, looking up the telephone numbers?'

'We're very short on resources, Mrs...' He glances at his notes before saying my name. 'As there has been no actual threat to your or your family's life or property, I'm not sure there's much we can do.'

'So this has to escalate before you can take any action?'

He throws me an exasperated look. 'I'm sorry, but my hands are tied. We have to assess crimes, and while I sympathise with you that these messages are unpleasant, there's nothing to suggest imminent danger to life.'

Well, this was a complete waste of time. I wonder if he had to memorise statements such as those in order to graduate police college.

'Look,' he says, softening, probably considering the dismay on my face. 'We'll give you a case reference, and if you're worried about anything in particular, just call 111 or 999 and we can look at it again. If your home security is lacking, then I suggest you improve it. Lock all your windows and doors and use security lighting and cameras.'

I grit my teeth. I'm not a bloody idiot.

'Right, thank you,' I say, as we both get up to leave. This was a total waste of time, and frankly, I should have known better than to waste my evening here at the police station.

'Your husband and children live with you, I assume?' he asks, as he accompanies me back down the corridor.

I nod, not bothering to tell him that my husband is I don't

know where and my children are twenty-five miles away with my parents.

'That's good,' he says, although it brings me no comfort.

Back at home, I double-check our security. We have only the Ring doorbell at the front of the house and no cameras on the exterior, although we have sensor lights all around the house. I send Jared a message.

> I'd be really grateful if you could come home.

I also send Stella a message saying I'm back. She offers to come over again, except I decline her offer. It's too much.

As I bolt the front and back doors, I realise Jared won't be able to get in if he does come home. But so be it. I double-check that all the windows are locked as well, and I put the alarm on, so that if anyone breaks in downstairs, it will chime and connect to the alarm monitoring station. I'm as secure as I can be.

Even though I'm bone-weary and exhausted, I'm wide awake at the slightest little creak, my heart pounding, my breath catching in my throat. I'm not sure I ever properly drift off to sleep, because for the first time in my life, I'm really scared.

CHAPTER FOURTEEN

I'm awake when my alarm goes off. I've been awake every hour of the night. My bones ache as I force myself out of bed. I lift my phone off the bedside table and scroll through my messages. There's nothing from Jared, and in fact, it looks as if he hasn't even read my message. I'm furious. Blood-boilingly livid. He's clearly off having the time of his life somewhere, completely uncaring about the kids and me. Or at least, me. Albie told me that Jared calls him and Rosie every evening to wish them goodnight and promises he'll see them soon. I've had enough. Jared and I need to talk.

Over my second cup of coffee of the morning, I call Erin. Her phone rings many times, and I wonder if she's going to ignore me, but then she answers, sounding slightly breathless.

'Hi, Erin. How are you?'

'Alright. Trying to wake the twins up and failing. They've got theatre club.'

I'm glad that she's sounding normal towards me. 'Is Jared staying with you?'

'Jared? No.'

'Oh,' I say. 'I assumed he was.'

'Why would he be with us?' she asks, with genuine surprise in her voice.

'He hasn't been home all week since we had a blazing row. I thought he'd be with you.'

'No, sorry. Goodness, I didn't know things were so bad between you.'

'So Jared has said nothing to Kieren?'

'Not that I know of. But he is okay, isn't he?' she asks.

'He's been talking to the kids every day but refuses to answer my calls.'

'I'm sorry, Kate. Men can be such jerks sometimes.'

I'd always assumed that Erin and Kieren had the perfect marriage, but perhaps she's just opened a small window to suggest I might be wrong. Or perhaps she's just being honest insofar as every relationship has its ups and downs. 'I'll speak to Kieren tonight and let you know if he's aware of what's going on.'

I thank Erin, for it sounds like she's being a genuine friend to me; hopefully, she's actually forgiven me. How I wish I hadn't hurt her by giving her such a low mark on my hateful list.

As I put the phone down, I think back to my discussions with Stella. If Jared isn't staying with his best friend, where else could he be? A hotel, perhaps? I log onto our online banking and check his credit card transactions. Except there's nothing out of the ordinary. Of course, Jared has a work credit card too, so potentially he could make transactions he doesn't want me to see on that. Or maybe he's staying with his lover. Assuming, of course, he has one. Although the more I think about it, the more likely it seems.

I race up the stairs and start going through all of his jacket pockets looking for crumpled credit card statements, notes with phone numbers scrawled on them, handkerchiefs stained with lipstick. Except I find nothing. My meticulous husband doesn't even have a sweet wrapper in any of his pockets.

My phone rings, and for a moment I'm hopeful, except it's Cole.

'Are you on your way?' he asks.

And then I remember. We have a meeting this morning with our business bank manager to discuss expansion plans. I've been pushing for this for months. Cole has produced all the projections, and today was meant to be the big day when we decide if we can open up two more offices. I'm not even dressed yet.

'I'll be there as soon as I can,' I say, grabbing a trouser suit from my walk-in wardrobe. 'Had a bit of an emergency at home. Please pass on my apologies for being late.'

I have a terrible day and I can't concentrate. I'm far from impressive with the bank manager, and Cole has to interrupt on numerous occasions, answering questions that make me tongue-tied. The chances we get the loan are close to zero now, and it's all my fault.

'Are you alright?' Cole asks after the man has left.

'Sorry, tired and distracted. Stuff going on at home.'

Cole hesitates as if he's going to say something and then seems to think better of it. I expect Stella has told him. Later, I send the wrong candidates to a client and find myself incapable of writing a pitch document, which I'd normally do in my sleep. Needing to hear the kids' voices, I telephone my parents. Dad answers and tells me Mum has taken them out for the day to play tennis with the grandchildren of a friend of hers. It leaves me feeling desolate.

Eventually, I realise there's no point in my staying at work when I'm doing more harm than good. Cole stares at me with concern when I say I'm leaving early, but I don't hang around for an introspective chat. I'm going to find Jared.

My husband is a partner in a venture capital firm based near Victoria Station. You'd have thought that with an office next to such good public transport, he wouldn't bother driving into work, but since he was made a partner quite a few years ago, he was given a parking space and a company car. He makes a big deal about feeling guilty driving in the city, contributing to air pollution, but still, he does it. Jared normally leaves work between 7 and 8 p.m., so as I'm childless with an empty evening ahead, I drive to Claffery Street. It's not easy finding parking, especially since most of the bays are for residents' parking only, but after driving around slowly, I get lucky. I find a metred bay with an excellent sightline of his office's parking garage. After paying online – an astronomical fee thanks to London's hefty parking charges – I turn on the radio and wait. Several fancy cars emerge from the garage. A Jaguar hovers on the steep ramp and nearly takes out a moped as it turns left. At 7.06 the garage doors roll up once again, and out comes Jared's Audi. I turn on my engine and slip down in the driver's seat so that he doesn't see me, except he's not glancing at any of the parked cars, just looking left and right to see if the road is clear for him to pull out. And then the car turns left. I almost lose him at the very first set of traffic lights. He slips through as they turn amber, and there is no way I can risk driving through a red light. But then I get lucky. He's caught in another traffic jam up ahead, and I'm only two cars behind him.

He turns onto the King's Road, continuing straight the whole way, until eventually he's crossing Putney Bridge and then driving along Lower Richmond Road. It's as if he's driving home. But when he gets to Barnes Common, he doesn't go along Rocks Lane as if he were heading home, but drives straight over. I follow easily, relieved that he hasn't clocked me in his rearview mirror. We're in familiar territory here, and for a moment I wonder if he's meeting one of our friends for supper. Except then he turns into Carrington Gardens and eases his car into a parking space. I slam my foot on the brake and hover at the end of the road. Jared gets out of the car, lifts out his coat, briefcase and a small bag with SpaceNK's logo on it, and strides across the road, a grin on his face. He removes a key from his trouser pocket and places it in the lock. Then the pale yellow door opens and he disappears inside.

I let out a little involuntary sob.

My husband has just let himself into Dakota's house.

The sound of a car horn right behind me jolts me into action. I drive forward and pull into the only free space on the long parking bay.

What the hell is Jared doing at Dakota's house? Why does he have a small bag from SpaceNK? The only reason I can imagine him staying with her rather than with Erin and Kieren is if he's sleeping with her. Why would he buy her some makeup or perfume unless they were extremely close? It also explains why Dakota is the only one of my friends who is still being so aggressive with me regarding the list. The crazy thing is that I listed Dakota at the top. I gave her 89 out of 100, which is significantly higher than Stella, who was next with a score of 71. Yes, I get it could potentially make her look unprofessional, but she's the victim. How I hate that word. But why would Jared be staying with her? He's always admired Dakota, telling me how impressive she is, how she made partner at such a young age and expressing his surprise that someone as stunning and clever as her has been single for so many years. I never took much notice of Jared putting Dakota on a pedestal because we all did. We still do. A brilliant single mother, beautiful, successful, and so together; of course we all look up to her.

And now what? I don't stand a chance if Jared and Dakota are in love. Should I confront them and accuse Jared of infidelity? Or what if I've got it wrong? Except I know deep down I haven't. They're a good match, those two. It's probably best if I head home and regroup, talk to Stella, and get myself a good lawyer. Except my hands are trembling so much, in fact, my whole body is shaking with shock and exhaustion, and I'm not sure I'm in a fit state to drive. I switch off the engine and squeeze my hands around the steering wheel. I sit there motionless for I don't know how long, trying to take deep breaths, to calm myself, all the while staring up at Dakota's darkened windows.

And then, to my surprise, Jared emerges from the front door. He's dragging his big suitcase and his golf clubs, with the little SpaceNK bag shoved over the top of the suitcase handle. And he looks so pale. He stumbles slightly as he tugs the case. What's happened? Have he and Dakota argued? Why is he leaving in what seems like a dishevelled hurry? He opens the boot of his car and hauls the case and his golf club bag inside. Then he rushes to the driver's side of his car without once looking back. He pulls out of the parking space with a screech of the tyres, and then he's gone.

He left so fast, I'm shocked. What just happened? He walked into Dakota's house with a smile on his face and left as if he'd seen a ghost. I could try to follow him, but that would be futile with the speed he drove away. After a few long moments, I get out of my car, lock it and walk across the road to Dakota's house. I'm not looking forward to this conversation, but it has to take place. I ring the doorbell. There's no answer. I wonder if Dakota has spotted me out of the window and is pretending she's not in. This time I use the door knocker, bashing the gold knocker with some force against the navy front door. To my surprise, the door swings open. Jared can't have closed it properly in his hurry to leave.

'Hello!' I shout as I step into the house. 'Dakota, it's me, Kate. We need to talk.'

There's a strange stillness. I step further into the hallway and catch a floral scent. Is that from the perfume Jared bought her? 'Hello!' I shout again, my heart flickering in my chest. I've been in Dakota's house many times and know my way around. I walk along the corridor and peer into the snug-type living room on my left. Some of Violet's toys are scattered on the carpet. 'Dakota, are you in?' I ask as I walk cautiously towards the kitchen. She has a fabulous kitchen in a new extension, all white marble and cream sofas and a large bespoke oak dining table. I step inside. The air is too still, and there's a strange scent in here. Normally, the countertops are bare except for a large bowl of fruit and a couple of decorative jugs, except today there are dirty dishes next to the sink, as if the normally fastidious Dakota hasn't gotten around to clearing up. Something doesn't feel right. I force myself to step farther forward.

And then I scream.

And scream.

Dakota is lying at the strangest angle on the marble floor, her head in a large pool of blood, her eyes closed.

I rush towards her, almost slipping on the shiny floor. But then I stop just a metre or so away from her.

'Dakota?' I say. I bend down on my knees, knowing I have to touch her, I have to help. 'Dakota,' I sob again as I lift her limp wrist and try to feel for a pulse. She looks so still, so very dead.

CHAPTER FIFTEEN

Is Dakota dead?

'Dakota, wake up!' I shout at her. She doesn't move but her eyelids flicker ever so slightly, and then I'm sure I sense the faintest of pulses. I grab my phone from my coat pocket, my fingers trembling so badly I can hardly jab 999.

'What's your emergency?' an operator asks in a low, steady voice.

'Ambulance, police!' I say, my voice shaking. 'My friend is lying in a pool of blood, and I think she's nearly dead.'

'What's the address of the emergency?'

'Carrington Gardens, Barnes. I don't know the number. About halfway along the street.'

'And what's your name?'

'Kate Pedersen. I'm a friend.'

'Alright, Kate. I've dispatched the emergency services, but I want you to stay on the line.'

It takes eight minutes. The eight longest minutes of my life. And then the sirens are blaring and blue lights flashing, and I rush out of the house, waving at the police car that screeches to a halt outside the door. An ambulance is right behind, and the paramedics in their green uniforms jump out of the vehicle carrying large cases.

'In the kitchen,' I say in a hoarse whisper.

Two hours later, Dakota has been rushed to hospital, barely alive. They wouldn't tell me anything, but it was obvious she was in a terrible way, with an oxygen mask over her face, IV lines in her veins. As for me, I'm at the police station. Again.

What I can't get out of my head is why Jared rushed out of Dakota's house? Was he responsible for her head injury? If not, why didn't he call the emergency services? It doesn't make sense, and my brain feels like it's going to burst open.

A detective is talking to me; an older man this time, not in uniform, who has introduced himself as Detective Kavi Patel. 'Kate, talk us through why you were visiting Dakota.'

I've already told them this at least twice. 'She's my friend, but we had a bit of a falling out.'

'Oh, yes?'

I immediately regret saying that. Will I now be a suspect, or am I anyway, as I'm the person who found her?

'Tell us about the falling out.'

'It's nothing major. I created a spreadsheet where I rated my best friends out of one hundred. Someone found the list and shared it on social media. It caused a fallout. Since then, I've been receiving threatening messages, and I lodged a report here only last night.'

'And what does this have to do with Dakota? Do you think Dakota sent the threatening message?'

'No, I don't think so. What's happened to her isn't related to me or my list. She was at the top of my list.' I realise I'm sounding confused and wish I hadn't mentioned anything.

'As far as you're aware, does Dakota have any enemies or problems?'

I want to scream, 'Yes.' That my husband raced out of her house just moments before I found her in a pool of blood. Except how can I do that? It would implicate Jared immediately, and as much as I dislike my husband right now, is he really capable of hitting someone? It hurts like hell that he looked happy as he walked into Dakota's house. But was he the reason Dakota is fighting for her life? Was there enough time for them to have an argument and for him to hit her over the head, or to push her so that she got that horrendous injury? He must have been in there for close on ten minutes, so the answer to that is yes.

'Kate?' Detective Kavi Patel asks.

'I'm sorry. It's all such a shock, and I'm exhausted.'

'Alright. Let's wrap this up for now, and we can talk again tomorrow. If you think of anything relevant in the interim, please call me.' He passes me his business card. 'Would you like a lift home?'

I consider asking him to drop me back at Carrington Gardens so I can fetch my car, but in the end decide I'd rather go straight home.

'Yes, please,' I say. I was brought to the police station to give my official statement in a marked car, so mine is still parked on Carrington Gardens. I can't bear the thought of getting an Uber home, having a chatty driver who might ask if I had a good night out, when all I want to do is blot out the memories of this evening. We both stand up.

'How can I find out how Dakota is, and whether her daughter Violet is alright?'

'According to the neighbour, Violet is spending half-term week with her cousins in Northumberland. Next of kin are currently being notified. Regarding Dakota, I will notify you if there are any changes in her condition.'

This time I'm ferried home in an unmarked police car. I'm grateful for that as I don't want our neighbours chinwagging about me, although as it's after midnight, I don't suppose many people will be up. To my surprise, as we pull in front of our house, I see that Jared's car is parked in the front. For a moment I freeze, and the young officer asks if I'm all right.

'Fine,' I say. 'Thanks for the lift.'

I wait until he's gone before walking slowly up our path. The house is lit up like a Christmas tree, which is ironic since Jared is constantly nagging us to switch off the lights. I pause, wondering what the hell I'm going to say to my husband. Wondering if I'm safe to confront him. Wondering if it might be better if I turn around and go to Stella's house. Except what would I tell her? That I'm fearful Jared might have hit Dakota? No, I can't do that.

I put my key in the front door, step inside and hang my coat up in the cupboard. The television is on with the sound down low. Jared comes out of the living room. He's wearing different clothes now, jeans and a polo shirt.

'Hello,' he says. 'You're home late.'

His tone of voice is completely normal. This catches me off guard for a moment. But then I realise he probably thinks I was out with friends, or like him, with a lover perhaps.

'Look, I'm sorry I went AWOL for a few days. You're right, we need to talk. Why don't I pour you a glass of wine, and we can have a chat?' He moves as if he's going to the kitchen, except I interrupt him.

'I don't want a glass of wine. I've just come from the police station.'

He freezes, his back to me. He turns around slowly, and I can see the blood has drained from his face. Goodness, I thought he was a better liar than that.

'Why were you at the police station? Is everything okay? With the kids?'

'The children are fine. They're at my parents.' I edge past my husband and walk into the living room, Jared right behind me.

I used to love this room with its tastefully neutral reclining sofas and gold and glass coffee table. I used to relish gazing at the paintings Jared and I chose together at great expense, and loved the feel of the heavy silk curtains in a coffee colour. But now I just see blood. I smell it, taste it. Even though our house hasn't been tainted.

I sink into an armchair.

'Where were you the past few days?' I ask.

'I stayed with a colleague,' Jared answers too quickly, as if the reply has been rehearsed.

'Don't lie,' I say.

He sits down on the sofa opposite me, perched forward.

'I'm not lying,' he says, his eyes skittish.

'Cut the crap, Jared,' I shout at him. 'I know you're having an affair. With Dakota. I saw you.'

'Saw me?'

I wonder for a moment if he's going to faint. His cheeks are the colour of parchment paper and his lips turn strangely pale. He clenches his fingers into fists.

'You can't have seen me because I have done nothing wrong.'

I know I'm taking a terrible risk by confronting Jared

directly, especially if he really did hurt Dakota, but what choice do I have? I glance at the door and wonder if I'd have enough time to dart through it if Jared decides to lash out at me. 'I saw you tonight. I saw you enter her house carrying your briefcase and a bag from SpaceNK, and then I saw you dash out of her house with your suitcase and golf clubs, and you drove away like a boy racer. You left her there, Jared.'

He jumps up from the sofa now. 'No, it's not how it looks. I didn't do anything.' Veins are sticking out of his forehead.

I tense up. 'I found Dakota lying on her kitchen floor in a pool of blood. So how can you say you did nothing?'

'Because I didn't. Have you told the police?' Jared bites the side of his lip so hard, a speck of blood appears on the surface. He licks it away, and my stomach clenches.

'Of course. I called an ambulance and the police.'

'Oh, God.' He places his head in his hands. 'And Dakota? Is she alright?'

'No, Jared, she's not alright. She's practically dead, and they don't know if she's going to make it.'

'I didn't do it, Kate. I promise you I didn't do it. I found her like that and I panicked.' And then Jared starts crying; pathetic, heaving sobs.

'But you didn't even call an ambulance!' I cry. 'You left her there to die. If I hadn't found her, she'd certainly be dead by now, and even so she'll probably die. How could you do that?'

Jared is sobbing hard – the first time I've ever seen him break down like this. Yet my heart feels hard towards him, devoid of an iota of pity.

'What were you doing at Dakota's house, anyway? I assume you were having an affair.'

'No,' he says, wiping his nose with the back of his hand.

I glower at him.

'So she was just giving you a room; you, your suitcase and your golf clubs?'

'I'm sorry, Kate. It didn't mean anything. I didn't love her; it was just opportunistic. You know, at the wedding, we'd argued, and then she said I could stay with her.'

'Stop the lying!' I shout. 'You've always had a soft spot for Dakota.'

'Maybe, but I promise you this was a new thing. I didn't want to hurt you.'

'A bit late for that,' I mutter.

And then Jared is on his knees in front of me, reaching out for my hands. 'Please, Katie. You're the only woman I love. You've always been my rock. I can't exist without you.'

I pull my hands away. 'You've managed pretty well the last week. And now you're going to be the police's number one suspect.'

'But she slipped, didn't she? That's what I assumed when I found her. You can't think that someone hurt Dakota deliberately?'

I shake my head. Jared is delusional. Of course someone 'did' it. The question is, was it him? And there are so many holes in that statement. If he just found her, why didn't he call for an ambulance?

I stand up and walk towards the fireplace to put some distance between Jared and me. 'You need to tell me the truth. Did you push Dakota? If it was an accident, I understand, but I need the truth.'

He stands up too and gives me his puppy-dog face, which right now makes me want to retch. 'I can't believe you're even suggesting that,' he says. 'Of course I didn't. I admit I walked in and found Dakota on the floor, and I was in such shock, I panicked. I grabbed all my belongings and ran out of her house. All I could think about was how I would be the number one suspect for hurting her as I'd been staying there and my DNA is on her bedsheets... well, everywhere, I expect.'

I screw up my nose in disgust.

'I need you to help clear my name, Kate. Surely you know I would never hurt anyone, let alone a woman.'

'You've done a pretty good job of hurting me.'

Jared winces. 'My DNA and fingerprints won't be on any police record, so there's no reason for them to suspect me,' he says.

'So why did you run away and leave her?'

'Because then they'd know I had been staying there. You must see how that looks!'

I'm trembling now, thinking about the full horror of Jared's involvement. 'You're really not going to go to the police?' I ask with disbelief. 'But people will have seen you going in and out; the neighbours, little Violet.'

'Violet hasn't seen me. She's been staying with cousins.'

'Surely it's better to be upfront and go to the police, and then they can rule you out of their enquiries. If you hide away, it's much more suspicious.' We're both quiet for a moment. 'Besides, *I* saw you, Jared, and I don't know if I can lie.'

He looks utterly startled now. 'Have you told the police that I was there?'

'No, but it's a lie by omission. You must come clean and go to the police.'

Jared paces up and down the room, his jaw clenched, constantly running his fingers through his hair.

'I don't know, Kate. I'm not on their radar at all, and surely it's better to keep it that way.'

'I disagree. If you're innocent, you've got nothing to worry about.' I stare at him, but Jared avoids my gaze. A nugget of fear grows in the base of my stomach for if he were genuinely innocent, he'd have nothing to fear, surely? Did Jared hurt Dakota in a moment of rage, perhaps? Has he got it in him? My husband is ruthless in business, but can he transfer that sharp edge to his personal life? I haven't ever witnessed it, but he could have cracked. What if Dakota was ending things and threatened to tell me about the affair? Could Jared have lashed out in fury, causing Dakota to fall and bash her head?

He groans. 'This is a complete fucking nightmare.'

'More of a nightmare for Dakota,' I mutter, except Jared doesn't appear to hear me say that.

'Let's sleep on it. Please, Kate. And if you still feel the same way in the morning, then I'll go to the police.' He's clenching his fists together at chest height, giving me that imploring look that I used to fall for. But tonight my heart has hardened, and I'm shocked all the affection and admiration for my husband has simply dissipated.

I also know for sure that I will feel the same way in the morning. I glance at my watch. It's gone 1 a.m., so I suppose a few hours will not make that much difference.

'Alright then,' I say reluctantly. 'You can go in the morning.'

He strides across the room, his arms outstretched as if he's going to draw me into a hug. I sidestep him. 'I'd like you to sleep in the spare room tonight,' I say. I wonder then whether I should have insisted he leave. Am I safe spending the night in the same house as a potential murderer? I consider this for a few moments, but this is my husband, the father of my children, and he's never shown any inclination of being violent before. I decide to give him the benefit of the doubt.

Upstairs, Jared has unpacked his suitcase, and all his belongings are back in our wardrobe, his wash bag on the side of the sink in our en-suite. But he does as I request and takes a fresh pair of pyjamas and slinks off into the spare room.

Despite my sheer exhaustion, I can't sleep, even with the bedroom door locked. I'm constantly seeing poor Dakota, lying there in the pool of blood, and Jared pushing her. I toss and turn for a couple of hours and then I switch the light on. I'm not sure what I'm looking for, but I search the pockets of the jackets and trousers he's hung in the wardrobe; I run my fingers inside the pockets of the suitcase, and find nothing. Then I unlock the door and tiptoe out of our bedroom and along the corridor, walking with bare feet down the staircase. Jared's briefcase is on a chair in the kitchen. I open it and search inside. There are two folders, each with spreadsheets and business plans, a few business cards, his laptop and a tiny umbrella. I consider trying to get into his laptop, but decide to leave that for now, as I'm not sure of his password.

And then I think of his car parked outside our house. Is there some incriminating evidence inside it? I've no idea what I'm looking for or whether I'm overthinking this, but I need to check. I take a set of car keys from the hook in the utility room, pull a coat over my nightclothes and slip my feet into a pair of trainers. Then, quietly, I exit the back door and walk along the path to the pavement. The night is still, all our neighbours' houses shrouded in darkness, the only light coming from a street lamp casting its orange glow. I press the open button on the fob, and the Audi doors unlock with a click and flashing of the lights. I glance back at our house to check no lights have come on, but it's also dark. The spare bedroom window faces the back garden, so Jared is unlikely to hear or see me. There's nothing in the car itself, so I walk around to the boot and press the button again. Jared has left his golf clubs here. I lift out the heavy golf bag, run my fingers around the empty boot and lock the car. I heave the golf club bag into the house, through the hallway and into the utility room, where I lean the bag against the wall.

I tried to learn golf a few years ago, except I soon realised I would have required so much practice, and even then, I would probably never be good enough to play with Jared and his friends, so I gave up. Something edges at the corner of my brain, a memory perhaps or something I've read. I unzip the top of the golf club case. Quite a few of the clubs have black covers over their heads. In fact, other than the irons, they all do. My eyes are drawn to the one that isn't covered.

I step away from the case, bile rising into my mouth. But then I force myself to look again, to stare at it more carefully. To be sure.

There is darkened blood on the driver. And hair. Black hair. Dakota's hair.

CHAPTER SIXTEEN

My hand rushes up to cover my mouth, and I have to swallow the bile and force myself to breathe, to stop myself from vomiting. These are Jared's golf clubs, the set I saw him remove from Dakota's house in a hurry, and one of them is most definitely smeared with dried blood. And now I'm sure.

My husband killed his lover.

I sink onto the floor of the utility room and bury my head in my hands. What the hell are we going to do? How can I protect our children from this catastrophe? How will they cope with having a murderer as their father? Our lives will be over. I can't turn him in. I just can't. But how will I live with myself knowing what he's done? What if he tries to kill me, or worse, the children? I debate this for what seems like forever, but deep down, I have no choice. Jared is a murderer, and we will all have to face the consequences of his horrific actions. Perhaps we can move away to another country, where no one knows us, change our names. Jared might have stolen Dakota's life, but he has also stolen my children's future.

I need to confront him, tell him I know the truth, except what if he gets violent with me? If he's done it once, there's every likelihood that he'll be violent again, and if he kills me, then Albie and Rosie will be orphans and my parents will have to bring them up. That doesn't bear thinking about. Time passes, and I've no idea how long, but I know I have to tell the police.

Eventually, I take out my phone and stare at it. What I'm about to do will change our lives forever, but I have no choice. I owe it to Dakota. Swallowing hard, I dial the number the police detective gave me yesterday evening. I hope he might not answer, that as it's the middle of the night, he's fast asleep with his ringer switched off. But to my dismay, the phone is answered on the third ring, and now it's too late.

'Hello, this is Kate Pedersen,' I speak as quietly as I can, all the time listening out for footsteps in case Jared has woken up. 'I have some news for you.'

'Go on,' Kavi Patel says.

'I didn't tell you the complete truth,' I admit. 'I witnessed my husband leave Dakota's house in a great hurry yesterday evening, and now I've found his golf clubs in the boot of his car. One of them has blood and hair on it.'

'And where is your husband now?' he asks.

'Upstairs, asleep in bed.'

The officer's voice comes in and out as if he's moving around.

'We will be with you in approximately thirty minutes. Do you feel safe, Kate?'

I look at the utility room door that doesn't have a lock. The house is still and dark, and I'm confident Jared is asleep.

'I think so,' I reply.

'If you feel you are in danger or your husband tries to leave the premises, please call 999.'

'Please don't arrive with sirens and lights,' I add.

'Don't worry, we won't. It's the middle of the night, so not necessary.' He ends the call.

I think about moving from where I've sunk to the floor in the utility room, except I can't seem to muster the energy. I'm terrified that Jared might get up, might use one of the other golf clubs. To run onto the road, I must be nearer to the front of the house. Hauling myself to my feet, I pad noiselessly through the darkened kitchen, lit only by the clock light on the oven, and through to the hall. Then I wait, sitting on the monks' bench seat next to the front door, my heart hammering, listening to the muted sounds of London at night, trying not to think about the future. Our devastating future. About twenty minutes later, I see car headlights. There are three police cars, and they park in the middle of the road, blocking traffic from both directions.

What have I done?

My hands are trembling so much, I can barely open the front door.

'Mrs Pedersen. As you know, I'm Detective Constable Kavi Patel, and we're investigating the grievous bodily harm caused to Dakota Solomon. These are my colleagues.' They both show me their badges, and I step to one side to let the officers in. Two other officers emerge from another car, and they stand on the edge of the pavement.

'Can you show us the golf club, please,' Patel asks in a low voice.

Standing in the doorway, they put on shoe covers and

rubber gloves, and I lead them through to the utility room. I'm sure Jared must have been awakened by the footsteps, but there's still no movement from upstairs. I point to the bloodied golf club. The officers look at it but don't touch it. Kavi Patel turns to face me.

'And where is Mr Pedersen right now?'

'Upstairs, asleep in the spare room. It's the second door on the left.'

He turns to his colleagues and cocks his head. 'Lead the way.'

A female police officer appears. 'Why don't you come with me?' she suggests. 'I'm Constable Lisa Lennon. 'Let's go and sit down.'

I lead her through to the kitchen, and that's when I hear multiple heavy footsteps running through the house, up the stairs, along the corridor. Someone is shouting, 'Police, open up!'

And I want to disappear. To be anywhere except here.

They arrest Jared. I don't see him because they take him from the bedroom straight downstairs and out to a waiting police car. I can only imagine how bewildered he must look, still in his green striped pyjamas, his hair ruffled up from sleep, or did they let him change into proper clothes? He will know that it's me who has shopped him, and I'm sure he feels utterly betrayed. But I have only done what I think is right. I hear voices outside and the revving of a car engine and wonder what the neighbours are thinking, but then Kavi Patel returns to the kitchen and sits down next to me.

He takes a statement from me where I explain I followed Jared home from work and that I saw him go into Dakota's flat and come back out again in a hurry with his belongings.

He gets me to repeat myself several times, and then I have to read through what he's written and sign it.

'Depending upon how the investigation goes and the interview with your husband, we will probably want to search your house in the morning,' Kavi Patel explains. 'And an officer will remain here for the foreseeable.'

'Do I need a solicitor?'

'No, but it is your right to have one.'

I am so out of my depth here, so terrified of what might happen next.

'My children are coming home today. They've been staying with my parents.'

'Might be a good idea to leave them there. There'll likely be a lot of upheaval.'

I nod, already dreading that conversation. 'What will happen to my husband?'

Kavi Patel stands up. 'It depends on his interview and the evidence. Do you think your husband is guilty?'

I shake my head. 'No. I don't think he has it in him.'

'Except you called the police.'

We're both silent for a moment. 'How is Dakota?' I ask.

'The last information I received was that she is in the operating theatre being treated for a traumatic head and brain injury. The doctors are not hopeful.'

I flinch. Poor, poor Dakota. I may be angry at her for sleeping with my husband, but she certainly doesn't deserve this.

If the leaking of my list caused upheaval, I know that I've just unleashed devastation. Jared will never forgive me for shopping him to the police, but how could I have lived with myself, seeing my friend's blood and hair on that golf club? Knowing that she is fighting for her life. All the police leave with the exception of one young officer, who tells me he'll be parked in his car at the front of the house. He explains that they've put tape around Jared's car and it might be removed in the morning. I lock the house and return to bed, trying to doze for a couple of hours, except it's impossible. At 8 a.m. I call Mum.

'Good morning!' she says brightly. 'What time will you be here?'

'I'm afraid I can't collect the kids today,' I say. 'Please, can they stay at yours until the weekend?'

Mum makes a sharp inhalation of breath. 'What's so important that you can't collect your own children?'

'I wouldn't ask unless it was critical.' In fact, I don't think I've ever asked my parents to step in when we've been let down by babysitters.

'Can't Jared take the day off work?'

I almost want to snigger. For a moment I'm tempted to tell Mum that her beloved son-in-law is currently being questioned at a police station for trying to murder the woman he's been having an affair with. Except I can't bring myself to say anything. Not yet. Not until I know more.

'You know we have lives too, Kate. I've got a fully packed diary for the rest of the week, as does your father.'

The former might be true, but the latter certainly isn't. Dad does little more than play the occasional round of golf and mow his beloved lawn.

'I'm sorry, Mum. I've got an emergency.'

'Medical or work?'

I hesitate for a moment, wondering which she'll be most sympathetic towards. It used to be work, but I think she's mellowed a bit, so I say medical.

'Nothing life-threatening, I hope.'

'No, but it would be great if the kids could stay with you.'

She huffs and puffs and finally agrees to keep them until the weekend. I can't ask for more.

A little later, I call the office and tell our receptionist that I'm sick and won't be coming into work. She's sympathetic, but I cut her short.

I'm exhausted but too wired to sleep, on edge, waiting for the phone to call, for the police to let me know what's going on. When, shortly after 9 a.m., the phone does ring, I grab it. It's Cole.

'Is everything alright?' he asks.

I wonder how he knows, or if he knows. I can't work out whether to tell him, but then if I can't tell Cole, who can I tell? We're together every day, probably spending more time in each other's company than I do with my husband. His wife is my best friend.

'Kate?' he urges.

'Dakota is fighting for her life, and Jared has been taken in for questioning. They were sleeping together.'

'What!' Cole sounds shocked. I hear him get up from his desk and walk over to the door, which closes with that familiar click. 'What's happened to Dakota?'

'I found her in a pool of blood in her kitchen. They don't know if she's going to make it.'

'God, that's terrible. But what has Jared got to do with it?'

'I saw him come out of her house.'

There's an endless pause during which I wonder if Cole is still on the line.

'You don't really think that Jared hurt her, do you?' he asks eventually.

'No. I don't know. It's all so confusing,' I cry.

'But Jared is a good man, isn't he?'

'Yes, he is. He's never laid a finger on me or anyone else as far as I know. It's probably all some horrible mistake.'

'Right. Well, keep me posted. Let me know if you want me or Stella to come over to your house.' Ordinarily, one of them would just come, and I wonder if this reticence is due to him wanting to distance himself and Stella from us.

'Thanks, Cole. We just need to keep all of this under wraps for now.'

'Of course. Speak later.'

Detective Kavi Patel doesn't call me. No one does. Not even Stella, my best friend. I wonder if Cole has said something to her, told her to step away from the shitshow that is my life. And Jared doesn't come home. Early afternoon, I try calling Patel, but am told he's in a meeting. Perhaps he's still interviewing my husband. I also call the hospital to find out how Dakota is, but no one can give me any information. I feel so alone, sick with fear, unable to do anything except pace my empty house.

And then the doorbell rings. I hurry to it and look through the peephole, except I don't recognise the man on the other side. Perhaps he's a plainclothes police officer. I open the door a few inches.

'Kate Pedersen?' he asks.

'Yes,' I reply.

'I'm a reporter from the *Evening Standard*.' And then a bright light goes off in my face, and I notice, too late, a photographer standing just off to the left. I slam the door shut in their faces and lean against it, trembling. How the hell do the press know what's going on? Have the police leaked the information somehow? It makes little sense. Or has Jared been charged, and that information is now in the public domain?

I rush into the living room and pull the curtains, then go around the entire house pulling every curtain and blind. Upstairs, I stand next to the window in our bedroom and sneak a look through the side of the blind. There are three men standing next to my car, staring up at the house. Are they all journalists?

I switch on the news on the television and go onto my phone, searching for Dakota and Jared's names, except I can't find anything recent, and there's nothing on the rolling news. What the hell am I meant to do? I'm trapped in my own home.

It strikes me that the one person who knows about handling the media is Lucia. She's hassled by them all the time and handles journalists with such aplomb. But will she help me? I vacillate for a while before eventually calling her. To my relief, she answers.

'I've just heard the terrible news,' she says. 'Dakota has been attacked in her own home, and she's in intensive care.'

'How do you know?' I ask.

'Stella called me and Erin.'

Of course she did. Cole will have told her, and it hurts that Stella hasn't reached out to me. I lean my head back against the wall and close my eyes. Not a good idea. I'm seeing Dakota in that pool of blood again.

'I found her,' I say eventually.

'Bloody hell, Kate. That's awful. Are you okay?'

'That's why I'm calling. Jared has been taken in for questioning.'

'Questioning for what?'

'For potentially being the person who hit Dakota.'

'No!' she says, as if that's the most preposterous thing she's ever heard. 'Jared wouldn't do that, would he?'

I find it ironic that all of my friends are more supportive of my husband than I am.

'I don't think so,' I say. 'But did you know he had a fling with Dakota?'

There's a heavy silence as this sinks in.

'Surely not!' she exclaims eventually. 'That doesn't sound like the sort of thing either of them would do.'

'He's admitted it. He slept with her at your wedding and then was staying with her afterwards.'

'Oh, goodness.'

'The thing is, there are a bunch of journalists outside my house, and I don't know how to deal with them.'

'Come to mine. You'll be safe here. I've got twenty-four-hour security and no one can get in.'

'But what about Hamish?'

'He's in the country all week. I was going to join him tonight, so it's no trouble for you to stay at mine.'

'Thank you, Lucia. It's so kind of you.'

'And the kids. Are they with you?'

'No, they're at my parents' until the weekend.'

'Perfect. I'll get the bed made up for you. You can park in the underground parking lot. Plug in the code 57632. I'll text you the number.'

'Thank you so much, Lucia. You're a lifesaver.'

I shove some clothes, toiletries and belongings into a rucksack. I wonder, do I need to tell Kavi Patel that I've left home? I decide not to; he can contact me on my mobile if necessary, if they have to search the house and need access. It isn't until I'm about to go out of the door that I remember my car isn't out the front, anyway. It's still parked on Dakota's street. Perhaps that's a good thing. I slip out of the back door and walk the few steps across our garden and through the gate that Rosie slipped out of only a few days ago. Hurrying along the path at the back of the houses, I pass the end of our street and glance down it, but no one is looking in my direction. I walk hurriedly towards Carrington Gardens, reaching it in about seven minutes. It's a different scene from last night; in fact, you wouldn't know anything was wrong, other than I catch a glimpse of a uniformed officer standing on Dakota's doorstep. No one looks at me as I slip into my car and pull away. It's only when I stop at the third set of traffic lights that I notice a black car two vehicles behind me. I'm sure it has been following me since I left Carrington Gardens.

My heart quickens. Not again. Surely not again. The black car is still there when I drive slowly along Putney Bridge Road, and it follows me as I go straight over towards Wandsworth. I try to reassure myself that this is London. Lots of people are going in the same direction. But I know this part of the city, along with all the shortcuts to avoid traffic. I turn onto a minor residential road, and still the black car follows me, but keeping a sufficient distance so I can't see who is driving. I decide to try to give it the slip. I turn back onto the main road and see that it does the same, still with a car in between us. I don't indicate, but at the next turning on the right, I swing hard into the road, driving fast along the residential street and then turning left and left again. If the lights are against the flow of traffic, I might just get to the main road to see who is driving that black car, perhaps to take a photo with my phone. I hope I don't get done for speeding. I put my foot down, and to my relief, I'm on the junction with the main road just as the small black car drives past.

I let out a gasp when I realise it isn't a journalist following me, or some stranger driving. The person at the wheel is Marilyn. Her hands are tightly gripping the steering wheel, and she's leaning far forward.

This cannot be a coincidence. Marilyn has been following me. But why?

CHAPTER SEVENTEEN

I'm shocked that Marilyn has been following me, and I can't work out why. Surely it has nothing to do with Dakota or Jared. Perhaps she's become obsessed with me, or is that presumptuous? Maybe she is also going to Lucia's place, although that seems very unlikely. Coincidences happen, of course, but London is a big place. If I was unsettled before, I'm even more so now, finding it hard to concentrate on the road, not least from exhaustion. It's a relief when I eventually arrive at Lucia's plush apartment block and turn onto a ramp that descends into the underground parking garage. I look in my rearview mirror and see that Marilyn's car has gone. The garage roller door is down, so I pull up to the console and plug in the code that Lucia gave me. The doors lift up. I edge in slowly, noting all the fancy cars. There must be millions of pounds of motor vehicles down here. There are three visitor spaces at the far end, and I park in one of them. Lights come on as I get out of the car, and at last I feel safe. I carry my rucksack and walk towards the exit door, noting cameras positioned in all the corners and above the doors. Previously, I might have felt uncomfortable being watched, but today it's a relief.

I walk into a small corridor with a lift, and when the lift doors open, I step inside and press the button for reception. Except the lift doesn't start. Eventually, I press the help button.

'Concierge,' a voice says.

'I'm staying with Lucia Highsmith. My name is Kate Pedersen, and I can't get the lift to work.'

'Yes, Ms Pedersen. Ms. Highsmith is expecting you. I'll start it for you. Please take the lift to the first floor and I'll give you a keycard.'

I do as instructed and emerge into the marble-lined reception area, which looks more like it belongs in a five-star hotel than a private block. The concierge asks to see proof of my identity and then he takes a photo of my face along with fingerprints. This is worse than being at a police station. Eventually, he supplies me with a key card that will let me get in and out of the building, but Lucia will have to give approval before my biometrics are added to her private entrance.

'Take the lift to the tenth floor,' the concierge says, although I already know the way.

The lift glides up slowly within a glass cage, affording stunning views of the River Thames and the buildings on the northern side, but I'm too preoccupied to take proper notice. I can't understand why Marilyn was following me, and I'm also increasingly scared that I've heard nothing from Jared or the police. What if he's already been arrested? Even worse, what if he's admitted to hurting Dakota?

The lift goes straight to the penthouse and emerges into Lucia's hallway. She's there waiting for me, dressed from head to toe in fawn cashmere, her feet bare and toenails painted black.

'Oh, Kate,' she says, throwing her arms around me. I dump the rucksack and take off my coat.

'Thank you for letting me stay,' I say.

'Of course. Come on. Let's get a drink in you, and you can tell us everything.'

It takes a moment to register that she's said 'us'. She leads me by the hand into her magnificent living room with its full wall of glass. To my dismay, Erin and Stella are also here, seated on large white boucle armchairs. I suppose I don't mind Stella is here, but Erin too?

'I wasn't expecting...' I wave at them.

'I thought it was important that we were all together,' Lucia says, reaching for a bottle of white wine standing in a cooler. She picks up a crystal glass and pours the wine into it. 'We need to be here for each other and Dakota in particular.' She hands me the glass.

'It's truly awful,' Erin says. 'But we don't understand why Jared has been arrested. Was he really having a fling with Dakota?'

I sink onto a chair opposite with a view of a feature fireplace, one of those egg-shaped types that hang from the wall and can be installed in houses that don't have a chimney flue.

'He's been taken in for questioning,' I say. 'I don't know what's happened.'

'Cole said you found Dakota.' Stella talks in a low voice.

'Yes. It was awful.'

The girls want to know the details, which I recount reluctantly. Except I don't tell them about the golf clubs, and I don't tell them I called the police and shopped my husband.

Lucia stares at me, nonplussed. 'I just don't understand what Jared has got to do with it. I mean, let's say he did have a brief fling with Dakota – which seems quite unlikely as he was so devoted to you. He wouldn't have hurt her.'

Stella is staring at me because, of course, she knows. She knows that I have suspected Jared of having an affair, and if Cole has recounted our conversation, she'll know that I believe that person was Dakota. I'm just about to speak when Erin says, 'I saw Jared coming out of Dakota's room at your wedding, Lucia. He was looking really dishevelled, and it was pretty obvious he'd spent the night with her.'

'What!' I exclaim, turning to face her. 'But why didn't you tell me?'

'How could I?' Erin retorts. 'I knew you and Jared were having problems; Jared told Kieren as much, and it's pretty obvious you've been unravelling ever since the list business. I didn't want to add to your problems or, even worse, be responsible for breaking you two up. For all I knew, it could have been a one-night stand regretted by both of them. Or maybe he just stayed in Dakota's room and nothing happened.'

I'm furious. How could Erin not have told me? I understand that she's been a bit cool towards me recently, and hurt by the list, and of course, she has her own issues, but surely a genuine friend would let something slip. Or perhaps Jared admitted his affair to Kieren, and Kieren told Erin, and they're both siding with my husband. That's the problem of being friends as a couple. When a relationship breaks down, everyone feels the need to take sides. Then again, what else can I expect from Erin? I shouldn't really be surprised that she doesn't have the backbone to tell me the truth. I take a large sip of wine and notice Stella giving me the eye. She's right. There's no point in shooting the messenger.

'Did you read that story about the man who pushed his girlfriend off the clifftop in Dorset?' Lucia says, breaking the frosty atmosphere. 'Luckily, she survived, but apparently she joked with him that she was having an affair with his brother, and he got so upset he pushed her.'

'I suppose even the mildest people can be capable of terrible things in the right – or wrong – circumstances,' Erin adds. 'Anyway, what are the police saying that Jared did exactly? He works such long hours, I expect he's got a good alibi.'

'I don't know the details,' I admit. 'I haven't heard from the police since last night.'

'That must be a good thing, surely?' Stella suggests. 'And whether Jared was or wasn't involved, couldn't Dakota have had an accident? What if she tripped over something, one of Violet's toys perhaps, and bashed herself?'

'Do we know how she was hurt?' Lucia asks. 'What did you see, Kate?'

All eyes are on me again.

'I found her lying in a pool of blood. It was around her head.'

'How awful!' Lucia says, her beautiful amber eyes wide and her manicured hand over her mouth. The others concur.

'Have the police actually said they think foul play was involved?' Stella asks.

'Not in so many words,' I admit, although by me telling them I saw Jared rush out of Dakota's house, that is certainly the presumption.

'So we're speculating like mad,' Lucia adds. 'It could have been an accident. Jared may or may not have been involved, or what if there was someone else? Dakota is always tight-lipped about her relationships. She could have a boyfriend for all we know.'

'You're right,' Erin says. 'Just because the police are talking to Jared, doesn't mean he was involved.'

I can't bear this. I can't bear the way my friends are discussing my husband almost as if I'm not here. How they're more interested in the whys of Dakota's injury rather than concerned as to how she actually is. This gossiping and speculating might have been something I would have relished just a few weeks ago, but today it feels trite and dirty. I need to make up an excuse to get out of here, perhaps tell them I'm exhausted and need to lie down. Except then Lucia speaks again.

'Could it be related to the person who sent a threatening note to Dakota?'

'What note?' I sit up straight.

Lucia frowns, although the crease in her forehead is so minuscule, it's barely there. 'Gosh, she shared it with me, but I was so caught up with my wedding and work I completely forgot about it.'

'But it could be vital!' I exclaim, putting my wineglass down on the table with a little too much force. The others are staring at me. 'Why didn't you tell us before?'

Lucia shrugs. 'I'm sorry, but it really didn't seem very important. I get nasty messages and threats all the time. I mean, I had one just before the wedding, which was particularly unpleasant. Someone sent me this grotesque collage of my face – at least I assume it was my face, made up of really ugly facial parts. A red, bulbous nose, hooded eyes, contorted lips and the like, along with a message threatening to tell the media that I've had plastic surgery done.'

My jaw drops open, as do Erin and Stella's. 'Is it normal for you to get sent something like that?' I ask.

'Well, no. I mean, I get nasty posts online but I've never received anything like this in the post.'

'Have you had plastic surgery?' Erin asks.

We all turn to look at Lucia. She pauses before replying, but there's a surprising redness in her cheeks. 'I might have had a few bits and pieces done,' she admits.

'But you've always been so against cosmetic procedures,' Erin says. 'I mean, you actually take a public stance against it.'

I interrupt. 'We're missing the point here. What did the threatening note to Dakota say?' I stare at Lucia. That's what's really important, not some silly threat made to Lucia.

'I'm really sorry but I don't know. I just recall that Dakota was quite shaken by it. I told her about my online hate messages, although the horrible collage and threat didn't arrive until after Dakota got her message.'

We're all silent for a long moment until Erin speaks. 'I also had a threatening message.'

I am completely still as the cogs turn in my brain. Surely this is all related?

'What did it say?' I ask.

'That I'm an unfit mother and that the anonymous sender has written letters to social services saying untrue things about my ability to be a good mother. They suggested that my mental health problems are affecting my children.'

I'm shocked. No, more than that, I'm horrified. That means that Lucia, Erin, Dakota and I have all received threatening messages. I turn to look at Stella, except she is staring at the carpet, tears welling in her eyes.

'Me too,' she whispers.

'But why didn't you say anything when I told you about my messages?' I ask, unable to keep the dismay from my voice.

'Mine are even worse. Please don't judge me.' She gives me an imploring look, and my heart sinks as I wonder what she's about to admit.

'I got a letter along with some bloodied baby clothes.'

'Bloodied baby clothes?' I ask, confused. Stella doesn't have children, so why did she receive baby clothes? It's one of the things I've admired most about Stella, how she's maintained her friendship with those of us who have children, despite being medically unable to have them. In fact, I bumped up her points on my list, adding in some extra for bravery and selflessness.

'The thing is, I could have had children. Probably still can. It's just that I don't want children.'

I stare at her, finding it hard to absorb what she's saying.

'I had an abortion in my early twenties before I met Cole, and I hated every second of that pregnancy. I never want to go through that again, so I told everyone that I couldn't have kids. It seemed easier to say that rather than the truth – that I don't want them. You know how judgmental people are.'

I suspect that comment is aimed at me, except no one is actually looking at me.

'Anyway, there was a note with the gross babygrow. It just said, "I know the truth, baby killer. Isn't it about time your husband knows too?"'

The room is so silent, I can hear the gentle tick of the clock in the hall. I feel really hurt that Stella couldn't have confided in me; that I didn't even know she'd had an abortion, let alone lied about not wanting children.

'Bloody hell, Stella,' Lucia exclaims eventually. 'So Cole thinks you can't have children when actually you can?'

She nods and wipes away a tear. 'I've lied to him, to everyone.' She turns towards me and murmurs, 'I'm sorry, Kate.' Then she takes us all in and says, 'I've told the story so many times, I've come to believe it myself. But the truth is, I secretly take the pill every day of my life.'

'And Cole doesn't know?' I ask.

She shakes her head slowly. 'And I don't want him to know. Not ever. It would break his heart.'

Oh, goodness. So many lies.

'That means we've all received threatening messages,' I say. I tell them about the dog poo through my door and the other anonymous text messages. 'Why just target us five? It must be related to my list.'

'Unless other people have been receiving them too,' Lucia adds. 'People we don't know about.'

'I doubt it,' Erin adds. 'I asked around some of the school mums to see if they'd received any threatening messages, and they all looked at me as if I'm mad. Perhaps I am,' she mutters as an afterthought.

'But what makes little sense is this person knows all about us, but at the same time they have demanded nothing,' Stella says. 'I mean, they could have asked for money or requested that we stop doing something – I don't know what – but it's like they've just been sent to unsettle us. Honestly, I'd have probably paid up if they'd asked for money in return for not telling Cole. Lucia, you'd probably do the same, wouldn't you, to stop the public knowing about your plastic surgery? So what's the rationale behind these notes?' Stella asks.

No one answers. She's right; it makes little sense.

'Have any of you been to the police?' I ask. 'Yours was particularly nasty,' I say to Stella.

'I can't go to the police. I just can't,' Stella exclaims, burying her face in her hands. 'What if they say something to Cole? He'd be devastated.'

I understand that, but equally, she's put me in an incredibly awkward situation. I work with Cole every day, and he's my friend, but now I know something fundamental about his wife that he doesn't know.

'Anyone got an idea who could be targeting us?' Lucia asks.

And then I think of Marilyn. How surprising it was to see her at Lucia's wedding. How I'm sure she was following me on my way here. How maybe she holds a grudge against us all.

'How well do you know Marilyn Tucker?' I ask Lucia.

It takes her a moment to place the name. 'You mean Marilyn the makeup artist?'

I nod.

'Not well, but she did a good job. Why?'

'She's got a son in the same year as Albie and the twins. She's got a grudge against Erin, but possibly against all of us.'

'Why has she got a grudge against me?' Erin pulls her neck back indignantly.

'We accused her of flirting with Kieren and then dropped her from our friendship group,' I say.

'Only because she behaved outrageously,' Erin adds. 'And that was years ago. I'd completely forgotten about it. Why does she want to take revenge now?'

'Oh, yes. I remember you and Dakota telling me about her,' Stella adds.

'She reached out to me a couple of weeks ago, after the

list was published,' I explain. 'And I'm sure she's been following me.'

But before anyone can say anything further, my phone rings. I stare at it for a moment, fearful of the withheld number, equally terrified of both answering and not answering it.

'Hello,' I say eventually. My friends' eyes are all on me.

'Kate Pedersen? This is Detective Kavi Patel. I'm calling to let you know that, sadly, Dakota Solomon died as a result of her injuries.'

CHAPTER EIGHTEEN

I burst into tears when Kavi Patel tells me Dakota has died. Our lovely, brilliant friend, the mother to such a bright little girl. It's so unfair.

'Kate,' Patel interrupts my snuffles. 'We've also formally charged your husband with her murder. I'm sorry.'

'But he can't have done it. He just can't.'

I feel arms around my shoulders. Lucia is perching on the arm of my chair and squeezing me gently.

'Unfortunately, the evidence suggests otherwise. We will need to interview you again, and we've got a warrant to search your house. We'll be at your home in an hour.'

'I... yes... I'm not there now... the press.' I can't get my words out. Is Jared's incarceration all my fault? Or do the police know something I don't? Surely Jared didn't hurt Dakota on purpose? My husband may have been foolish, but a murderer?

'We know that the press is outside your house. It's been reported by some of your neighbours. We'll do our best to move them along. In the meantime, I must reiterate that under no circumstances must you tell anyone that Dakota was hit with a golf club. We're holding back that piece of evidence from the media until we're further along with the investigation.'

'Right,' I say. I haven't told anyone, and I have no intention of doing so. Just imagining that bloodied golf club fills me with horror.

'I'll see you in an hour.'

The phone slips out of my fingers and lands on the soft, shaggy rug by my feet.

'What is it?' Stella asks.

'Dakota has died, and they've charged Jared with her murder.' My voice catches.

There's another heavy, long silence as we all try to absorb the enormity of what Patel has told me.

'And now I've got to go home because they've got a warrant to search our house.' I stand up, but I wobble violently and grasp the back of the armchair to steady myself.

'You're not going alone,' Lucia says. 'I'll come with you.'

'We can all come,' Stella adds.

'Thanks,' I say weakly, so grateful that my oldest friends appear to be supporting me. And they have every right not to, considering my husband has been charged with killing our friend. 'You do your own thing. I'll take up Lucia's offer, assuming I can still stay here?'

'Of course you can, sweetie. It's all such a shock.'

Ten minutes later, Lucia and I are in my car, except I'm finding it hard to concentrate and nearly rear-end a black cab.

'Think it's best if I drive,' Lucia suggests. I agree and stop the car behind a stationary red London bus. My lovely friend takes over.

I simply can't order my thoughts. My entire world has collapsed, and none of it makes sense. We don't talk as we head back towards Barnes, and it's just as well, as I doubt I could string a sentence together. All I can think about is how Jared must be feeling and how our children will cope growing up without their father. As we pull onto our road, Lucia slams on the brakes.

'Shit,' she mutters and immediately puts the car into reverse.

'What's going on?'

'The paps. There's a whole crowd of journalists gathered outside your house. They can't see me; it would be a disaster.'

And what about me? I think, but I say nothing. Lucia finds a parking spot in a bay on the next street over. 'I'm sorry, sweetie, but I'm going to have to leave you here. I can't be seen with you. I hope you understand.'

I don't, really, but I suppose I should be grateful she got me home. 'Thanks,' I say weakly.

'Message me when you're on your way back to my place.' She places a quick kiss on my cheek and says, 'Courage. Lots of courage.' And then she's out of the car, and I watch her jog to the end of the road, before she disappears.

I lock my car and walk slowly towards my street. Lucia is right. There's a load of press, and I don't want them to see me. I edge along the street until the opening to the little path that runs behind the houses, then I run. Just as I reach our gate to enter the garden from the back, there's a woman's voice.

'What the hell's going on, Kate?' my neighbour shouts. It's not nice Janice, but the woman from three doors down, whose name escapes me.

I don't have the energy to tell her, so I just say sorry, then I run across our garden, open up the back door and hurry inside.

I put my bag down, and immediately my phone rings. It's Mum, so I send her call to voicemail. Except she calls again, just a second later. Worried about the children, this time I answer it.

'What the hell is going on?' Mum's voice is shrill.

'What do you mean?'

'It's all over the media, that your friend Dakota somebody or other has been murdered and that Jared Pedersen, venture capitalist and father of two, married to MY daughter, is being held in custody accused of her murder! Didn't you think you might tell us?' Mum snaps.

'I've been busy,' I say, which even to my ears sounds trite.

'You need to come immediately,' she says. 'Come and collect the children.'

'I can't. I'm expecting the police. They've got a warrant to search the house.'

'Bloody hell, Kate! I'm a leading judge. Didn't you think it might be sensible to ask my opinion, to talk to me, get my expert advice?'

I grit my teeth and don't reply. For starters, Mum is retired, and secondly, her speciality was European law; she had nothing to do with the criminal justice system.

'Can you keep the kids a bit longer?' I ask. 'Please.'

'Out of the question. Your father's blood pressure is dangerously high, and I need my own space.'

Selfless as ever, I want to say, except I stop myself from uttering any sarcastic retorts. 'Don't you think we need to do what is best for the children?' I suggest.

'What is best is for them to be with their mother in their own home.'

I know I'm going to lose this argument, and frankly, the thought of her turning up at my house and depositing the kids in front of the bevvy of journalists is inconceivable, so reluctantly, I agree to drive to collect them, but not until later.

It's only when I've finished the call that I wonder how Mum knows. Has the information been released to the media, or does Mum get told things through her old lawyer network?

Before I can search on my phone, there's a banging on the door, which makes me jump. I tiptoe into the hallway and look through the peephole. Detective Kavi Patel is standing there with four people behind him.

I open the door just a smidge. 'You need to let us in, Kate,' he says.

I do as he says, and immediately flashlights go off in my face. 'Get off the path!' one of the police officers shouts at the journalist. 'This is private property.'

A few seconds later, the officers are inside. Our decent-sized hallway feels crowded, even airless. Patel shows me a piece of paper, which he says is the warrant, and I sign where he indicates.

They take three hours to search the house. During that period, I get two messages from Mum asking where I am; I ignore them. By the time the search is finished, the house feels different, violated. The officers take some papers from

Jared's office and some clothes from the laundry basket. Perhaps they were the clothes Jared was wearing when he rushed into Dakota's house; I really can't remember. Perhaps there'll be splatters of blood on them, vital bits of incriminating evidence. I wonder what would have happened if I'd run a load of washing. Too late now.

As Detective Patel is getting ready to leave, I say, 'There's something you need to know. Dakota received a threatening note, and I'm wondering if it had something to do with her murder.'

I expect him to grill me on this, to want to know more, except he doesn't. He just thanks me and says he'll be in touch when they want to interview me again. It's as if they've decided they've got their culprit and no further evidence is required. It makes my stomach clench.

If I assumed I could slink out of the house via the garden and not be spotted, I was wrong. There are two journalists hovering on the other side of the garden gate, one with a camera.

'Kate! How do you feel about your husband being accused of murdering one of your oldest friends?'

I try to ignore them, except the journalist is constantly in front of me, trying to block my route. And then there's a shout, and more people appear at the end of the path.

'Let me through!' I cry. Fear clasps my chest. I feel claustrophobic; my breath is shallow, my heart pounding.

'Get out of the bloody way!' a well-spoken female voice shouts. 'You're trespassing, and if you don't move this instant, I will call the police.'

I see Janice flinging her arms from left to right, not caring who she's hitting in the process. 'Come here, love,' she says, as she kicks out at a journalist. Somehow, Janice and I push through the crowd, and she escorts me to my car.

'What a bunch of bloody predators,' Janice says. 'Are you alright?'

'Not really,' I admit.

'I thought as much. It's all over the media, but don't worry, I know your lovely Jared hasn't got it in him.'

I smile weakly at her. I hope Janice is right.

I make the mistake of switching the car radio on just as the news has started. 'A woman has died after being found in her own home with a traumatic head injury. Dakota Solomon, a partner with law firm Sterling Peters, passed away in hospital earlier today. Jared Pedersen, a family friend and venture capitalist, is being held in custody, charged with her murder.'

I switch off the radio. It seems inconceivable that we have made the headlines; that Dakota is dead; that the man I share my bed with is accused of killing her.

'Mummy!' Rosie shouts as she rushes towards me, careening out of my parents' kitchen and into the hallway. I don't think I've ever been so happy to see my little girl. 'I've missed you, Mummy,' she says as she flings her arms around my midriff.

'I've missed you too. Where's your brother?'

'Watching telly.'

The children's bags are standing ready and packed next to the staircase in the hall as if my mother can't wait to be shot of them. It brings back all of those suppressed memories of abandonment whenever it was time to return to boarding school.

'Let's go and find your brother,' I say, taking Rosie's hand. We walk towards the snug, and I pull open the door. I expect Albie to be watching a film; he's not. He is watching the news.

The second he sees me, he has hysterics. 'What are they saying Dad has done?' he cries. 'It's all lies, isn't it? What's happened, Mum?' He is sobbing, hunched over as if he's in physical pain. I grab the remote control and turn the television off.

Mum appears. 'What's all the fuss about?'

'How could you?' I spit at her. 'He's just turned thirteen and you've let him watch the news! To discover that his father has been–' I let the words die on my lips.

Mum appears startled. 'He's a young man. It's not for me to censor what he watches, and the news is hardly X-rated. Not my fault that you married a murderer.'

'Mother!' I exclaim.

Rosie is staring at both of us with big eyes, and Albie is still sniffling on the sofa, his arms wrapped around his torso.

'We're going home, both of you.' Albie doesn't need asking twice, and five minutes later we're back in the car.

'Where's Dad?' Albie asks. 'Is it true, what they're saying?'

'It's all a horrible mistake,' I try to reassure him, praying I'm right. 'He'll be home in no time.'

'What's a horrible mistake?' Rosie asks.

I don't answer. 'So Grandma said you played tennis. How did it go?' I change the subject, which is sufficient for Rosie to stop asking any more questions. Albie, on the other hand, doesn't utter a word.

As we're driving at a snail's pace along the A3, I realise I haven't checked with Lucia if it's all right for me to bring the children to her place. I call her.

'Oh, babe, how are you?' she asks.

'You're on loudspeaker and I've got the kids with me. They can't stay at my parents' any longer. Is it alright if the three of us stay with you?'

There's a moment's pause and then she replies, 'Of course! The more, the merrier.'

CHAPTER NINETEEN

The children seem unimpressed with Lucia's fancy apartment. Albie is miserable without his games console, and there's nowhere for Rosie to play outside. And they're both unhappy that they need to share a room. But I feel safe here, and that's most important.

Lucia orders in supper for the three of us and then announces that she's leaving us to go and stay with Hamish. Perhaps that's for the best.

My phone rings shortly after 7 p.m. It's another withheld number, and I brace myself in case it's a journalist.

'Mrs Pedersen?' My heart sinks.

'My name is Jeff Ward, and I'm your husband's solicitor.'

The name sounds vaguely familiar.

'I would like to meet with you to discuss the statement you made to the police. Time is of the essence, so I was wondering if we could get together this evening. I can come to you.'

'Yes, okay. I'm staying at a friend's place in Battersea.'

'Excellent. I can be with you in the hour.'

I suspect everyone at the moment, and when I put the phone down to Jeff Ward, I wonder if he really is Jared's solicitor. I call Detective Kavi Patel.

'Am I able to speak to my husband?'

'I'm afraid not,' he says. 'Not until after the remand hearing. Everything has to go through his solicitor or ourselves.'

'And can I confirm that his solicitor is Jeff Ward?'

There's a moment of what sounds like shuffling papers. 'Yes, Ward is his solicitor.'

'Thank you,' I say, before ending the call.

Jeff Ward is exactly the type of man my husband likes. Tall, broad, with a full head of hair and a suit that likely cost the average person's monthly salary. He talks with a plummy voice and unwavering authority. I send the children to their bedroom, and Ward and I sit in Lucia's living room with the door closed. I offer him a cup of coffee, but he declines.

'I understand that you reported your husband to the police, so I need to get a sense as to what you're thinking,' Jeff Ward says.

'What do you mean?'

'It would be good to know if you're supportive of your husband's defence. It would make things easier all around.'

'If he's not guilty, then of course I'm supportive.'

'Right,' Ward says, although I get the sense he's going through the motions and isn't that interested in what I've got to say. 'I've been talking to Jared about the best approach. As expected, his DNA has been found on the golf clubs, and his prints have been found in Dakota Solomon's house. This is to be expected, as he was staying there. But there is no actual evidence to suggest that he hit Solomon with that club. We're still waiting for analysis of his clothes to check for blood splatters. As such, the only really incriminating factor is that Jared left the scene of the crime when he discovered Ms. Solomon. This, of course, can be explained by blind panic. Consequently, the whole of the prosecution case hinges on your statement.'

'Mine?' I ask, frowning.

'But here's the thing. The prosecution cannot compel you to testify against your husband due to spousal rules. The only exception to this is in the case of assault or injury to the spouse or a sexual offence against a child under the age of sixteen. As this does not apply here, the police cannot force you to give evidence against Jared. So where does that leave us?' This is clearly a rhetorical question as he doesn't pause for breath. 'All the police evidence is circumstantial. I am reasonably confident that I can get your husband off this charge; however, it would help enormously if the police had someone else to concentrate on. Right now, they think they have their man, and they're not even considering an alternative scenario. They could of course turn their focus onto you. Perhaps you went into the house to confront Dakota for being with Jared. Maybe you became angry and hit her with the golf club, then put it in Jared's bag before calling the police.'

I stare at him, horrified. No one has suggested that scenario.

'But that's not true,' I exclaim. 'And my fingerprints won't be on any of the golf clubs.'

Jeff Ward leans towards me. 'I'm not suggesting that is the case, Kate, but it's my job to consider all possible scenarios. I'm on your side.'

I realise it's Jeff Ward's job to get Jared off the charge, whether or not my husband is guilty, but the thought that anyone might think I hurt Dakota is horrifying.

'Is there anyone else you can think of who had a grudge against Dakota Solomon? Anyone else in her life causing her problems? I will, of course, be talking to her family, but I understand you knew her well.'

'Actually, yes.'

Ward's face lights up. I tell him about the threats that we have all received, although I can't tell him the nature of the threat against Dakota, as I don't know it.

'This is excellent news,' he says, clapping his hands together. 'Gives me something to work on, and if we can show that someone was pursuing Ms Solomon, that should be enough to create reasonable doubt in the minds of a jury. Of course, if we can get something substantive, that would be better still, as it would avoid your husband going to trial.'

Jeff Ward stands up. 'Could you speak to your friends and get me details of these unpleasant threats that you've mentioned? I would like to take statements from all your friends as soon as possible, please.' He hands me his heavily embossed business card.

I call Stella.

'Are you alone?' I ask.

There's a pause. 'I can be.' I hear her footsteps and the closing of a door.

'Alone now.'

'Jared's solicitor has requested that we all make a statement to the police about the threats we've received. He says the evidence they have on Jared is circumstantial, and if we can prove that someone else was threatening Dakota, as well as us, it would shift the blame. Would you do it?'

'Tell them about the bloodied babygrow?' she asks in a whisper.

'Yes.'

There's a long silence before I speak again. 'Please, Stella. You'd be doing it for me. I've no idea what the future holds for Jared and me, but I don't want the father of my children to be convicted of a murder he didn't commit.'

'But if I make a statement to the police, Cole might find out about my lies.'

'We can ask them to keep it completely confidential. This must happen all the time with witnesses.'

'I don't know, Kate. I'd do anything for you; I hope you know that. But this could destroy my marriage.'

'Will you at least think about it? It's so important.'

'Alright. I'll think about it.'

I put the phone down, demoralised. I just hope I can persuade Stella to tell the truth to the police. Next, I call Lucia and ask the same question.

'Bloody hell, Kate. If the media finds out, I'll be decimated. Crucified. Let me have a word with my publicist, and I'll come back to you.'

Lucia returns the call about fifteen minutes later.

'I'm sorry, babe, not great news. I know this isn't good timing for you but I'm going to have to ask you to leave my apartment.'

'Why?' I ask.

'My publicist is really worried. You must understand that I can't be seen to publicly support you, and having you hanging around my place, it's just too dodgy. You're potentially the wife of a murderer. But I will make a statement to the police, so long as they can guarantee my anonymity. A fair compromise?' she asks.

I have no response. I understand Lucia needs to look after herself, but it feels like she's abandoning me and the kids.

'How soon do you need me to leave?' I ask, unable to banish the coldness in my voice.

I'm expecting her to say tomorrow or the next day, but she says, 'As soon as you can, please. Again, I'm really sorry, babe.'

I groan after ending the call. *Thanks, Lucia, for nothing*, I think. I feel so weary as I get off her comfortable couch and, with heavy feet, walk along the corridor to the children's room.

'I'm sorry, kids. Change of plan. We're going home.'

CHAPTER TWENTY

I've been dreading the children returning to school; dreading the stares at the school gates and the unpleasant comments that will no doubt be directed towards Albie and Rosie. Rosie doesn't really understand what's going on but Albie is withdrawn and obviously unhappy. I message both of their headteachers, asking them to look out for my children, but I don't suppose there's anything in a teacher training handbook that explains how to protect children whose father has been accused of murder.

The kids are eating breakfast, although Albie is just pushing the cereal around in his bowl, when my phone rings. It's Stella.

'Have you seen the papers today?' she asks.

My heart sinks. What further negative things are going to be written about my husband?

'I'll send you a link.' A message pops up on my phone, and I click on the hyperlink.

'Is cruel friend ranking list the reason that top lawyer was battered to death?' the headline screams.

'What the hell!' I exclaim as the words sink in.

'I'm sorry, Kate, but the article even mentions your name.'

I read the first paragraph. *'The brutal killing of top lawyer Dakota Solomon has taken a further twist. Dakota was a long-standing friend of recruitment boss Kate Pedersen, whose venture capitalist husband, Jared Pedersen, is accused of murdering Ms Solomon. In the days before her death, Dakota discovered Kate Pedersen had compiled a spreadsheet ranking her so-called friends. According to this paper's sources, the list was brutal, grading Pedersen's friends on a range of qualities from kindness to sense of humour, intelligence to attractiveness. Pedersen, who runs Pedersen Domestic Staff Agency, may use psychometric testing for her recruitment, but how appropriate is this for her friends? The friend list has gone viral on social media and has now hit stratospheric levels as the news has broken that Kate Pedersen's husband has been accused of the vicious murder of her friend.'*

I can't read any more. 'I've thought about what you asked,' Stella says. 'And I will make a statement to the police. For you,' she adds. 'But they need to promise that it won't get back to Cole.'

'Thank you,' I say, wondering if the police really will give such a reassurance.

'I'm going to get the bus,' Albie interrupts me.

'No, love. I'll take you to school.' I don't want him to be bullied on the bus. 'Sorry, Stella, but I've got to go.'

'Alright, but shout if you need anything.'

By last night, the journalists had disappeared from our street, and I was relieved that we were yesterday's news, but today, when I open the front door, a man and a woman appear, both holding voice recorders.

'Is it true that you rate your friends, Kate?'

'Does your friendship list have anything to do with Dakota Solomon's murder?'

I slam the door shut again. This is a nightmare.

'What do those men want?' Rosie asks, her voice sweet and high-pitched. I hate that this will be destroying the kids' innocence. We could walk out the back, but it doesn't help much with the car being parked at the front of our house.

'They're not very nice, those people, so we're going to rush straight to the car and ignore them.'

'The journalists?' Albie asks.

I nod.

'They're only doing their job,' Albie says. I'm shocked at the maturity of that statement. To be fair to the media crowd, when they see me with the children, the cameras are lowered and there is no heckling. They let us pass through and walk to the car without any comments or flashes of cameras. I'm beyond grateful.

IN THE CAR, I let Albie sit in the front and give Rosie my phone, along with my earbuds, so she can listen to music. It gives me the chance to talk to Albie.

'There's so much that's been written online about Dad and about us,' I say. 'I know you're going to read some of it, or your mates might say stuff, but I don't want you to believe what's been written.'

Albie's head is turned away from me, and he's staring out of the window. It seems so wrong that I can't protect him from the media storm, but even if I confiscate his phone and stop him from using my iPad, he'll only be told about his father by his school friends.

'Your dad is a good man, darling, and the police have made a terrible mistake. You know that, don't you?' I just pray I'm right. I reach over and squeeze his hand, but he sits there rigidly and says nothing.

It's busy at Albie's school, with parents dropping children off and a bus disgorging kids up ahead. He reaches for the car door.

'If there's any trouble, go to your teacher or call me,' I say.

'I'm not allowed the phone on at school.'

'There's always an exception to that rule. Be strong, sweetheart.'

Albie throws me a strange look and hurries away. I want to wait until he's safely inside the gates, but the car behind me hoots, so I pull away. I can only pray that the other kids are kind to my boy. Traffic is bad, so by the time we get to Rosie's school, we're late. I find a parking space a couple of roads away, grab her school bag and hold her hand as we hurry along the pavement. Parents are walking away from the school, some huddled together deep in conversation. If I had felt I had been stared at before, this is far, far worse. I feel eyes on me from every direction.

'What are you doing here?' a strident female voice asks.

'Kate!'

I stop. It's Martina, Tessa's mother, the woman who stopped her daughter from being friends with Rosie after the list debacle. My heart sinks.

'What are you doing here?' she asks again, her hands on her hips, as if she's the school policewoman.

'Taking my daughter to school.'

'But you're not wanted here,' she says.

For a moment, I'm speechless. Who is Martina to say whether we can be or can't be at the school? She's just another mother, not even the class rep. I desperately want to come up with a suitable retort, except my mind goes blank and Rosie tugs at my hand. 'Come on, Mummy!'

I throw Martina what I hope is a killer stare and carry on walking. But it's shaken me, and now I'm doubtful about whether Rosie should be at school. We jog towards the entrance, where to my relief, I see the school secretary, who is about to lock the gate. She's a kindly woman whom I've spoken to on numerous occasions when the kids have been sick or needed to leave school early for an appointment.

'Mrs Smith,' I say breathlessly. I brace myself for a scowl or a stiffening.

'Mrs Pedersen, and Rosie. Did you have a lovely half-term?' There's a wide smile on her face as she bends to talk to Rosie.

'I'm sorry we're late. I wasn't sure if I should bring Rosie to school, what with everything that's been happening.'

'I think this is the best place for her. Rosie, why don't you hurry along to your classroom so Mum and I can have a little chat.'

'Have a lovely day, darling,' I say, blowing Rosie a kiss.

She waits until Rosie has disappeared and then says, 'Children need routine, Mrs Pedersen. I can't begin to imagine what you're going through, but rest assured, school is the best place for Rosie. We'll make sure we keep an eye out for her, so please don't worry.'

I want to hug this woman, but all I can do is muster a weak smile and say thank you.

'Good luck with everything,' she adds.

I've just got in my car when the phone rings. At long last, it's Jared.

'I've been released on bail,' he says, his voice loud and cheerful. 'Jeff Ward is the best.'

'Oh,' I say. I know I should feel relief, except I don't. Do I really believe that Jared is innocent? Logically, I know I should do but there's still a niggling doubt. Perhaps it's because he's lied to me rather than a belief that he's really a killer. I lean my head back against the car seat and close my eyes, trying to order my thoughts.

'I'm staying at Kieren and Erin's house. Thought it would be better to be there rather than caught in the middle of the media circus. I assume our house is surrounded?'

'Yes, there has been a lot of press.'

'We'd better have a chat though. Do you want to come over?'

Ten minutes later, and I'm ringing Erin's doorbell. Jared opens the door. We stand there looking at each other awkwardly before Jared steps back and waves me in. How are you meant to react to your husband when he's admitted having a relationship with one of your best friends? When he was accused of her murder? When he's turned your life upside down? It all feels completely surreal and overwhelming.

'Do you want a coffee?' he asks, leading me into the kitchen.

'Okay. Are Erin and Kieren not here?'

'No. We've got the house to ourselves.'

He makes me a coffee in silence, and I stare at the back of this man, whom I thought I knew better than myself. My hands are shaking slightly as I take the pretty white cup from him; exhaustion and confusion combined, I suppose.

The Meddings' kitchen is a bit smaller than ours, and its oak finish makes it seem more outdated than many of the houses I've seen in the area. Unlike us and many of our friends, who have done major refurbishments or DIY after moving into our houses, Erin and Kieren haven't even repainted any of the walls. But what shocks me is how messy it is. Once upon a time, Erin kept a spotless house, almost clinical in fact, but now every work surface is covered in clutter; piles of paper, dirty dishes in the sink, boxes of cereal and tea bags littered on the kitchen counters. I haven't seen a kitchen like this since our student days, and I'm taken aback but try not to be judgmental. I wonder how Kieren feels about this or whether he's used to it.

'I wouldn't wish what I've just been through on my worst enemy,' Jared says as he sits heavily on a pine chair, seemingly unconcerned by the cluttered kitchen. 'Look, I've been thinking. It's horrible what's happened, but we shouldn't let it affect us too much. You said before that we should do counselling, and I agree. I don't want to lose you, Kate. The fact is, I only slept with Dakota after you and I had an argument and I was drunk. It didn't mean anything, and it's the biggest regret of my life.' Surely his biggest regret should be leaving Dakota to die on the kitchen floor? He holds his hands together in a prayer pose, and his eyes fix onto mine. 'I've never cheated on you before, and I never will again. I promise. I love you and the kids so much.'

He stares at me with a puppy-dog look, but surprisingly, I find myself able to look at him dispassionately. Jared's hair is too long, and he seems tired, with a grey pallor and rings under his eyes. Yes, he is a good-looking man, but that supreme confidence now seems like cockiness. Where's the contrition? Where's the concern and sorrow for Dakota?

Where's the consideration for our kids and how this affects them? He should be grieving for his friend and lover. He should be feeling the very deepest regret for causing so much pain.

'Did you do it?' I ask.

He jerks his head back, and his eyes widen.

'Did you kill Dakota? Even if it was done in a moment of passion or was a terrible mistake. Did you do it?'

'No, Kate!' he exclaims, leaning really far forward towards me. 'How can you even think that? You have to trust me!' His breath smells a little sour, as if he was drinking last night or hasn't cleaned his teeth.

I don't know what to say. Do I still love this man? Probably not. Objectively, I can see he's attractive, but do I want his arms around me? No.

'You won't testify against me, though, will you? Jeff Ward told me about spousal privilege.'

I shrug. 'I won't testify against you if you're innocent.'

'Of course I'm innocent!' He's almost shouting now. 'I just want us to be together. You, me and the kids. For everything to get back to normal.'

'I don't know, Jared. Our friend is dead, and frankly, I feel broken.'

'I'd like to come home and be with you,' he says, as if he hasn't heard a word I've just said.

'I don't know,' I murmur. 'It's too soon.'

'But I haven't seen the kids in two weeks.'

'That was your choice,' I say.

'It wasn't my choice that I was locked up in the cells.'

'You chose not to be there for Albie's birthday,' I remind him.

We stare at each other, and in this moment, I know I

can't forgive Jared. What decent man would leave someone to bleed out on the floor?

I stand up. 'I think we should keep our distance for the time being,' I say.

Jared looks at me with an expression of disbelief. 'No, Kate. I want to come home.'

'Sorry, Jared. Not yet,' I add. In my gut, I know it's not now and it's not ever. I walk out of the Meddings' house, and as I softly close the front door behind me, I hear a yell come from inside the house. Jared has lost his cool.

I can't decide what to do. To go home and wallow or go to the office and try to distract myself with work. In the end, I decide the latter might be preferable. I head towards Hammersmith and switch on the radio. It's *Woman's Hour* on BBC Radio 4, and the presenter is introducing her next interviewee.

'Today our guest is Lucia Highsmith, the supermodel and influencer who has been caught up in the friend ranking debacle. Lucia, we understand that you're a friend of Kate Pedersen, the woman who wrote the now infamous friend ranking list.'

Lucia laughs. 'I wouldn't say I'm a friend,' she says. 'But yes, I am on the list.'

'And what was your score?'

'Fortunately for me, I didn't come last.'

'How do you feel about your inclusion and being judged?'

'Honestly, it's water off a duck's back. I barely know the woman who wrote this list. She's a friend of friends of mine; just someone I went to university with a decade ago who has a chip on her shoulder.'

I blink away the tears in my eyes, and then, because I'm

not concentrating, I slam my car into the rear of the white van idling at the traffic lights in front of me.

'Bloody idiot!' The driver storms out of the van and yells at me, and as I'm close to sobbing anyway, I burst into tears.

'Turn off the bloody waterworks, woman,' he mutters, before walking to the front of my car and examining the damage to his van. I try to pull myself together and eventually get out of the car. The traffic is mounting behind us, and I can sense everyone's frustration.

I rub my eyes and study his rear bumper. It's dented, but the damage is a lot less than I'd feared.

'I'll give you my details,' I say. 'What's your phone number?'

He gives me his number, and I text him my name, number and email.

'Blow me down!' he says, as he stares at the incoming text. 'You're the wife of the chap who's accused of murdering that solicitor, aren't you?'

'Contact me when you've got a price for fixing the damage,' I say. 'I accept full responsibility.'

'More than what your f-ing husband has done.'

I need to end the conversation fast, so I return to my car and lock the door. After a bit of arm-waving and mouthing obscenities at me, he gets into his van and pulls away. It isn't until I've also eased into the stream of traffic that it strikes me I've just given an angry stranger all of my contact details.

CHAPTER TWENTY-ONE

This morning, the van driver texted me the quote for the repairs to his vehicle. It's less than I had feared, so I agree to pay in full rather than putting it through our insurance. I just hope that once I've transferred the money, that will be the last I hear from him.

Today, it's Dakota's funeral. It's being held in a church near The Strand, and the wake is in a wine bar next door to where Dakota used to work. I know this only thanks to Stella. Stella has been the one friend who has rung me every day, who has dropped off dishes of lasagne and quiche and sat with me until midnight as I wailed about my bastard of a husband. She's brought gifts for the children and even offered for us to go and stay with her if I get scared being alone in our house.

'I don't think you should go to the funeral,' she had said.

'But Dakota was my friend. I really cared about her.'

'Please tell me Jared isn't thinking of going?'

'I don't know, but I doubt it. He might be out on bail, but he's still a suspect,' I say.

'I know this is harsh, but you're the suspect's wife. I doubt Dakota's family will want you there.'

I groaned. It feels like I'm damned if I do and damned if I don't.

Perhaps it's selfish of me, but I want to say goodbye to Dakota. I want to pay my respects to her family. Is it egotistical of me to go? I put on a black dress and black coat, along with large, dark sunglasses, and set off for central London. I take the underground, wanting to be anonymous. By the time I arrive at the church, it's just five minutes until the start of the funeral. It goes against every one of my instincts being this late and makes me feel nervy and uncomfortable. The hearse has already arrived, so I slip in through the open doors, my head lowered, my coat done up to the neckline, and my oversized dark glasses too big for my face. The church is large, but it's crowded with people sitting on all the pews, murmuring. There are a couple of men standing right at the back, and I recognise Detective Kavi Patel, who is sitting at the end of the second-to-last pew. Perhaps I shouldn't be surprised that the police are here. There's a space on the end pew, so I shuffle past a few people, muttering my apologies, and sit down.

The service is desperately sad. Dakota's brother gives a reading, and there are lots of stifled sobs. Tears run down my face, and I dab at my eyes with a tissue, trying not to remove the sunglasses, even though I suspect I look ridiculous. Poor Dakota. I can't stop seeing the image of her lying in that pool of blood. As the service ends, her parents follow the coffin, her mother supported by Dakota's brother, little Violet looking bewildered as she grasps her grandfather's hand. Dakota's mother is stooped, her father trembling, and my heart bleeds for them. There are white lilies everywhere. On the coffin, on the pews and at the front of the church in flamboyant floral displays, and the sweet scent is stifling. I don't think I'll ever buy a lily again. The congregation leaves in an orderly way, with the front pews departing first. I slink back into the pew as Stella, Erin and Lucia leave together.

As I exit the church, I see Lucia standing to the side of the wide steps, surrounded by paparazzi. She's talking into a microphone with two cameras angled towards her, but I can't hear what she's saying.

'Kate!' Stella spots me and waves me over. Cole is standing next to her. 'So you came?' she says.

'I had to,' I say quietly.

'Are you coming to the wake?'

'I'd like to, but I'm not sure.'

'I'm going back to work,' Cole says. 'Will you be in later?'

'Not sure. My diary's pretty empty. But I'll call you.'

Cole nods, gives Stella a quick kiss on the cheek and waves at us as he walks away.

Erin appears at my side. 'I think you should come to the wake,' she says. 'You and Dakota were close, and with Jared having been released...' She lets her words peter out.

'What do you think?' I ask Stella.

She shrugs her shoulders. 'You're here now, so you might as well come. Besides, I've done the catering for the wake, and we've got your favourite mushroom vol-au-vents. Dakota's brother asked me to do it as the wine bar doesn't serve food. My team is there now, so I'd better get a move on.'

'Alright,' I say, relieved that Stella and Erin are being supportive. 'I'll come with you.'

Just as we're about to walk down the church steps, I

catch a glimpse of Marilyn. She's wearing a black raincoat and is hurrying away from us. What the hell is she doing here? I didn't even think she knew Dakota. I run down a few steps, about to call her name, but she's disappeared into the crowd.

Dakota's family has taken over the whole wine bar for the wake. It's a large space, with tall tables pushed back against the walls and a long bar with a black marble top. There are servers handing out glasses of wine and delicate nibbles. There must be a couple of hundred people here, and I'm glad for Dakota's parents that there's such a large turnout. But then there's a commotion at the door and the flashing of lights. Lucia is standing in the entryway talking to one of the journalists, a television camera just inches from her face.

'Well, this is turning into a bloody media circus,' Erin says, with surprising venom. 'What the hell is Lucia doing, using Dakota's funeral to promote herself? I'm going to talk to her.'

'Erin!' Stella shouts, but Erin ignores her and strides towards Lucia. 'Oh no,' Stella murmurs. 'I don't know what's got into her recently, but Erin appears to have regained her self-confidence.'

I wonder if she's on some new medication.

We edge nearer to the door, just in time to see Erin place a hand on Lucia's shoulder. Lucia says something to the cameraman and turns to Erin.

'This is a funeral, not a bloody media circus!' Erin spits at Lucia.

'Sorry,' Lucia says to the paps, and turns her back to them.

'Erin's right, Lucia,' Stella says, as we draw up level with them. 'Couldn't you have thrown them off? It doesn't seem appropriate.'

'Or not come at all,' I mutter, although the irony of that statement isn't lost on me.

'Come on, girls,' Lucia says, pushing her shoulders back and adjusting the collar of her black coat dress. 'Dakota was my friend too. And it's not like the funeral was a secret. The media knew about it and would have been here even if I wasn't.'

'But apparently I'm not your friend anymore,' I hiss.

Erin frowns at me.

'You didn't hear the Radio 4 interview?' Stella asks her.

'No,' Erin replies.

'Look, I had to distance myself, Kate,' Lucia says. 'You must understand that. I've got a public persona to consider.'

'I was really hurt, Lucia,' I say. 'I mean, I've been staying in your apartment. My daughter was a bridesmaid at your wedding. How can you say you barely know me and that I've got a chip on my shoulder?'

'Did you want me to tell the truth?' Lucia's eyes are darker now. 'That you were one of my best friends and I was horribly hurt by your pathetic list, as were the rest of us?'

'Oh, come on,' I add. 'That's all been forgiven. We've got bigger things to worry about.'

'Actually, I'm with Kate on this one,' Erin adds, surprising me. 'It feels completely shit to be dismissed, and although I hate what Kate wrote, you can't pretend that she isn't a close friend.'

'Come on, everyone,' Stella adds. 'There's a time and a place, and it's not here or now. We might have hurt or upset each other–'

Lucia interrupts Stella. 'Oh, don't tell me you're still

upset about my not giving you the wedding catering?' She wriggles her fingers at the server just to our left, who is carrying a platter of nibbles. 'What you've done here is hardly A-list.'

'You're such a bitch,' Erin says.

'Well, I can tell I'm not wanted,' Lucia adds. 'See you around.' She hoists her black Birkin handbag into the crook of her elbow and looks around the room. Being several inches taller than the rest of us, helped by high-heeled knee-length boots, she has a good view. She stalks across the room to where Dakota's parents are huddled together with the pastor.

I know nobody here, and the conversation between Erin, Stella and me is strained. We're all drinking too much, but I guess we're trying to dull the pain of losing one of our closest friends at such a young age. At some point, a huge television screen above the bar springs to life and photos of Dakota appear from all stages of her life.

'This is so sad,' Stella says, wiping tears from her cheeks.

Erin appears to have got hold of a bottle of white wine, and she pours some into my empty glass. At some point, the photos seem to become blurry, and the room begins to spin. I've drunk too much on an empty stomach. I look for the servers to find some more food, except there appears to be none left. I find myself talking to some older man who explains he's a friend of the family and then gives a speech about the crime rates in London, and I soon zone out. I have an overwhelming urge to go home. I glance around the room, trying to locate Erin or Stella, and see that they're deep in conversation with Dakota's brother. I mutter some apologies to the man who is still talking at me, and head towards the door.

The cold, damp air does little to mitigate my feeling of drunkenness, although I take in great big gulps of it. Unsteadily, I walk towards the station. My emotions are all over the place; sometimes I feel like giggling, other times like bursting into tears, except I try to control myself, conscious I'm surrounded by commuters, their heads down, minding their own business. I'm waiting at a set of traffic lights, cars and taxis passing by slowly, tyres sloshing up filthy water from the puddles. And then a Rolls-Royce drives past slowly, and there is Lucia staring out of the back window. She sees me, I'm certain of it, except she doesn't ask her driver to stop.

I walk straight across Waterloo Bridge to the south side of the river. The air is heavy with rain, and the wide river is grey and fast-flowing. I feel a little nauseous and increasingly unsteady on my feet but determined to get to the station. I'm drunk, stupidly drunk. Inside Waterloo station, it's swarming with commuters striding briskly towards waiting trains and tourists pulling large suitcases on wheels. I know my way without having to study the departures board; just as well, because when I look up at it, the words merge and wobble. Platform one. I head towards it, holding my phone over the electronic barrier, waiting for the gate to open and then moving unsteadily through it. The train hasn't arrived yet, so I head down the platform, weaving in between the waiting commuters. God, I'm so drunk, I can barely put one foot in front of the other. Halfway down the platform, I come to a halt. My head is throbbing now, and all I want to do is sink down onto a seat. I see the train coming towards us quite fast, the air whooshing, the acrid smell of diesel making me nauseous. The clunking of the wheels on the track is so loud, I want to put my hands over my ears. And then I feel the most enormous shove.

I wobble. My knees give way. I hear a scream. More screams.

I can feel the air, the nothingness. And weirdly, I accept it. That this is the last second of my life. That someone has pushed me to my death.

CHAPTER TWENTY-TWO

They say that your life streams through your head in that final second, except it doesn't. Or maybe it doesn't for me for this wasn't my last second on earth. I had expected to feel agony and then a nothingness.

The pain is there, and it's coming from my knees and my head. I reach up to touch the side of my head, and it feels sticky. The ground is grey and hard. Dirty too.

'Are you alright?' A man is kneeling down next to me. He's got very white hair and wears tortoiseshell glasses and a red tie.

'Call an ambulance!' someone says.

I see lots of shoes all around me. Trainers, stilettos, brogues, boots. So many feet.

'I'm a doctor! Let me through!'

A woman kneels down beside the white-haired man. 'What's your name?' She is grey-haired, with small eyes and a long, aquiline nose. I can't speak. All I want to do is shut my eyes and sleep. I let my eyelids close.

'You need to stay awake.' The woman is holding my wrist

now. It feels nice and secure. I force my eyelids open, and she's just inches from my face. 'I'm a doctor, and you need to tell me your name.'

'Kate Pedersen,' I say, although my words sound distant and fluffy around the edges.

'Kate, you've had a fall and are in shock. The paramedics are on their way.'

'Someone pushed me,' I say in a slurring voice.

The doctor woman glances up at the white-haired man and frowns. She then turns back to me. 'What hurts?'

'Dunno,' I say.

'Do you think you can sit up?'

I nod. I place the palms of my hands on the concrete platform and lever myself upwards. That hurts. A lot. All those feet seem further away now, but I'm dizzyingly close to the edge of the platform and can see straight under the carriage of the train that is now parked in front of me.

'Bloody hell,' the white-haired man says. 'I thought she was a goner.'

'What happened?' the doctor asks.

'She slipped. I managed to grab her just in time and pull her back from the edge.'

'I was pushed,' I say again.

As my eyes begin to steady, I see a huge crowd has gathered around me. I don't want to be seen, to be peered at, to be pitied. And then the fear strikes. Someone tried to push me, and that person is probably still here.

I'm not safe.

There's a loud announcement over the tannoy. 'Could all customers on Platform One move away from the edge. The train doors will not be opening. This train will be delayed until further notice.'

Legs start shuffling backwards. A guard appears, wearing all black. His heavy boots are dusty, though. 'Move back, everyone. Move back.'

Is this all for me?

The grey-haired doctor is on her haunches now. 'Kate, I'm going to give you a quick check over. Is that alright?'

I nod. She opens her briefcase and takes out a stethoscope. She checks my pulse, listens to my heart and puts that little instrument thing on my index finger. 'Where does it hurt?' she asks.

'I think I'm okay. Just a bit bruised. My hands, the side of my head.'

She moves the hair away from my right temple. 'Okay, that's not too bad. Just a graze. Do you think you can stand up?'

'Yes.' Slowly, I lever myself up until I'm standing, but I feel woozy. She holds my arm. 'What happened?' she asks.

'I was pushed.'

She looks doubtful. 'Are you sure?'

I nod. I am 100 percent sure. I can still feel the sensation in the middle of my back.

She stands up and walks over to the train guard, who is talking in low tones into a walkie-talkie. I hear the word *police*.

I realise that the white-haired man is still supporting me. The doctor returns, and together they guide me towards a bench. I sink down onto it and look at my knees. They're scraped and bleeding, as are the palms of my hands.

'Thank goodness you're okay,' the white-haired man says. His face is so pale it's almost translucent.

'Thank you for saving me,' I say, trying but probably failing to smile at him. It feels like my facial muscles aren't working properly. And then there's a *beep, beep, beep* as the train doors open and people pour out of the train, and commuters huddled together on the platform surge forwards, climbing onto the train.

'She's here,' a man's voice says. I turn to look. The train guard is accompanied by two police officers. They're in full uniform.

'What's your name?' one officer asks.

'Kate Pedersen,' I reply

She sits down next to me, which feels strange somehow. 'This gentleman says you think you were pushed. Can you confirm that?'

'Yes, I was pushed.'

The second officer turns to the white-haired man. 'Did you see her being pushed, sir?'

'No,' the white-haired man says with some authority.

'And you?' the officer asks the doctor lady.

'No. I just saw Kate fall to the ground, and this gentleman grabbed her and pulled her backwards onto the platform.'

'Have you been drinking, Kate?' the female officer asks me.

I feel a wave of shame, wondering if my breath smells that bad, but I have a reason to have been drinking. 'Yes, but not that much. I've been to the funeral of a friend of mine. Dakota Solomon.' The officer narrows her eyes, clearly recognising the name. 'Kate Pedersen, did you say?'

I nod.

She stands up and beckons to her colleague. They step away from me, out of earshot. And then suddenly, everything is too much. Tears spring to my eyes, and I can't stop them from rolling down my face. Someone just tried to push me to my death. Dakota is dead, probably murdered. Jared is a suspect. Through my blurry eyes, I see the officers talking to both the white-haired man and the doctor. After a moment, the doctor walks over to me and bends down again. 'I'm going home now, Kate. It might be a good idea for you to get a check over at the hospital. I hope you're not too bruised.'

'Thank you,' I say. 'You've been very kind.'

The white-haired man doesn't say goodbye, but I watch them both climb onto the waiting train. And then the doors beep to signal they're closing, and the train slowly pulls out of the station. I feel bereft. As if my guardian angels have left me behind, left me to a horrible, unknown fate.

The female police officer returns to me. 'Can we call anyone to help you home?' she asks.

'Are you going to check who tried to push me?'

I recognise that expression of disbelief and doubt. They don't believe me.

'You said you'd been drinking, Kate. We can check the CCTV, but we think you slipped, probably because you're a bit unsteady on your feet.'

'No!' I exclaim. 'Someone has been threatening me. It's all on record. You need to talk to Detective Kavi Patel. Everything is related.'

I can tell she thinks I'm talking nonsense, and once again, the tears come. God, I'm being pathetic, but I don't know how to keep it together. 'Please talk to the detective.'

'Alright,' she says, but there is zero conviction in her voice. 'Who's your next of kin?'

'My husband,' I say automatically.

'And what's your husband's telephone number?'

I recite it, but it isn't until I've given it to her that I realise

I don't want to talk to Jared. I don't want to see him, and I certainly don't want his pity.

It's too late. My reflexes are too slow. The officer has stepped away from me and is on the phone.

'Good evening, Mr Pedersen. There's nothing to worry about, but I'm a police officer, and we have your wife here at Waterloo Station. She's had a minor accident, nothing that requires hospitalisation, we think, but she needs to come home.'

There's a long pause. 'Oh, I see. Right. Yes, of course you can't leave them.'

I glance at my watch and realise to my dismay that it's nearly 7 p.m. Who collected Rosie from school? Are the kids with Jared? I've never just left them before.

The officer turns back to me. 'Your husband is looking after your children at home, so he can't leave them.' She hesitates for a moment. 'Come along then. We'll get you home.'

This is my second, or is it my third trip in a police car in the past few days? It feels so strange, sitting in the back of a police car. I also feel extremely sick and have to concentrate not to throw up. It's not quick driving from Waterloo Station to Barnes, and the officer is driving carefully, sticking steadfastly to the ridiculously low London speed limits.

Parking outside our house, she gets out of the car and accompanies me up to the door. Not waiting for me to extract a key from my bag, she rings the doorbell. It's answered almost immediately by Jared.

I'm dismayed he's in our house when I'd chucked him out, but then my hazy thoughts regroup and I realise he has to be there for the children.

'Go straight up to the bedroom,' he says in a tight whisper, as if I'm some errant child. 'Thank you, Officer, for bringing her home.'

I don't wait to listen to the conversation. Gripping tightly onto the handrail, I lever myself up the stairs. I can hear the television blaring from the living room and assume the children are there. I'm glad they're not seeing me in this state, with my torn stockings and bleeding head. I go straight into the bathroom, sit on the closed toilet and lean against the sink. I look dreadful. There's dried blood on my temple and black mascara smudged down my cheeks.

The door swings open behind me, and Jared strides in, shutting it behind him. He leans with his back against it.

'What the fuck!' he exclaims. 'You get completely pissed, fall down at Waterloo Station and have to be brought back by a copper. What the hell are you playing at, Kate?'

I look at him through the mirror. The compassionate Jared has disappeared again. 'Someone pushed me. Someone put the palm of their hand on my back and shoved me just as a train came alongside the platform.'

'Yeah, right,' he says dismissively. 'That's not what that officer said. She said you're drunk and got lucky thanks to some guy who grabbed you.'

'That's not true. The officer wasn't there. I was pushed.'

'What were you doing at Waterloo Station, anyway?'

'I went to Dakota's funeral. The woman you may or may not have killed.'

'I didn't fucking kill her, Kate! I've been released. I'm shortly going to be completely exonerated. You need to pull yourself together for the sake of the children, at least. And where were you at pick-up time? I was rung by Rosie's school that you hadn't tipped up, and when we got home, Albie was sitting on the doorstep waiting for us. I thought you'd want to prove yourself to be an exemplary mother, that you'd be fighting to get custody of the children.'

'What are you talking about?' I exclaim. What's this about getting custody? My head feels like it's about to split open, and it's hard to get my thoughts straight. I asked Amara to collect Rosie from school, didn't I? I stand up unsteadily and shove my way past Jared into the bedroom. I lift my handbag off the chair. Fumbling inside, I find my phone and pull up my WhatsApp messages. Shit. I wrote a message to Amara this morning, but I didn't actually send it. And with all the drama at Dakota's funeral, I completely forgot to check. Could Jared be right, that I'm losing it and I am a terrible mother?

Jared has stormed back into the bedroom again and is standing near the door with his arms crossed. 'You need to pull yourself together, Kate. You're an embarrassment to us all.'

'Get out!' I completely lose it. 'Just get out of the bloody room!'

CHAPTER TWENTY-THREE

Our marriage is broken. All respect I have for Jared has dissipated. We are meant to be a team, except it feels like we're on opposite sides; he simply isn't listening to me, and frankly, considering he's the one who has cheated and the person who is still the main suspect for murder, he should be doing everything he can to press for forgiveness. His arrogance disgusts me.

As I'm drifting off to sleep, I wonder who pushed me. Was it the white van driver whom I rear-ended? Unlikely. Could it have been the person who is threatening me with those messages? Or one of my so-called friends, perhaps? Lucia could have followed me into the station.

But I'm so utterly exhausted, I sleep. It probably helps that I know Jared is in the house and if anything happens, I won't be looking after the children alone. Except I don't want Jared here.

I wake early, tentatively check my bruises and realise I feel much, much better. I pad downstairs to the kitchen to make myself a pot of tea. Jared appears about ten minutes later.

'We need to talk,' he says as he sits down at his normal place at the kitchen table.

'We do,' I say. 'I want you to leave. Our marriage is over.'

He clearly wasn't expecting me to say that, and he swallows hard, his Adam's apple bobbing up and down. 'I'm sorry. I'm really sorry, Kate. I shouldn't have cheated.'

'It's not only that,' I hiss. 'You've been completely unsupportive towards me and you treat me like I'm a fool. It's clear you've lost respect for me, and I've certainly lost respect for you.'

'That's not true!' he exclaims.

'I can't trust you, Jared.'

'But I didn't do anything wrong.'

From the expression on my face, he quickly backtracks. 'Well, obviously I did, but–'

I cut him off. 'You left the woman you were sleeping with to die on her kitchen floor. I will never be able to forgive you for that.'

We're both silent for a moment. I try to take a sip of tea, except my hand is shaking too much.

'Are you going to testify against me?' he asks, his voice cracking slightly.

And here we are. My husband is showing his true colours. All he cares about is getting off the hook, and he needs me to do that. My heart hardens further.

'No. I won't testify against you, but if you even think about trying to get custody of the children or try to take me to the cleaners in our divorce, then I can't promise anything.'

'Divorce. You want a divorce?'

I shake my head in disbelief. What the hell does he think

is going to happen? That I'm going to forgive him for everything and that we'll ride off into the sunset for a happily ever after?

'We can wait until things settle down regarding the investigation into Dakota's death, but yes, I want a divorce. You will get half of everything and shared custody of the children. I want you to be in their lives, but they'll live with me, either here or somewhere else.'

Tears well in his eyes.

'Please, Kate.'

I stand up. It's gone 7 a.m. and I need to wake the children.

'It's too late, Jared.'

And then he gets up too and anger flashes in his eyes. 'You will not get all my money. Do you hear me?'

'I don't want all your money, Jared. I want what's equitable. Fifty percent of everything. But that's for our lawyers to sort out. For now, you need to move out of the house. You can see the kids at the weekend.'

He shakes his head. He's clearly livid.

'And we are going to have a good breakup. This divorce will not affect the kids. Do you understand?'

I don't hang around for an answer and hurry upstairs. Albie is already in the bathroom, so I wake Rosie. She's thrilled that Jared is in the kitchen for breakfast, which makes me really sad, because I know we're about to ruin our children's futures.

Back at work, it's a relief to return to some degree of normality. Not that I'm able to concentrate. I spend the first hour researching divorce solicitors before remembering that one of my clients is top of her field.

I leave the office at 1 p.m. as I always do and head

towards the sandwich shop. And that's when I spot her. Marilyn is strolling along on the other side of the road. What the hell! She glances over at me, and when our eyes meet, she does a little wave with her fingers. Is she stalking me? Or worse than that, is she the person sending the threatening notes? She's the obvious culprit, having been ostracised from our group, and I haven't helped matters by not being overly friendly to her. Her cheeks look flushed, and she hovers outside a pharmacy, obviously unsure what to do. I make the decision for both of us.

As the pedestrian light turns green on the zebra crossing, I hurry towards her.

'Hi, Kate,' she says, as if it's perfectly normal for her to run into me here.

'Are you here to see me?' I ask bluntly.

'No, not at all,' she blusters. 'I've got a client just up the road, but I was wondering if we might run into each other again. Are you on your lunch break?'

'I need you to be honest with me. Are you behind the threats?'

'Threats?' She frowns and scratches her forehead.

'The messages and notes that have been sent to me and all my friends.'

'I'm sorry, Kate, but I haven't got a clue what you're talking about.'

I stare at her, looking for any sign that she might be lying. Except she doesn't touch her nose or her ears, and her gaze remains steady and directed on me, her forehead wrinkled, her head tilted to one side. She appears genuinely confused. Or is she? I don't trust my own judgment anymore.

'The threats have been reported to the police,' I say. 'We've all given statements, so they're on to you.' I'm not sure if that's strictly true, but at least it's true that I formally reported the threats made to me.

Marilyn takes a step backwards, away from me. 'Look, I'm sorry about what's happened to you,' she says, waving her hands around. 'How your friends have turned against you, and that your husband is a suspect for Dakota's murder. I can't imagine what hell you've been going through, but I don't know what you think I've got to do with it.'

'Someone has it in for me and my friends, and I know you have a grudge against us.'

'You've got it all wrong, Kate. It's not me you need to be worried about.'

I narrow my eyes at her. What does she know that she's not telling me?

'But you've been following me, and you can't deny it. I saw you following me in your black car when I was driving to Lucia's.'

'Oh, Kate. I'm looking out for you, that's all.'

'Well, don't!' I exclaim. 'It's creepy and unsettling, and I've got enough going on in my life without having you trailing me around.'

'You need to watch your back, Kate. And look after your children. Keep them close.'

'You stay away from me!' I say, jabbing my finger at her. 'I'm going to report you to the police for harassment. Just stay away!' I turn then and have to restrain myself from breaking into a run to get away from her. When I glance back over my shoulder, she's still standing in the middle of the pavement, staring in my direction. The woman has totally creeped me out. I forgo a sandwich and head straight back to the office.

I debate whether to ring Kavi Patel, to let him know that

Marilyn has threatened me to my face, except Cole accosts me as soon as I step back into the office.

'We've got a problem,' he says, tilting his head towards his private office. I follow him inside, and he closes the door.

'Unfortunately, Pedersen is an unusual name, and word has got out that your husband has been arrested on suspicion of murder.'

'And released,' I add.

Cole ignores me. 'We have won literally no new business this month, Kate. And we're losing clients hand over fist. Our reputation is taking a battering, and Donna has handed in her notice.' Donna, who is our best salesperson by far.

'Oh, God,' I say, sinking into the chair opposite Cole's desk. This is exactly what I feared might happen. 'What are we going to do?'

'You won't like this, but I think you should take a sabbatical for three months or so, just until Jared's name is completely cleared and hopefully the police find the real culprit. We'll tell our clients that you're stepping back from the business. Combined with Dakota's murder and the list ranking your friends, the optics aren't good. I'm sorry, Kate.' And Cole really does look sorry. He knows how much I've given to this business, my third baby. We had so many plans to grow the business and eventually, hopefully, sell out to a larger firm. Jared, of course, was going to facilitate that.

I close my eyes and bite my lower lip. Cole is right. Of course he is, but it breaks my heart. It seems that I've lost my marriage and my business all in the space of a few days. Eventually, I open my eyes and lean forward, my elbows on my knees. 'I assume I can work from home, behind the scenes?'

'Yes, but nothing client- or employee-facing. You'll need to do everything through me.'

'And you can cope?' I ask.

'I'll have to. We can't afford to employ an interim director to replace you.'

I nod. 'And what do you suggest we change the company name to?'

'As it's your company, I thought I'd leave that up to you. But something generic, ideally.'

'And you'll put out a statement to our customers and staff?'

He nods.

It takes such a lot of effort to lever myself off Cole's chair, and it's not due to my hip and shoulder being bruised and my hands, head and knees grazed. My back feels rigid as I walk out of his office and look around at everything I've built. This is my place, my success story, and I have to swallow hard to stop myself from crying. I think back to six years ago, when Cole was made redundant and Stella was beside herself, wondering if they would end up defaulting on their mortgage. Pedersen Domestic Staff Agency was going through such rapid growth, and I was flailing. My part-time bookkeeper wasn't giving me the financial information I needed, and our IT systems were overloaded. I was nervous about Cole joining the business, wary of mixing friends and business, but I needn't have worried. Much of our recent success has been due to him. Cole is the most organised person I know, good with the team and a genuinely nice person to have around. I made him a director of the business two years ago and gave him a shareholding. I know the agency will be in expert hands in my absence, but it doesn't make me feel any better.

I do a supermarket shop before collecting Rosie from school – as always, keeping my head down and not talking to anyone. Back at home, Rosie sits at the kitchen table to do her homework, and I sort out the groceries before making a start on supper. It isn't until 5 p.m. that I realise with a start that Albie isn't home. I check the weekly planner on the fridge and see that he doesn't have any after-school activities today, so he should be home by now. And then I remember Marilyn's words. 'Look after your children. Keep them close.' My stomach plummets. Has she done something to Albie? I drop a glass, which shatters onto the kitchen floor. Rosie frowns at me, and I hurry to get the dustpan and brush, rapidly shoving the broken shards into a single pile. I need to call the school, check that Albie's actually left school before I go into a blind panic.

I ring the main number and am eventually put through to the school secretary.

'This is Albie Pedersen's mother. He hasn't arrived home. Please, can you tell me what time he left this afternoon?'

'Of course, Mrs Pedersen. I'll check the system.' The phone goes silent for a while. Too long. Eventually, she's back. 'Albie left the premises at 4.02 p.m. I shouldn't worry, Mrs Pedersen. You know what these lads are like. They get distracted, have a natter with their mates. I'm sure he'll be home any minute.'

I thank the woman. Except Albie isn't like that. He always comes straight home. And then I remember his new phone and the tracking app I put on it. I navigate to it on my phone, but his phone must be switched off because the last known location was at school at 3.58 p.m. and since then, nothing.

Without thinking, I race up the stairs and hurtle into Albie's room. At first glance, it's neat and tidy, and that's thanks to Pavlina cleaning here this morning. His navy duvet is pulled up and his pillow plumped, shoes neatly lined up in front of the freestanding wardrobe, books in perfect piles on his desk. It smells fresh in here, of fabric conditioner and furniture polish; no whiff of teenage boy. But then I see a piece of paper lying on the floor, next to the bed. I pick it up. There are just two words written on it in Albie's scrawling writing.

I'm sorry.

CHAPTER TWENTY-FOUR

What the hell does Albie mean, writing *I'm sorry* on a piece of A4 paper? And who is he saying sorry to? My stomach does cartwheels. This could be something completely innocuous, but I get a spidery sixth sense that it's not. I call Pavlina.

'Hello, Mrs Pedersen. Is everything alright?' Pavlina speaks with a heavily accented voice.

'You did a great job of cleaning the house, thank you. Did you see a note in Albie's room? It says, "I'm sorry".'

'Yes, Mrs Pedersen. I did. It was on the floor near the door. I picked it up and put it on the bed after I'd changed the sheets. I hope that was the right thing to do?'

'Yes, absolutely. Many thanks. That was it. Have a lovely evening.'

I hear the confusion in Pavlina's voice as she says goodbye. I scratch my head. Did Albie purposefully leave the note on the floor, wanting me to find it, except he forgot that Pavlina was cleaning the house this morning? Or was it something he'd done for some homework?

With some hesitation, I call Erin. I don't particularly want to talk to her, but her boys will know if Albie was on the bus.

'Hi, Erin,' I say, trying to keep my voice light. 'Are the twins at home?'

'Yes, why?'

'Albie hasn't come back from school, and I'm worried. Can you ask them if he was on the bus?'

'Of course,' Erin says. I can hear her footsteps as she moves through the house. 'Teddy! Seth! Can you come here?' There's a lot of clattering and then muffled voices before Erin comes back on the line.

'Teddy says Albie wasn't on the bus. Apparently, he told Teddy he was going somewhere else this evening.'

'Going where?' I ask. My throat feels tight but then relaxes again. Perhaps Albie has gone somewhere with Jared. That would make sense. 'Is he with Jared, do you think?'

'Unlikely,' Erin replies. 'Jared and Kieren are out together. They both skived off work early to play golf in Cobham or somewhere. Some corporate thing to which Jared invited Kieren.'

So where the hell is Albie?

'I'll question the boys again, and I'll call you if I find out anything. I'm sure he'll be home any minute,' Erin adds.

I stand in Albie's bedroom, but it's Marilyn's words that are echoing in my head. Keep your children safe, or however she put it. Was that a threat? Has she acted on it? My stomach cramps. I glance around Albie's room and I notice there are a few things missing. His rucksack, which is normally on the back of his chair, is gone; not the school one but the one with some trendy label given by a friend. The pig-shaped money box is standing upside down on his desk. I pick it up and realise it's empty. All the money that he's been saving up to buy new video games has gone. In the bathroom, his toothbrush and toothpaste are missing, as are his newly acquired hair gel and deodorant. I realise that Albie has done what Rosie did; he's run away. Except Rosie only went out onto the back path, and Albie could be absolutely anywhere. For a split second, I feel relief that he's run away and hasn't been abducted, but still, he's a young boy, and he's so vulnerable. Fear makes my stomach clench.

Back in the bedroom, I pick up the note. What is my boy sorry for? Is he still upset about the incident at football and sorry about that, or is it something more? I glance around the room, desperately looking for any clues. He has a wall full of posters, and photos, and pictures of games that he intends to buy, and that's when I see several new photos which he's printed out on ordinary printer paper. They're of the four of us on family holidays — happy, bronzed faces in Italy and Greece, with azure seas or sparkling swimming pools in the background. Photos of us down on the south coast, near Littlehampton, where we regularly stayed at Jared's parents' holiday house overlooking the English Channel. Memories of happier times.

I try calling Albie's phone and, to my delight, it's no longer switched off. The phone actually rings several times until it goes to voicemail.

'Albie, sweetheart,' I say breathlessly. 'Where are you? Please let me know. I'm really worried about you.' I'm about to hang up when I add, 'You're not in trouble. I just want to know you're safe.'

I then navigate to the tracking app, and to my relief, it's working now. It takes me a few moments to understand what

I'm seeing. The little dot that is Albie's phone is moving, surely and steadily, right over the top of a grey line. Albie is on a train. A train that is rapidly approaching Gatwick Airport. That realisation sends me into a further panic. What is he doing? What if Marilyn has abducted him and they're about to fly somewhere far away, a place that has no extradition policy with the UK? But for that, Albie needs a passport, and I keep the passports locked in the small safe at the bottom of the wardrobe in the spare room. Does he even know the code? Possibly. I race into the spare room, get down on my knees and punch in the code. I grab the pile of passports and count them. There are four, and Albie's passport is in my hand. Thank goodness for that, at least. Except then I wonder if Marilyn might have acquired a fake passport. Could she get him out of the country on that?

I try calling Albie again, but once again it goes to voicemail. I send him a text message.

> Albie, please call me. You're not in trouble. I just want to know you're safe. Mum xx

Unsure what to do first, I call Marilyn, except she also doesn't pick up. Of course she doesn't. I leave a breathless message. 'Albie's gone missing. I don't know if you have anything to do with it, but I'm calling the police to tell them about the threats you made.' I'm about to ring Detective Kavi Patel but reckon I'd better check that Jared really is playing golf and that Albie isn't with him. I'd look a complete idiot if that were the case. Unsurprisingly, my husband doesn't answer either. I also send him a message.

> Is Albie with you?

Two little blue ticks appear next to the message, followed by dots.

> No. Don't say you've lost our children? I'm sure my solicitor will love that...

The bastard.

Detective Kavi Patel has to be next. I call his number, but it also goes to voicemail. Why is everyone ignoring my calls? I feel a desolate sense of desperation. 'Please, can you call me back? I think a woman called Marilyn Tucker might be behind all the threats, and now my son Albie is missing, and he's at Gatwick Airport, and I'm worried she's got him. Please call me.' I know I sound panicked and desperate, but that's exactly how I feel.

My next call is to Stella. 'Hey, babe,' she answers. What a relief that she answers.

'Are you able to have Rosie? Albie's run away and I need to get him.'

'Shit,' Stella mutters. 'Of course. I'm at home.'

And now what? I have to get to Gatwick Airport. I have to rescue my boy.

I run downstairs, almost slipping, bash my thigh on the bottom spindle of the staircase, and then hurtle into the kitchen. 'Rosie, collect up your things. I'm going to drop you off at Aunty Stella's.'

'Why?'

'I'll tell you later.'

But Rosie is too slow, so I grab her schoolbag and the few toys that are scattered around the room and cajole her out of the house and into the car. How the hell am I going to get to Gatwick Airport quickly? If I take public transport, I might get there faster than if I drive, but then again, maybe not. I decide to drive, praying that the traffic won't be too bad, praying that I'll get there before Albie gets on a flight. At Stella's house, I double-park the car and almost shove Rosie through Stella's front door.

'Keep me posted, yeah?' Stella says, wrapping her arms around Rosie.

'Will do.'

I plug Gatwick Airport into Waze, hoping the app will help me avoid any traffic jams, and then I go back onto the phone tracking app. It takes a moment to realise that Albie is no longer at Gatwick Airport. He's back on the train, a train that is moving steadily southwards. I follow the grey train track southwards and realise that he might be heading for Littlehampton station. Of course, it makes sense. I remember the photos on the wall in his bedroom. Albie is probably hoping to get to Jared's parents' holiday home, where we've spent so many happy half-terms and long weekends. Except his parents sold the house a few months ago. Does Albie even know that? Would we have had any reason to discuss the sale with the kids? But actually, this is a relief. He's not jetting off on a plane, and I think I have an idea of where he is heading. Now, all I need to do is intercept the train. Except how likely is that? If he reaches Littlehampton before me and turns up at the house, what will the new owners do? Turn him away?

I'm not sure how I manage to drive. My mind isn't on the road, except somehow I find myself on the A3 heading south, almost as if I had been teleported there. My thoughts drift back to Marilyn. Could she have my boy? But why would she choose to take Albie to the south coast, unless Albie had shared that it's one of his favourite places? Or maybe Marilyn isn't involved at all and Albie is alone. Except I'm sure she is. Every few minutes, I try calling his phone again, and each time the phone goes to voicemail. I ask my sophisticated car how long it takes to get by train from Gatwick to Littlehampton. One hour and ten minutes. And then I ask which stations the train stops at en route. Thirteen different stations. That's a lot of stops, but the train is already so far ahead of me it would be physically impossible for me to reach any of the stations in time. I pull off the A3 and onto the A243 and realise with a pang that I'm passing Chessington World of Adventures. I'll bring the children here soon. Really soon. At the next set of traffic lights, I look at the tracker app. But Albie is motionless now. The train looks like it's stopped somewhere outside of Crawley. Why? Is it just for a red light, perhaps?

I carry on driving, but at the next junction I sneak another look at the app. Albie is still in the same place, on the train line in the middle of nowhere. My mind starts catastrophising. What if something terrible has happened? Is he all right? Could he have jumped from the train? No, that's ridiculous. A train might have broken down, like they regularly do.

I ask Google if the train from Gatwick Airport to Littlehampton is on time and, to my relief, the answer is no. There are significant delays on all lines south of Gatwick Airport due to an incident on the line. I pray that the incident has nothing to do with my little boy. I'm speeding now, but honestly, I don't care. The next station stop for the train is Haywards Heath. I need to make a decision. Do I continue south to Littlehampton or do I divert off to Haywards Heath in the hope of reaching there before the delayed train gets in? I decide to risk going to Haywards Heath.

I switch on the local news and there's a traffic update.

The reporter says there are delays of up to two hours because of a fatality on the line between Crawley and Balcombe. I try to calm myself, concentrating on my breathing. It will be a coincidence; devastating for the family of the bereaved, but helpful for me if my boy is caught up on a delayed train. That's what I tell myself repeatedly as I reset my SatNav destination for Haywards Heath. Albie won't have done anything stupid; I'm sure of that. At least I pray he hasn't. The SatNav directs me onto the M25, the motorway most notorious for traffic jams. Except today I'm lucky. The traffic is flowing steadily. And then I'm on the M23 heading south.

I'm flashed by at least two speed cameras, but I don't care. My knuckles are white as they grip the steering wheel, my head bent forward as I navigate the roads, driving in the fast lane, driving way too quickly. It's far. Much farther than I anticipated, and the minutes tick over and over until it's been more than an hour since I left Barnes. I'm too focused on the road to risk looking at the app to see where Albie might be. My little boy, barely a teenager. So young and vulnerable.

And then I'm off the motorway and see signs for Haywards Heath train station. It's such a relief. I swerve into the car park with screeching tyres. There's a big Waitrose next door and a few cars parked in front of the station; a pick-up zone. There are no free spaces, but I don't care. I park up in a zigzag area, where you're forbidden from parking. Someone shouts at me as I race out of the car, running full pelt into the station, but I ignore them. I buy a ticket for Littlehampton at the machine, jiggling from foot to foot, desperate for the machine to hurry up and disgorge the ticket. And then I'm running through the barrier, and I see a train guard. 'Which is the Littlehampton train?' I ask breathlessly.

'Delayed train pulling into Platform One right now.'

I'm not sure I've ever run so fast. As I reach the platform, there are hordes of people, many disgorging from the train, others trying to get on it. I don't even know if this is the right train, whether Albie is here, but I elbow my way through, eliciting a few swearwords in the process. But I'm on the train. It's packed, with every seat taken and people standing in the corridors and in the link sections between carriages. The train chugs out of the station.

'Good afternoon, everyone. This is the delayed service to Littlehampton. Apologies for the severe delay to this service due to a fatality on the line. This train will be stopping at Burgess Hill, Hassocks...'

I zone out. I'm panting as I look at the app and realise, to my relief, that the dot that signifies me is in exactly the same place as the dot that signifies Albie. My boy is on this train. I make my way towards the front of the train, having to ease my way past standing passengers, apologising as I go through, stepping on people's toes, edging past bulky suitcases, all the while looking left and right, desperate to find Albie. When I reach the first-class carriage at the front of the train, I feel desolate. He's not here. Now I need to go back the way I came to the other end of the train. I make my apologies. A man in a dark suit mutters, 'Can't you wait until the next station?' I ignore him.

The train weaves from side to side, and I have to hold on to the edges of the seats to stop myself from falling into seated passengers. And then I let out a small cry, covering my mouth with my hand. Albie is sitting next to the window on the right-hand side of the train. He's got earphones over his head, the pair that came with the expensive games console Jared gave him for his birthday. There's an older woman sitting next to him, and Albie is staring out of the window.

'Excuse me,' I say to the woman. 'That's my son. Is it possible for me to sit next to him, just for a quick moment?'

She lifts her handbag off her lap and stands up. 'Of course, love. I'm getting off at the next stop, anyway.'

I slip into the vacated seat and tap Albie on the arm. He turns to look at me, and it takes a second for him to register it's me. He tugs the headphones off his head. His eyes widen with fear.

'Oh, darling!' I say, throwing my arms around him. Albie is tense and unyielding.

'What are you doing here?' he asks.

'I've come to find you. I was so worried. Are you safe?' I glance around, expecting to see Marilyn slipping between the standing passengers, except I'm looking at a sea of strangers' faces. Frustratingly, my phone rings, and I see it's Kavi Patel.

'Can I call you back later?' I ask before he can speak. 'I've found my son and I'm on the train.'

'Right,' he replies, and I hang up before he can ask me anything further.

'Are you angry?' Albie asks. He can't bring himself to look at me.

'No, not at all. Just worried.'

'I'm sorry, Mum.' And then my boy bursts into tears.

'Hey, it's okay.' I put my arm around him again, and this time he softens and leans his head against my neck. 'Where are you off to?'

'Gran and Gramps' house by the beach. I just thought you'd be so angry.'

'You left a note saying *I'm sorry*. What are you sorry for?'

'Everything's my fault,' he says through hiccupping tears.

'Of course it's not, darling. Adults argue all the time.'

'But if I hadn't leaked the list, you and Dad wouldn't have argued. And maybe Dakota wouldn't have died.'

'You leaked the list?' I ask, unable to keep the shock from my voice. It had never crossed my mind that Albie could have been behind it.

'I knew you'd be angry,' he says, sniffing hard. 'I'm sorry. I didn't mean for any of this to happen.'

I squeeze his hand, unable to talk for a moment.

'I found your spreadsheet and thought it was really funny. I sent it to a couple of my friends, and they thought it was funny too, so then I sent it to Leo Buckmaster.'

'Who's he?' I ask.

'He's in Year Nine. Mister Popular, and one of the coolest guys in the school. His elder brother is head boy. But Leo's kind of a bully too, and he'd started picking on me, and I thought...' Albie lets his voice taper away. 'Anyway, it went viral after that. The whole school saw it, and then it went to Rosie's school and other schools too. Tessa's mum got her hands on it, and it went completely viral after that.'

'Oh, Albie,' I say.

'And the thing at football... I wasn't bullying another boy, Mum. I really wasn't. I was trying to protect you. Ethan Berry said you were a bitch, and he said other really horrible things about you, so I kicked him. I'm sorry, Mum.'

'No, I'm the one who's sorry. I should never have created that list in the first place. It was a horrible thing to do, and it's really upset my friends.'

'Well, I don't have any friends anymore either. To begin with, everyone thought it was funny, but then they turned on me and said I was a snitch. That's why I didn't want a birthday party.'

'Oh, sweetheart,' I say, placing a kiss on the side of his head. 'I wish you'd been able to tell me all of this.' How I wish I could take away all the hurt and misery he's suffered.

The train is beginning to slow down now, and the conductor talks over the tannoy system. 'This train is approaching Burgess Hill. All passengers for Burgess Hill, please leave the train at the next station stop.'

'Come on,' I say, tugging at Albie's hand. 'Let's get off here and take the next train back to Haywards Heath. Then we can get something to eat before driving back to London.'

His face falls. 'Can't we go to the seaside?'

'No, love. Besides, Gran and Gramps have sold that house. There'll be strangers living there now.'

'Oh,' he says forlornly.

At Burgess Hill station, we sit close together on a bench, waiting for the next train to take us back the way we've just come. I feel absolutely terrible. With everything that has been going on, I've neglected Albie. It's been so hard for him, starting a new school, navigating new friendships, and all the while, I've been wrapped up in my own drama.

'Do you think Dakota was killed because of the list?' Albie asks.

'Absolutely not,' I say, injecting as much conviction into my voice as I can. 'I can promise you it's got nothing to do with it.' Although I don't know that for sure. 'By the way, how well do you know Marilyn Tucker's son?'

'Joey?' Albie says. 'We don't have much to do with each

other. He's a bit of a nerd, and we're not in the same classes for any lessons.'

'And do you know his mum?'

Albie looks at me askance. 'No.'

That, at least, is a relief. We're quiet for a while, watching the passing scenery of fields and woodland, being lulled by the rocking of the train.

'I know you and Dad are getting divorced,' Albie says weakly. 'I overheard you.'

I sigh. So much for trying to keep it from the kids. 'If Dad and I split up, it's absolutely nothing to do with what you've done or said. It's because we've fallen out of love with each other. These things happen, and no one is to blame.' Not exactly the case here, but I'm not going to start shaming Jared. I wonder if Albie has twigged that his father had an affair; I really hope not. 'And it doesn't mean we love you or Rosie any less. We want you to be brought up in a happy home, and sometimes that's easier when parents live apart.'

Albie seems to accept that explanation, and we chat easily on the way back to London. I feel like I've got my boy back again as he tells me all about the kids in his year and his new teachers, the subjects he's enjoying and those he's struggling with. When we're approaching Roehampton, I call Stella. 'I've found Albie and we're nearly home.'

'Oh, that's fantastic news,' she exclaims. 'I'll drop Rosie back at yours. How long will you be?'

An hour later, both Rosie and Albie are getting ready for bed. Stella is sitting at our kitchen table, nibbling on some pistachios. I open a bottle of wine and remove two glasses from the cupboard.

'What an afternoon!' I let out a whoosh of breath as I pour two full glasses.

'What actually happened?' Stella asks.

I explain that Albie ran away, and he admitted he had leaked the list. It seems to me that a very large piece of the puzzle has slotted into place, except Stella instantly brings me back to earth.

'Still doesn't explain who is threatening us all.'

'Or who killed Dakota,' I add.

'Cole is so worried about you,' Stella says. 'He told me that you're stepping back from the business.'

I nod. 'I've really dumped him in it,' I say. 'Don't know what I'd do without your husband.'

Stella laughs, although it sounds strangely forced. I glance up with surprise.

'He's off playing golf again.'

'Like Jared and Kieren. Ironic how we're all golf widows. I didn't know Cole was that into golf.'

'It's a new thing. I reckon it's so he can get in with Jared and Kieren. Keeping up with the Joneses,' she says rather bitterly. Stella takes a large sip of wine. 'Not that I can bring myself to look at a golf club ever again.'

We're interrupted by Rosie shouting from upstairs. 'Mum! I'm ready for bed.'

'I'll be back in a moment,' I say, chewing on a pistachio nut.

It's when I step onto the stairs that it hits me. What did Stella mean by saying, 'Not that I can bring myself to look at a golf club ever again'? The police never released any information to suggest that Dakota was hit with a golf club. And I haven't told anyone either. So how the hell does Stella know? Or did she mean something completely different?

I pause mid-step and then clutch the bannister, staring up at the console table in the hall where Pavlina has placed a small vase of pale pink scented roses. It triggers something in the back of my brain. The floral rose scent. I remember being hit by the scent of flowers in the entryway to Dakota's house. It was familiar, but I couldn't place it, and following all the horrors, I'd forgotten all about it. It's a perfume that I know all too well as Stella wears it every day.

With a terrible realisation, it hits me. Is Stella Dakota's killer?

CHAPTER TWENTY-FIVE

It's instinctual. I turn around and move back down the stairs just as Stella walks out of the living room with her handbag over her shoulder. But I'm too quick. I stand before the front door, blocking her exit.

'Going somewhere?' I ask.

'Something came up. I need to go home,' she says. She's flustered, and there are pink patches on her cheeks. We stare at each other.

'You were there,' I say. 'You were at Dakota's house.'

'I don't know what you're talking about!' Stella's face betrays her. She's skittish, her eyes darting all over the place, her fingers tugging at the strap of her bag.

'How did you know that Dakota was hit with a golf club?' I ask. My legs are trembling as I stare at this woman who has been my best friend for so long.

'You must have said something,' she replies hurriedly. And now I know for sure that Stella is lying. Detective Kavi Patel asked me not to mention the golf club, and I haven't done. I'm ninety-nine percent sure that Jared won't have said anything either, so how else could Stella know, unless she was there?

'Did you hit Dakota?' I ask. And then I'm paralysed by fear. If Stella killed Dakota, then what's stopping her from hurting me or the children? The air is so still, it feels like it's been sucked out of the house. And then I'm startled. Stella makes a run for it, except she doesn't dart into the kitchen to head for the back door, or try to weave past me to get to the front door. She completely takes me by surprise by running up the stairs, taking them two at a time.

'Where are you going?' I exclaim. I race after her, watching as she turns left into the hallway, pushing Rosie's bedroom door open and slamming it closed behind her.

'No!' I shout. 'Leave Rosie alone!' I'm just seconds behind, and turn down the handle, trying to push the door open, except Stella has already wedged something behind the door, and I can hear her shifting furniture, barricading herself into the room. In the room with my daughter. All the while, Marilyn's words are echoing in my ear. 'Keep your children safe.'

I have failed my children. Completely and utterly.

'Let me in!' I shout, pushing the door handle down in vain.

Albie appears in the corridor behind me, dressed in his pyjamas. 'What's going on, Mum?'

'Get back into your room right away and wedge the door shut. Don't let anyone in under any circumstances. Okay?'

He stares at me with wide eyes.

'Just do it!' I cry.

I can hear Rosie sobbing inside the room. 'Hey, it's alright,' Stella is saying. Except it's not all right. My best friend has barricaded herself in my daughter's room. And the chances are she killed Dakota.

'You need to tell me the truth, Stella,' I say, rapping my knuckles on the door. 'If you don't tell me immediately, I'm going to call the police.' That isn't strictly true, as I realise I've left my phone downstairs.

'I can't.' Stella's voice cracks.

'Can't what?' I ask. Rosie is still crying, and Stella says *shush* repeatedly.

'You've got ten seconds,' I say. 'Tell me everything.'

'Alright, alright,' Stella says. I can hear movement from within the room, and her voice sounds stronger now. I guess she's right up against the other side of the door. 'I want to explain, I really do, but it's all so terrible.'

'Spit it out,' I demand. 'You're running out of time.'

'I had an affair with Jared.'

My gasp is audible.

'I'm really sorry, Kate. It lasted for a long time, and I feel dreadful about it. I never wanted to betray you like that, but there was something so magnetic about Jared, I couldn't stay away from him. I wasn't stupid. I knew he'd never leave you for me. I mean, I'm just some little cook whereas you're a high-flying businesswoman with a successful firm. For a while, I hoped we could do some friendly husband-swap thing. You'd fall for Cole so I could be with Jared, except it didn't work out like that. I could see that I'd always be the bit on the side for him, his naughty pleasure as he described it. Anyway, I didn't want to be responsible for Jared leaving you and the kids.'

I snort with derision. 'What did you do to Dakota?' I ask.

'I discovered that Dakota was sleeping with Jared. It was one thing him staying married to you, but quite another for him to cheat on me as well. Honestly, I was devastated. I confronted Jared, and he admitted it, and then he called things off between him and me. It was humiliating and soul-destroying.'

I shake my head in disbelief. Two of my supposedly closest friends were sleeping with my husband. Two of them. What a bastard my husband is.

'What happened with Dakota?'

'I went over to her house to talk to her. I wanted to tell her that she was just one in a long line of women that Jared was sleeping with. I wanted to warn her not to fall for him, that he's a user of people and heartless. Except the conversation didn't go well.' Stella sniffs loudly, and I can still hear Rosie crying gently in the background. My poor little darling girl. 'I didn't mean to hurt her, Kate. I promise you. It was a terrible, terrible accident.'

'Don't hurt Rosie,' I say. 'Please don't hurt her. Do what you like to me but leave my children alone.'

'I'd never hurt Rosie,' Stella says. 'And I'd never hurt you. I love you like a sister.'

'Except you lied and cheated. Is that how you treat your sister?'

'I'm so sorry. Please forgive me, Kate. I beg you to forgive me.' She sounds as if she's crying.

'What did you do to Dakota?' I ask again.

'It was an accident.'

'You need to tell this to the police.'

'How can I? They won't believe me. They'll throw me into jail, and my life will be over. Please, just let me go, and you'll never see me again. I'll come out of here and walk away quietly. I promise.'

I think about this, except how can I trust Stella?

'How long?' I ask. 'How long were you sleeping with Jared for?'

'Four years,' Stella replies in a whisper. 'Except I don't think I was his only bit on the side. There might have been other women besides Dakota.'

I close my eyes. I need time to digest this, to fully absorb the terrible betrayal. And then I realise that my little Rosie will have heard every word that Stella has been saying, and the chances are that Albie has his ear up against his bedroom door and can hear us too. My heart shatters with the realisation that I've been unable to protect my children. In that regard, perhaps Jared is right. I'm a terrible mother. Can I really stand back and let Stella leave? Surely she must know that the second she's out of the door, I'll call the police, and she'll be arrested. But if I refuse, can I trust her not to hurt my little girl?

'Will you let Rosie out?' I ask.

'Rosie's fine,' Stella replies.

'I want to talk to her.'

I can hear some whispering and shuffling, and then Rosie's voice is close to the door. 'Mummy,' she says. She sounds scared, and I just want to scoop her into my arms.

'Is Aunty Stella being kind to you?' I ask.

'Yes,' she says, her voice barely a whisper. 'I want to be with you, though.'

'You will be very soon.'

I know what I need to do now. 'Do you want a hot chocolate, sweetheart?' I ask.

'Yes, please.'

'This is too much for Rosie,' I tell Stella. 'I'm going to make her a hot chocolate, and you can give it to her. Do you promise me you won't hurt her?'

'I love Rosie. I'd never hurt her.'

I have to believe Stella. I think back over the thousands of interactions she's had with my children over the years, and she's always been the kind, fun Aunty Stella. Whatever else she's done, I have to trust that Stella genuinely loves my little girl.

'Stay there, sweetheart, and I'll be back in a minute.'

As quietly as I can, I tiptoe downstairs. My phone is in the kitchen. I walk to the utility room and close the door, the furthest room away from Rosie's bedroom. And then I call the police and beg them to come as fast as possible.

CHAPTER TWENTY-SIX

It takes eight minutes. When the police arrive, I explain they need to go upstairs quietly. I'm so scared for Rosie, terrified that Stella might hurt my little girl. I lead them up the stairs, worried about every creak on the staircase. Then I stand silently with my ear up to Rosie's door. The only sound coming from her bedroom now is Stella singing a lullaby, a tune she might have sung to Rosie when she was a toddler, hardly appropriate for a nine-year-old. Except there's something soothing about it, and when I ask, 'Rosie, darling, are you alright?' Stella answers.

'She's asleep, Kate. In bed, fast asleep.'

And I just pray that Stella is telling the truth.

One of the uniformed officers knocks on Rosie's door.

'Stella, I'm a police officer, and I want you to open the door so we can make sure no one is hurt. Not you, not Rosie, not Kate. Can you do that for me?'

Stella lets out a sob, except then there's a lot of shuffling and movement.

'Stand back, Kate,' the officer says, and I edge backwards

down the corridor. Stella opens the door and steps outside. She looks so pitiful. Mascara smudged down her face, her cheeks blotchy, her head hanging low.

'It was an accident,' she says. Her voice is choked. 'I didn't mean to hurt Dakota, but yes, I was there. You can take me away now.' She holds out her arms, ready to be cuffed, except there are no handcuffs. Tears are dripping down Stella's face, but as I look at her, I'm not sure I recognise my best friend. How could she have killed Dakota and then pretended to us that she knew nothing at all? How could she have lived with herself? It just doesn't make sense to me.

'We'd like you to come to the police station for a formal interview. Are you willing to do that?'

Stella nods. I follow them as they go downstairs and watch as they escort her out of my house into a waiting police car. Another car arrives, unmarked this time, and Detective Kavi Patel climbs out of it and strides up our path.

'I'd like to take a short statement from you now and then a more detailed one in the morning.'

My voice trembles as I explain what happened. He nods sympathetically as he scribbles in his notebook, and then places a hand on my arm as he stands up.

'I'll call you first thing,' Kavi Patel says.

I nod and watch them all leave. A wave of gut-wrenching sadness comes over me. This is my best friend. Was my best friend. Such betrayal and so many lies.

I hurry back upstairs. Unbelievably, Rosie is still fast asleep, but the light is on under Albie's door. He must be terrified.

'Albie,' I say. 'You can let me in now. Everyone has gone.'

I listen as he shifts furniture away from the door, and

then he's standing there, his face so pale and eyes so large. I throw my arms around him, and he hugs me back.

'Did the police take Stella away?' he asks.

'Yes.'

'So Dakota's death was nothing to do with me?'

'Absolutely nothing whatsoever. You don't need to feel bad about anything.'

'Even leaking your list?'

'Even that. Although I'd rather you didn't do anything like that again.'

He unwraps himself from me and gives me a wry smile.

'Fancy a hot chocolate before going back to bed?' I ask.

When Albie has gone to sleep and I'm alone, I sit in the darkened living room and try to think. Stella's betrayal hurts even more than Jared's. It honestly feels like some deep part of me has been wrested from my body, leaving me empty and scared. I trusted her completely, shared all my private thoughts with her, and with hindsight, I made it so damned easy. If Jared and I had an argument, she knew all about it. She knew our schedule, knew if I was away or working late. How could I have misjudged my best friend that badly? I try to think through why she did it. Why she wanted my husband, why she was so devastated when my bastard of a husband dumped her for Dakota. And why wasn't lovely Cole enough for her? I wonder now about all those threats. Although she didn't mention them earlier, they must have been her. She's clearly been eaten up by jealousy for so long, and I guess my friend ranking list pushed her over the edge. I can see how, from the outside, my life might seem more fulfilled than hers. As a family, we are wealthier – much wealthier. We have the two children and the fancy holidays and the businesses, and yet none of that has brought true happiness. My marriage is over. My trust in everyone destroyed.

As I lie in bed trying to settle my thoughts, I console myself that at least the kids and I are safe. With Stella locked up, I realise her threats were empty. I doubt she would have really hurt us. I suppose it was some weird kind of power game, making me feel vulnerable and unsafe in my own home. I wonder if it was her way of getting me to listen to her, to hear her side of the story. It just goes to show that however well we think we know someone, we really don't.

The next morning, I'm awakened by my phone ringing. It's Jared. I almost don't answer it, but at the last moment, I sit up in bed and hit the accept call button.

'Have you heard the news?'

'What news?' I ask groggily.

'Someone's been arrested for Dakota's murder. I was worried it might be you. I assume it's not?'

'Of course it's not me. Why would you think that?'

'Because you were there. You saw me leave. And you were the scorned wife.'

'The scorned wife!' I snort with derision. 'Is that how you see me?'

I sense that Jared realises that is a step too far. 'No, but...'

'It was Stella.'

'What was Stella?'

Why is he being so dumb this morning? 'Stella was arrested for hitting Dakota.'

There's silence on the other end of the line.

'Stella?' he asks. 'Why would Stella hurt Dakota?'

'I know, Jared. I know you had an affair with Stella for years before dumping her for Dakota. I suppose if Lucia hadn't been so out of your league, you'd have made a play for her too, and Erin? Did you leave her alone only because Kieren is your best friend, or perhaps she turned you down?'

'It wasn't like that,' Jared says.

'Oh, really?' I can't stop the sarcasm.

'I didn't mean to hurt you or lie to you. I'm really sorry. I think I might have an addiction problem. You know—'

I cut him off. 'No, I don't know. And frankly, I don't care.' That is, of course, a lie, but I'm not going to give him the satisfaction of knowing how I'm really feeling. 'You'll be hearing from my solicitor. Don't call me again.'

I end the call and slam the phone down on the bed, unable to stop the tears springing to my eyes. I want to pull my duvet up and over my head and blot out everything that's happened. The thought of seeing anyone today except my children fills me with dread. I decide to let the kids sleep in and give them the day off school. They must be both emotionally and physically exhausted, Albie particularly. And it's not like I've got anywhere to go today. I haul myself out of bed and pull on my dressing gown. Albie's alarm clock has sounded, and I can hear him pottering in his room. I knock on his door.

'Fancy a day off school?' I ask.

He looks a bit nervous, but I reassure him there'll be no repercussions. Rosie is delighted by the news, and we agree to spend the day watching films and baking.

Later in the morning, Albie is with me in the kitchen, measuring out ingredients. 'If Stella has been arrested, does that mean Dad's off the hook?'

'Yes, I assume it does.'

'I knew he wouldn't do anything bad like that. I just knew it,' Albie says, spilling a little flour. I'm glad that he has such conviction about his father, although at some point I fear he'll come to realise Jared is really a cad. But we don't need to destroy that illusion for now. 'Does that mean you guys are going to get back together?'

'Oh, Albie,' I sigh. 'I'm sorry, but no. Your dad and I just aren't getting along anymore. Sometimes grownups fall out of love and don't want to be together.' I have to really bite my tongue not to say anything negative about Jared. 'I understand how difficult this must be for you, how disappointing.'

I watch all the emotions flash across his face, but then he wipes his flour-covered hands on the front of his apron and throws me a wide smile. 'It's alright, Mum. I get it. And you don't need to worry as I'm going to look after you and Rosie from now on.'

'Sweetheart, you don't need to do that. Dad will still be around, even if he's not living here, and it's my job to look after you and your sister.'

'Yeah, well. I want to.' He picks up the baking powder and carefully measures out a teaspoonful. Rosie comes running into the room, so that's the end of the conversation. Except my heart feels broken all over again. Have we ruined Albie's childhood? It tears me to pieces that he's had to grow up so fast.

The three of us have a lovely day at home, pottering, watching two films, eating the cake we made and creating crazy toppings for our homemade pizzas. I'm so grateful for my children and promise myself I will do everything I possibly can to protect them from any fallout as a result of the divorce. I expect Detective Kavi Patel to call me, but he doesn't, and in many ways that's a relief. I don't want to think about everything that has happened. As evening approaches, I send the kids to bed early because tomorrow will definitely be a school day.

I'm sitting in the kitchen nursing a glass of wine, watching the evening news on the television. Although Stella's name hasn't been released to the press, there is a bulletin stating that a 38-year-old woman has been arrested and charged with the murder of Dakota Solomon and that all charges against Jared Pedersen have been dropped.

I'm jolted when the doorbell rings. I'm not expecting anyone other than perhaps the detective, so I walk cautiously to the front of the house and peer through the peephole in the door. To my surprise, it's Erin, holding a bottle of wine.

I open the door. 'Hello,' I say.

'I hope you don't mind my just turning up, but I heard that Stella got arrested, and Jared is out celebrating with Kieren, so I thought you might like some company.' She lifts the bottle high in the air.

'That's so kind of you,' I say, opening the door wider to let her in. As I follow Erin into our kitchen, I realise with a slight stab that she's my only friend left. Dakota is dead, Stella is probably in a cell somewhere, Lucia has publicly rejected me, and so there's just Erin, the friend I felt the least affinity to, if I'm being honest to myself. I wondered if Erin would be on Jared's side and not want anything to do with me. Clearly not.

It seems strange to think that only last night, it was Stella and me sitting here at my kitchen table. How can life have changed so much in such a short period of time? Erin unscrews the bottle as I find another wine glass.

'I see you've started without me,' Erin jokes, pointing at my half-filled glass.

'Yes, but it's much nicer drinking with someone else.' I rummage in the larder for a packet of crisps and empty them into a bowl, carrying it to the table.

'I can't believe that Stella was capable of killing Dakota,' Erin says, leaning back in the chair.

'She said it was an accident, that she didn't mean to kill her. What have you heard?'

'Only what the detective told Jared – that he's off the hook and Stella has been charged. I just can't imagine Stella had it in her. And why did she do it? That's what I don't understand.'

I sense Erin is fishing for information from me, but I'm not going to provide it.

'The crazy thing is Stella has been acting totally normally ever since Dakota's death. It's shocking.' Erin takes a sip of wine. 'And she was probably the one who leaked your dreadful list, too. I guess she had the opportunity because she was around your house a lot, wasn't she?'

There is no way that I'm going to tell Erin or anyone who really leaked the list. Maybe one day they'll find out it was Albie, but not a soul will learn that from me.

'The list was nothing to do with Dakota's murder,' I say.

'But how can you be so sure?'

'Stella was here when she confessed.'

'Oh, my God! She confessed?' Erin is practically off her seat. 'So why did she hit Dakota?'

'I don't know,' I lie. It's up to the police to release the details. I don't trust anyone now, not even Erin.

'And you and Jared? He's been tight-lipped about why you've split up, but is there any chance you might get back together again?'

'No chance,' I say. I feel disappointed to realise that Erin is only here to snoop, and I wonder whether she's been set up by Jared to pump me for information. That initial joy I felt when I saw her on the doorstep has completely evaporated.

'So how are you feeling?' I ask, trying to steer the conversation back onto neutral territory.

'Oh, I'm fine. I'm on some new drugs and, honestly, I've never felt on such an even keel. I'm thinking about going back to work and was wondering if I could ask you to look over my CV.'

'With pleasure,' I say.

'So what are you going to do about this house? Will you have to sell it?'

I grimace. 'I've no idea. That's something for the future.'

We talk a bit about the children, how the twins are settling into secondary school, the type of work that Erin might look for. I excuse myself to go to the bathroom, and when I'm upstairs, I peek into the children's rooms. Rosie is lying in her normal starfish manner, stretched out across her bed. I pull the duvet back over her. Albie is cocooned inside his duvet, facing away from me. I worry about him more. My boy, who has had to grow up too quickly.

Back downstairs, Erin has topped up my glass, and I take another sip. I need this. Even if Erin is here to pump me for information, it's better than sitting in my house mulling over everything alone. Her presence gives me a smidge of normality in what has been the hardest fortnight of my life. She's talking to me, except I'm finding it hard to concentrate on what she's saying. I yawn and yawn again, overcome by a wave of sheer exhaustion.

'I think I need to go to sleep,' I say to Erin, except I'm not sure the words are coming out properly.

'Really tired,' I try again. I push my hands against the table and shove my chair backwards, except the effort of it is utterly overwhelming. I try to stand up, but my knees are jelly and I sink straight back into the chair. Something isn't right. I know what it feels like when I've drunk too much. It envelops me slowly like a fog; I feel light and happy, and then the room starts to spin a little, and my limbs feel languid. This is too quick. Much too quick. This doesn't make sense.

It's hard to hold on to my thoughts. They arrive like little wisps of smoke and dissipate almost immediately. But one thought I try to keep hold of.

I've been drugged.

Erin has drugged me.

And the children are upstairs. Too vulnerable. I look up at Erin, and she's smiling. Except her smile contorts across her face like a slash. Such a very big smile...

CHAPTER TWENTY-SEVEN

I cannot lose consciousness. I must not. Albie and Rosie need me. I dig my fingernails as deeply into the palms of my hands as I can.

'Feeling sleepy?' Erin asks. She laughs, except it's not a laugh I recognise. It's cold and harsh and terrifying, just like her slash of a smile. Wasn't Erin pretty? She's not now. She looks like a monster, a clown monster. And why is she looking at me so clinically? I bite the side of my cheek, drawing blood, weirdly grateful for the pain.

'You never really saw me, did you, Kate? None of you did. I've been struggling for years, always the one in the background. Poor little Erin with her silly little depression. And do you know what that list did?' She jabs a finger towards me. 'You ranked me last, Kate. Last on your fucking list! 43 out of 100. And you said I had no sense of humour. Well, the last laugh is on me. You drove me to the very depths of despair. You made me feel utterly worthless. And I didn't need you to do that; I already felt it myself. Except then something amazing happened. When the attempt to take my life failed, I realised that I had nothing to blame myself for. It's not my fault that my brain works in a different way from everyone else's, or that I'm low in certain chemicals. It's you who is the problem. You and your judging, bitchy attitude.'

My breath feels shallower now, and the edges of my sightline are blurring. I have to stay awake. I have to.

'What have you done to me?' I ask, although I'm not sure my words are intelligible.

She ignores me anyway. She's up and pacing the kitchen now, and it's hard for me to keep my eyes on her.

'My so-called friends are all selfish and self-centred. You've never really been there for me, have you, Kate? No, you just judge me as being not enough. You're so sanctimonious, full of your own success. Well, fuck you. You don't actually know me at all.'

She reaches over for her wineglass and tips the remaining liquid down her throat.

'Would you even have cared if I'd died? There you were at Dakota's funeral, all false tears. If you'd had any heart, you'd have stayed away. Imagine how awful it must have been for her parents to see you there, the wife of the man accused of his murder.'

'But...'

She ignores me. 'It's always about you, isn't it, Kate? What Kate wants.'

I wither at her words. Is that what she really thinks?

'The thing about this drug,' she says, pointing at my wineglass. 'Is that your body will give up sooner than your brain. I chose it especially because I want you to listen to me, to hear me.' She walks close to me, and I try to shrink back into the chair.

'After my suicide attempt, I realised I was directing my anger at the wrong person. I always blamed me. But it wasn't my fault. You made me feel terrible. And yes, I sent all of those messages and the dog shit, and I slashed your dress. Oh, and I sent the messages to my other supposed friends too. But ultimately, it's you who is to blame. How dare you set yourself up as a judge of other people? What gives you the right to do that? You always think you're better than everyone, except you're not.'

She takes a deep breath and then carries on. 'You ranked me low on intelligence, didn't you? But you were wrong. So very wrong. You're going to die soon, Kate, and the world will think you've taken your own life. I'll be leaving this empty packet of pills on the table.' She holds up something, but my eyes are unable to focus on it.

As hard as I try, I'm losing my grip on consciousness. The edges of my vision are completely blurred now. I want to hold on, except I don't know how to. Erin pulls out a chair and drags it so that she's facing me, her back to the door. But as I watch her, I see something else – a figure appearing in the doorway, moving soundlessly across the kitchen, reaching to pick something up off the hob. I force my eyes open. Force myself to look and, more importantly, to see. I make myself blink and try to focus. There is my boy. My Albie, and he's holding a cast-iron saucepan, his face so pale and his eyes so wide, a look of sheer terror on his young face. He lifts the saucepan up into the air. But I can't hold on.

My world goes black.

CHAPTER TWENTY-EIGHT

SIX MONTHS LATER

'Do you want to keep these?' Marilyn asks me. She's holding up a box of waffle wool blankets that I inherited from my grandparents. Blankets I'll never use.

'No, they can go,' I say.

'Actually, I think we might have done enough for today,' Marilyn suggests. 'You're looking tired.'

'You're right. I'll make us a pot of tea.'

The house is going on the market next month, so I'm making a concerted effort to sort through all our belongings. It's not easy discarding things, but there's so much from my old life that I need to get rid of. Not just my blankets or clothes or paintings.

When I regained consciousness, I was in hospital, with tubes coming out of both arms. I have never felt so scared and confused, unable to work out how I got there. It turns out Albie saved me. He hit Erin on the head with a heavy saucepan, and then he had the wherewithal to call an ambulance. Fortunately, he didn't hit her hard enough to do any lasting damage, but the truth has come out now. Apparently, my stomach was pumped, and the doctors saved my life. Erin had poisoned me with some crushed-up drugs she stole from Kieren. She wasn't that clever, as Kieren rapidly worked out what was missing and was able to tell the hospital what she'd poisoned me with, so they could inject me with the antidote. They say I got lucky. If Albie hadn't called the ambulance when he did, I might have lost my life. Erin has been charged with attempted murder, and she's locked up in a secure unit for psychological assessment prior to her trial. Apparently, she's admitted to pushing me at Waterloo Station, although there's talk she might have made that up to get more attention. I can still sense that imprint of a hand on my back, so I'm positive she did.

It seems impossible that two of my closest friends were charged with such terrible offences. Stella was held in custody for several weeks whilst the forensic evidence was studied. Eventually, the evidence backed up her story. The killing of Dakota wasn't premeditated but happened in the heat of the moment. When Stella went to see Dakota, they got into a verbal fight. Dakota screamed at Stella and demanded she leave her house. Jared's golf clubs were in his bag next to the patio door in the kitchen. Dakota grabbed one and went for Stella. Dakota's prints were discovered on one of the other clubs in Jared's bag. Stella also grabbed a club and lashed out with it, catching Dakota on the side of her head. Dakota fell, hitting her head on the side of the island unit as she went down. Stella panicked. She picked up both clubs and put them back in the bag and fled Dakota's house. The irony is, she probably only missed Jared by a couple of minutes. He walked in, and according to his testimony, went straight upstairs, expecting Dakota to be there. He took a quick shower and didn't discover the devastating scene in the kitchen until about ten minutes after he'd walked into Dakota's house. Panicking, he grabbed his bags without noticing that one of the clubs had blood on it. It's at that point that I saw him and rushed into Dakota's house.

Jared is also being charged with leaving the scene of a crime. And so he should be. The coward left his lover to die on her kitchen floor.

Stella has been released on bail as the prosecution has accepted that she was acting in self-defence. It will be up to the jury to decide whether her actions were reasonable and proportionate to the threat she faced from Dakota. Although I will never forgive her for sleeping with my husband, I do genuinely think that Stella didn't mean to hurt Dakota, let alone kill her. She has very strict bail conditions and has lost everything. Not least Cole, who is divorcing her. He told me he might have been able to forgive Stella for hitting Dakota in self-defence, but he could never forgive her for pretending that she couldn't have children. So many lies. To my disappointment, Cole handed in his notice two months ago. He wanted to distance himself from me and our friendship group. I don't blame him. It's given me the chance to reevaluate my work-life balance. I'm recruiting two new directors to take over Cole's role and to allow me to take a back seat. Let's hope it all works out because money will be tight after our divorce.

And so it is that Marilyn has become a friend. She was the last person I wanted to see two days after being released from hospital, but I let her in, largely due to the guilt I felt from having misjudged her.

'These are for you,' she said, handing me a gigantic bouquet of brightly coloured flowers and a Victoria sponge cake. 'It's shop-bought because who the hell has time to bake these days?' She laughed, and I found it rather refreshing. I made us a pot of tea and led her into the living room.

'I knew there was something wrong with Erin,' she said, her hands wrapped around the mug of tea. She shifted uncomfortably on my sofa, and I had to stop myself from being concerned that she might spill a bit. 'I mean, I don't want to say bad things about anyone, except I want you to know what really happened.' She leaned back and took a sip of tea. 'It was years ago when the boys were really little. I got a telephone call from Erin, who was in a bit of a panic. She told me that Kieren was working late. I think he'd been called out on some emergency house visit, or maybe he was in the hospital. But whatever, he wasn't at home. She'd also just got a call from her mother. Something had happened, and she needed to rush over to look after her mum. Erin asked me to babysit the twins, which I was happy to do. My husband was at home, so he could look after our Joey, and as I wasn't doing anything else that evening, it was no problem. Erin left as soon as I arrived, so immediately I went upstairs to check up on her boys. Straightaway, I knew something wasn't right. They were falling asleep, but not in the normal way kids do. I sensed they were drugged or something. I was really scared, but Erin was long gone by that point. I went into the twins' bathroom and found some sleep-inducing antihistamine tablets. There were only a couple left in the pack. I deduced that she'd given them more than the prescribed dose, so I sat in their bedroom monitoring their breathing until Erin got back an hour or so later.'

'You think she drugged them?' I asked.

'I'm positive she did. Anyway, when Erin returned, I confronted her about it. I asked what she'd given the twins. She got super-aggressive, accusing me of putting my nose into something that wasn't my business. Threatening to go to social services over my parenting skills.'

'Oh my goodness,' I'd said. It clicked into place then. That afternoon at Lucia's apartment, when we were talking about the threats we'd all received, Erin invented hers so it looked like she'd also been threatened. Of course, she knew that none of us would ever find out if social services had investigated her or not.

'Anyway,' Marilyn continued. 'The very next day, Erin accused me of flirting with her husband, which was absurd. But she was clever. She made that preemptive strike, and she knew that none of you would believe me over her. And of course, she was right. Solid, dependable, slightly boring Erin would never lie.'

I had blanched when Marilyn told me that, for she was right. We just assumed Erin was telling the truth, and Marilyn, who hadn't gone to university with us, who was a bit different to us, was the liar. How deeply I regret that.

'I thought about going to the police to report Erin for giving her kids drugs. In fact, my husband really wanted me to, but in the end, I reckoned it had the potential to blow her life apart. Besides, it might have been a one-off. Maybe the twins were playing up that night, and she just needed them to settle quickly. I kept an eye on those boys for a while, and they seemed to be normal enough.'

'That's so shocking,' I'd murmured. 'And I'm very sorry for the part I played in it.'

'You see, the thing is, I saw through Erin. I think I was the only one. I had a feeling she'd try to wreak revenge on you over that list. That's why I tried to befriend you, tried to keep an eye out for you. I probably went about it the wrong way, and with hindsight, I can see I came across as creepy.

But when I told you to watch your back and keep your children close, I was being genuine. If I'd told you I thought Erin might have it in for you and your kids, you'd never have believed me.'

I nod. I wouldn't have believed Marilyn over Erin, ever. More fool me.

But now, six months later, I see Marilyn for who she really is. A woman with a kind heart. A little needy, perhaps, but I am too.

So much has changed. Both Jared and I have appointed divorce lawyers, although we've instructed our solicitors that we wish the divorce to be as minimally combative as possible. That's not easy, but we're trying. Yes, even Jared is trying. A fortnight ago, when the kids were at school, we spent a couple of days going through the house together, marking what will be Jared's and what will be mine. I've accepted that we need to sell up, and I'm looking for a smaller house somewhere near here in Barnes. I don't want the children to move schools or for Albie to have to find another football club. The other thing I've done is consciously take a step back from my parents. It's clear to me now that they think I was never good enough for them – Mum particularly – and I probably never will be. But that's their problem, not mine. In reality, it was Mum and Dad who let me down, not the other way around. I don't need to be perfect. Indeed, I'm about as far away from being perfect as is possible, but if they can't love me unconditionally as I am, then that's their issue. But I haven't severed relations. So long as the kids still want to visit them, I'll take them to stay, but it doesn't mean I need to hang around.

Of course, I'm more guarded now. Those women whom I've known since my university days, whose lives were so entangled with mine, are no longer my friends. Lucia hasn't once reached out to me, and honestly, I don't care. Good luck to her. I realise now that I hung onto my old friends because I thought it was easy. Except it wasn't. They made me feel lesser, and I was never able to break free of their perceptions of me from when I was a naïve, insecure twenty-year-old girl. And so that insecurity perpetuated. Now I can be truly myself, and I accept that friends will come and go.

'I meant to tell you,' Marilyn says. 'I saw Martina the other day, little Tessa's mum.'

'Oh, yes.' I brace myself as I recall how foul she was to Rosie and me.

'She asked me to pass on her best wishes and to say how sorry she is for the way she reacted towards you.'

'Really?' I ask, surprised. 'I still see her across the schoolyard, but she never approaches me.'

'Maybe she's embarrassed,' Marilyn suggests.

'Maybe.' I think about how I might have judged her previously, have come out with some bitter comment and made my so-called friends laugh. I don't do that anymore. None of us knows what struggles or insecurities other people have. Although our tendency is to assess others based on our own knowledge and experiences, that's dangerous. Not as dangerous as a scorned woman with a golf club, but dangerous, nevertheless. I've promised myself to be kind, not just to my friends and family, but above all to me. We all make mistakes sometimes. The important thing is not to make the same mistake twice. No more spreadsheets for me.

A LETTER FROM MIRANDA

Thank you so much for reading *One Little Mistake*.

I got the inspiration for this book from a newspaper article. It cited a British celebrity who was being harangued for admitting that she ranked her friends. Apparently, she creates lists of who she likes in order of how much she likes them and then sends the list to her assistant to schedule time to talk to these friends. This admission got her many column inches in the media and proved to be quite controversial. With my overactive imagination, I wondered what the fallout of this could be and so Kate and *One Little Mistake* was born!

Recipients of my newsletter and members of my Facebook Group have the opportunity to name characters in my books. Thank you to the following people who suggested the names I used in *One Little Mistake*. I'm so grateful for your support.

Noreen Dane, Sherrill Dennison, Brenda Iddins, Peter Karabin, Denise Little, Erin Meddings, Rob McLean,

Mandy Simon, Karen Stojanac, Sara Tedesco Tagget, Thrillers_chillers_and_killers, Zirafka Vyskov, Cheang Wai Kuen, Marilyn Wright and Jessica Highsmith.

I'd like to extend a special thank you to all the awesome book bloggers who take the time to review my psychological thrillers and share their views on social media. I try my best to thank them on Instagram and Facebook but if I've missed a mention, please know that I'm grateful beyond words.

The team at Inkubator Books is simply the best! Thank you to Brian Lynch, Garret Ryan, Stephen Ryan, Jan Smith, Alice Latchford, Claire Milto, Elizabeth Bayliss and Ella Medler. You make dreams come true.

Most importantly, thank *you*. If you have a moment to leave a review on Amazon and Goodreads, I'd be massively grateful. It helps other people find my books.

If you would like a **FREE** copy of my novella, The Cheat, and the chance to name characters in my future books, please sign up to my newsletter at: **https://bit.ly/The-Cheat-Signup**

You'll also get exclusive access to new releases, giveaways and more!

My warmest wishes,

Miranda

PS – Here's that FREE thriller for you: https://bit.ly/The-Cheat-Signup

www.mirandarijks.com

ALSO BY MIRANDA RIJKS

Inkubator Books Titles
Psychological Thrillers
THE VISITORS
THE INFLUENCER
WHAT SHE KNEW
THE ONLY CHILD
THE NEW NEIGHBOUR
THE SECOND WIFE
THE INSOMNIAC
FORGET ME NOT
THE CONCIERGE
THE OTHER MOTHER
THE LODGE
THE HOMEMAKER
MAKE HER PAY
THE GODCHILD
EVERY BREATH YOU TAKE
THE HOUSE SWAP
VIOLETS ARE BLUE
YOU CAN TRUST ME
ONE LITTLE MISTAKE

The Dr Pippa Durrant Mystery Series
FATAL FORTUNE
(Book 1)
FATAL FLOWERS
(Book 2)
FATAL FINALE
(Book 3)
FATAL SERIES BOX SET

Titles Published by the Author
GASPS
I WANT YOU GONE
DESERVE TO DIE
YOU ARE MINE
ROSES ARE RED
THE ARRANGEMENT

Printed in Dunstable, United Kingdom